SCIENCE FICTION

This is a volume in the
Arno Press collection

SCIENCE FICTION

ADVISORY EDITORS

R. Reginald

Douglas Menville

See last pages of this volume
for a complete list of titles

USELESS HANDS

Charles Bargone

(Claude Farrère, pseud.)

ARNO PRESS

A New York Times Company

New York — 1975

Reprint Edition 1974 by Arno Press Inc.

SCIENCE FICTION
ISBN for complete set: 0-405-06270-2
See last pages of this volume for titles.

Manufactured in the United States of America

———◆———

Library of Congress Cataloging in Publication Data

Farrère, Claude, 1876-1957.
   Useless hands.

   (Science fiction)
   Translation of Les condamnés a mort.
   Reprint of the 1926 ed. published by Dutton, New
York.
   I. Title. II. Series.
PZ3.F2484Us6 [PQ2611.A78]   843'.9'12   74-15969
ISBN 0-405-06289-3

USELESS HANDS

USELESS HANDS

BY

CLAUDE FARRÈRE

Author of "The House of the Secret,"
"Thomas the Lambkin," etc.

Authorized Translation from the French

by

ELISABETH ABBOTT

NEW YORK
E. P. DUTTON & COMPANY
681 FIFTH AVENUE

TO
MY WIFE

CONTENTS

PART I
THE HEADS

PART III

MECHANISM VS. ORGANISM

PART IV

THE AXE

PART I

The Heads

CHAPTER I

ARTIFICIAL PARK, NATURAL PARK

QUARTER to five in the belfry tower!
In the Moorish courtyard the antique barouche
made a wide turn, grazed the porphyry steps and drew
up with a flourish in front of the Gothic door—the
door that was never opened for anyone but the Governor himself. Fifteen minutes more and His Excellency
would come out of the Palace to take his daily drive.
Not one of the thirty footmen in attendance had ever
seen the Governor ten seconds behind time—nor for
that matter ahead of time either! Men who are great
workers have to have their lives ruled as regularly as
bars of music. Now the Governor, of all men, was
James Fergus MacHead Vohr—"MacHead Vohr, the
Wheat King"! And the Wheat King had been and
still was the best worker in the world, as he had been
and still was the richest man in the world, and his
eighty billions made him king of kings!

In front of the Gothic door at the foot of the porphyry steps, the horses pawed the ground impatiently.
For this was a real barouche, a good old-fashioned
barouche drawn by a pair of horses, a magnificent team
for that matter—two golden chestnuts, so alike that

3

not even their groom could tell them apart.   The finest
zoological collections might well have been proud to
include these beautiful specimens of a race well-nigh
extinct.   Since the middle of the twentieth century
horses had become scarce, and forty years later the
last of the horse-breeders, Lord Katrine, regularly sold
the products of his stud for three and four times their
weight in gold.   The Governor's team had cost more
than that and had set all America in an uproar.

Bizarre luxury of a multi-billionaire, no doubt, but
more especially a bit of paternal folly: the Governor
idolized his daughter.   This man, feared by the whole
world, the hardest of the hard, had never softened
except in response to the smile of his adored child, but
then—to the last degree!   To MacHead Vohr his
billions were only a fairy wand to be placed at his
daughter's service.   The horses had been nothing more
than a birthday present.   Miss MacHead Vohr had a
weakness for everything that was old, archaic, out of
date.   Achilles, living, would not have had as much
value in her eyes as a dead cowherder.   And she loved
horses precisely because there were no more horses.

A birthday present too, the wide steps of the same
porphyry, from the Ural Mountains, from which
Alexander II had taken the rocks he offered Napoleon
III as a tomb for that Other Emperor!   A present,
also, the Gothic door from the ruined cathedral of
Sainte-Foy-les-Spire which MacHead Vohr had pur-
chased from the Rhine Republic!   He had had the
stones torn down one by one, packed separately and

transported to the States, each one in its padded box with a tag, position number and place on the plan. And stone by stone the arches were rebuilt in the period of a single night so that Miss MacHead Vohr might have a surprise on waking up in the morning. Still another present, the Persian faiences with which the Governor had decorated the Moorish court—half-Moorish that is, since four of the arches had been removed to make room for the Gothic door! This door, to be sure, was somewhat out of place. But for that matter was not all the High Palace a harlequin affair, with its tall and spindling basement arches, its Corinthian columns on the first floor, the Franco-Assyrian mixture of the rear façade and, weighing heavily on the whole, the formidable wall of unbroken granite? A blank wall this, for the architect had lighted from the ceiling the reception rooms, the theatre and the Roman bath which occupied the entire second floor from one end of the horse-shoe to the other. All that taken together was not of the purest taste. But so much granite, so much porphyry, so much marble, so wonderfully chiseled, fretted, notched and in such profusion too, could not be ugly. It expressed too much power, and at the same time, a power too proud and too regal. Those who had built the High Palace— the men of America—had truly fashioned it in their own image; in the image of their nation, the youngest, therefore the crudest and the most barbarous, the least civilized of all, perhaps; but also the strongest and— who knows?—the greatest?

No, the palace was not ugly. It was even beautiful in its way, for after all it was what it was intended to be, what it should be; "the right place for the right man"—the superhouse of a superman. That man was James F. MacHead Vohr. And he was Governor—Governor for the Sixty United States of America, for the Dominion of Canada, and for Mexico; Governor for the Six Central Republics, for Lima, Santa Fé and La Plata; Governor for Buenos-Aires and Rio de Janeiro: in a word, for the Three Americas—Governor of the A. S. M.; of the "American Siturgic Monopoly"; all-powerful Governor of this all-powerful factory into which poured all the wheat of America, out of which came all the bread of America. And James F. Mac-Head Vohr, sole miller, baker, pieman and pastryman from the Horn to Behring Strait, was also called, more familiarly, the Wheat King.

The hands of the clock pointed to five minutes of five. Then, swiftly but in absolute silence, the thirty footmen lined up in the inner court, and ranged themselves on the steps in double rows. And this was done with the correctness and precision of a military parade. Two buglers, with silver trumpets embannered with azure, joined the footmen and took up their positions behind them. Two lackeys, powdered as white as hoarfrost, mounted behind the antique barouche; the coachman gathered up his reins and raised his whip; the groom, at the horses' heads, hung on to the two bits with both hands. To all the moment of waiting was one of terrible anguish, for few men dared to look the

Governor in the face and even fewer had risked it fearlessly or without mishap.

Emblazoned liveries, white perruques, coachman, horses, carriage, all symbolized the allegory of bygone centuries—centuries long since past which saw man almost the conqueror of nature, almost master of animals, standing indeed on the very threshold of most of the present-day sciences, but not yet daring frankly to plunge into any one of them, and not having discovered, or divined, or even anticipated, the ultimate paths which join them all one to the other: therefore still ignorant of Nature's Supreme Secret, of this law of interchange which is the basis of the universal edifice; ignorant too, and with much more reason, of all the corollaries of the Sovereign Theorem, which gradually, and one by one, reduced to naught the clumsy mechanisms of former days—motors, generators, dynamos, who knows what all!—to substitute in their place the thousand artificial arms of our contemporary humanity; our Machines; the Machines—or rather, the MACHINE: for there is mathematically only one, while appearing to be legion.

Legion!

Machines of child-training, of education, of teaching; birth machines, nursing machines, training machines, directing, correcting and perfecting machines, an arsenal of adapting machines: machines of apprenticeship; machines of feeding; wheat machines, meat machines, preserve machines; dressers, builders, fitters; machines of euphony and euphóry; perfume machines, harmony machines; thermofactors, imbrofactors; electro-regulators; machines for constructing, designing, calculating, solution machines and solving machines; machines of assembling, forging, founding, hammering, hollowing, pestle polishers, mangle polishers; unskilled machines, skilled machines, and boss machines; muscle machines; adders and multipliers, utilizers and transformers; inversors, conversors, perversors; machines for books; machines for instruments; medical machines; scientific research machines, historical research machines and ideal machines; physio-psychurgic machines; euthanasian machines, last of all! Who, in our day, could imagine the world without all this—without the Machine?[1]

Five o'clock in the belfry tower! On both sides, the Gothic door was flung wide! The row of footmen stood at attention. The buglers sounded the pibroch of a Scottish clan famous for its loyalty to the Stuarts, for in spite of his half-Saxon name—Head Vohr instead of Penn Vohr[2]—the Governor had had some bare-kneed ancestors, Highland chieftains.

Then the first clapper touched the bell and, as it swung back to strike again, James F. MacHead Vohr stood on the threshold. His daughter, Miss MacHead Vohr, was with him. Together they descended the flight of stairs, he leaning one hand on her shoulder. And in this simple gesture all the immense tenderness

---

[1] The author apologizes for the torrent of barbarisms dictated by the exigencies of verisimilitude.

[2] *Penn* in Gallic: *Head* in Saxon; *Tête* in French, all have the same meaning. *Wohr, Great, Grand,* same meaning also: *Head Vohr* should therefore be, correctly, either *Great Head* or *Penn Vohr;* or in French, *Grandchef.*

of the father for the daughter was revealed, proclaimed. The young girl entered the antique barouche
first; the Governor, before following her, arranged
the shawl which served as covering over her summer
dress—the air might be cool on the Hill. Then, following his invariable custom, he took his place beside
her at last, seating himself on the right as etiquette
demanded. For that matter it was he, MacHead Vohr,
who had established this etiquette. The father, de-
voted as he was, had never taken precedence over the
Governor.

The coachman snapped his whip smartly about the
horses' heads, according to the best coaching rules of
bygone days, and they were off with a start. They
crossed the Moorish courtyard in the twinkling of an
eye; and, down the avenue of sycamores, nearly two
miles long, the antique barouche rolled swiftly towards
the Artificial Park.

Artificial Park, Natural Park: this is what they
called the two halves of the garden adjoining the High
Palace; a garden equal in size to an English county.
These two parks were separated by the Eighth Mouth,
a river at least two hundred yards wide, from twelve
to thirty feet deep and navigable by the largest
steamers. And this was, besides, the most direct route
between New Orleans and the Gulf. But as this route
dated from only about fifty years ago, and as it takes
longer than that for navigation to become accustomed
to a change, few ships other than those belonging to
the Siturgic passed this way. Moreover, the Siturgic,

which had built, one might almost say, created, the
Eighth Mouth overnight, and which had borne all the
expense of this creation, had no intention of working for others to reap the benefit; only the boats carrying wheat and bread passed between the Natural Park
and the Artificial Park, to go and dock, twenty miles
upstream, at the wharves of the shops.

And all the Eighth Mouth, created by the Siturgic,
was therefore the possession, the property, the territory of the Siturgic, which extended on either bank
from the juncture of the two streams to the mouth—
territory one hundred miles long, covering twelve hundred square miles, or half a million acres. Upstream
were the laborers' quarters—for there were still laborers' quarters and there were still laborers in the year
199—! In fact there were even a great many laborers,
millions, dozens of millions, hundreds of millions. Upstream therefore were the laborers' quarters—the
Blocks; downstream, the Residences—houses of engineers, vice-president and other heads of departments;
and, between the Blocks and the Residences, the Shops:
six hundred and twenty-six factories out of which came
the vital nourishment of three hundred million men;
the daily bread of every man, woman and child from
the Horn to Behring Strait.

The Residences here; the Blocks over there; and the
Shops between the Residences and the Blocks: this had
been MacHead Vohr's plan for protecting Capital from
an ever menacing uprising of Labor. Sixty miles of
neutral territory, of No Man's Land, were more of a

protection than ten regiments. At least so the Governor had calculated. For that matter the whole Siturgic was his work; and if the price of bread had gone down, in twenty years, to the amount of one cent for four pounds, America and the World owed it to him alone. In presenting him with the two parks, which had become his personal property, the Sixty States had paid him only a small, a very small, part of the enormous debt of gratitude contracted by the whole world toward this man—a debt quickly forgotten, besides. Ten years had not passed since the founding of the Shops, when the American press, forgetting the Governor's old nickname, Breadgiver, was beginning to call him the King of Famines.

—And down the avenue of sycamores, the antique barouche was rolling swiftly toward the Artificial Park.

Avenue, park, the High Palace, and the greater part of the Residences occupied the right bank of the river. This had not always been the case, for the right bank was of recent origin. At first the Eighth Mouth had flowed between its left bank and some muddy dikes which separated it from the Gulf of Mexico. At that time MacHead Vohr was living in the Low Palace on the left bank—then the only bank. But the necessity of having quays on both shores had led him to build a right bank from beginning to end. And, as in everything he undertook, he built it on a big scale. Three hundred thousand acres had been reclaimed on the Atlantic; and, since reclaimed lands are seldom healthy, the Governor, to prevent malaria, had raised the height of all this right bank which he had "created." When completed it towered above the old bank, the left— the natural bank.   Before he built the High Palace and moved into it, MacHead Vohr finished off his bank by dotting it with several valleys, a stream, a forest, and even with a hill whose crest was four hundred feet above sea level.   In the entire bank, hill and valley included, there was not a grain of sand which had not been brought by boat from the quarries of Mexico or Alabama.   And now, there on the very spot once washed by the waves of the Gulf, the avenue of sycamores stretched its century old trees the length of the orange colored macadam, between the double border of ancient greensward on its lower slopes.

At the end of the avenue the antique barouche entered woods.   A moist, stifling heat fell from the tops of tall trees stretched in a shadowy vault above the passersby.   The avenue of sycamores was followed by a forest road.   And had this highway not been irreproachably maintained, the timbered lands it crossed might very well have been taken for a virgin forest, for it had all the wildness and all the exuberance of one. It was not more than ten years old, however: even to the last blade of grass, everything had been planted by the hand of man.   This work had required no less than four million trees, one third of them over one hundred and twenty years old.   But the very vastness of the operation assured its success: so and so many cedars, oaks and pines spreading out over miles and miles of soil especially prepared for them, became ac-

climatised at once; ferns, hanging vines, moss, thorns,
brambles, bushes, thickets, and that lacy parasite
which in Louisiana is called Spanish Beard, had, in
less than one season sprung up out of the ground at
the foot of these trunks so favorable to their growth.
Then the forest had grown, impetuously. Wild beasts
now multiplied there rapidly, and Man would have had
to blaze a trail with a hatchet. From the cushions
of the antique barouche, MacHead Vohr, stiffly erect,
cast his eye over this spectacle of nature unchained
—by him—and, smiling with pride, stretched himself
slowly. Staled as he was to success, he could not refrain from a feeling of satisfaction at remembering
what had been and comparing it with what now was.

The antique barouche rolled swiftly along behind the
quick-stepping chestnuts; the road wound about, rising
little by little to the first slopes of the hill. The forest,
denser here than in other parts, enfolded the road in
a close embrace, perfumed, sensual, like the embrace of
a woman in love. For the first time since she had sat
down beside the Governor, Miss MacHead Vohr raised
herself from the cushions; and her nostrils dilated as
she breathed in the pungent odor of trees in leaf. At
the same time with a graceful gesture, a little studied
perhaps, she put her arm about her father's shoulder,
then closed her eyes as if overcome by a delicious sense
of wellbeing and pleasure.

After the dense forest came a stretch of woods less
thickly settled; meadows intersected it, as clearings

on the Jura Mountains intersect pine forests. The
road mounted now, scaling straight up one of the crests
of the hill. To right and to left the country stretched
away to the ends of the island; the ocean on the west,
the Eighth Mouth on the east, with its left bank
beyond. The horses quickened their pace. And, passing the tenth mile, the carriage suddenly emerged upon
a platform surmounted by a circular colonnade, the
Belvedere. This was the summit of the Artificial Hill.
But, from the Belvedere, thousands of square miles
appeared, majestically encircling this colonnade which
MacHead Vohr had dedicated to the Mother of Men,
Eve, the wife of Adam.

Miss MacHead Vohr was named Eva. At this
moment her father called her by name. Since his
daughter had put her arm caressingly about his
shoulder, MacHead Vohr had not stopped smiling.
And there was no stranger sight than the smile on this
mouth—a swordcut, as it were, in the terrible hard-
ness of a hatchet face. As the barouche, obeying
orders, stopped abruptly at the foot of the steps
leading to the little latticed temple, after a curve as
brilliant as the one described on leaving the Moorish
court, this smile of steel turned towards the rosy smile
that had never left Miss MacHead Vohr's lips, and
that made her appear more beautiful than ever, ac-
centuating, as it did, her pallor:

"Eva, would you like to get out and walk around
your temple a bit?"

The platform was an English greensward surrounded

by marble balustrades, broken at intervals by Pom-
peian benches with arms and backs. As a rule, Miss
MacHead Vohr liked to sit here, yielding her supple
body to the carefully modeled curves of this marble
warmed by the sun, marble that was more comfortable,
for that matter, than a cushioned divan.

But at present this did not strike her fancy.

"No, Governor!" she replied. (She always called
him "Governor," liking, as much through pride as tender flattery, to recall the rank and power of this man
who to her was only a cringing slave.) "No, Governor!
I would rather—but only on condition that it does
not displease you, or make you late?"

"What is it, dearest?"

"I would like to come back through the Natural
Park, and stop on the bridge between the two rivers,
to get a breath of fresh air from the water."

MacHead Vohr glanced at his watch. Not even his
daughter could make him forget that at quarter past
seven the Board of Chief Engineers would meet at the
High Palace. But it would not take any longer to return by way of the left bank than by the right bank.
And the horses had trotted so fast that they were
ahead of schedule time.

The Governor touched the coachman's shoulder with
the tip of his cane and ordered:

"Natural Park."

In speaking to his daughter, MacHead Vohr's voice
was full of tenderness. Lovers, in their most intimate
moments, have the same tones. But, in giving orders

to one of his men, the Governor, without even noticing
the change, spoke in his usual voice, a voice that was
like his face, sharply metallic; a voice that no one
had ever heard without experiencing a feeling of fear
or uneasiness. At the command the horses themselves,
even before the whip could touch them, were off with
a start as if they were running away.

CHAPTER II

THE BLOCKS

ONTO the footbridge the barouche dashed without slackening speed. The platform vibrated and gave out a clear sound. The footbridge was like a violin string which the barouche ran across like a bow.

No bridge spanned the Eighth Mouth, for a bridge would have interfered with navigation. But thirty tunnels connected one bank with the other, all beneath the riverbed. And these tunnels, built to accommodate the needs of traffic or of manufacturing, all opened in the neighborhood of one quay or the other, that is to say, on the very lowest level of the land. On the other hand, the Governor most often drove to such and such a height, either natural or artificial, in his domain; especially to his Artificial Hill. To pass from one island to the other, through the tunnels, when the fancy seized him, would have meant more or less monotonous driving uphill and downdale. The foot-bridge saved him this annoyance.

Forty years earlier, on the eve of the celebrated experiments in Strasbourg, whence the science of radio was to emerge, so to speak, fully armed—in the time when its very existence was unknown and the world still believed in the efficacy of very high antennae of wireless telegraphy—they had built, on what was afterwards to be called the Natural Island, a metal tower eighteen hundred feet high, and much sturdier than necessary for its purpose. This tower one third higher than the Artificial Hill itself, was only two miles from the Hill as the bird flies. To throw from the crest of the Hill to the fourth floor of the tower (both being exactly on the same level), a hollow beam, elastic and yet strong enough to withstand the force of even the worst Mexican cyclones; this had been the problem; a problem, however, that the engineers of the Siturgic had solved irreproachably. The beam was a trellis of Martium steel and of glass infiltrated with gold in a proportion of three to a thousand. The eastern end —the natural bank—was riveted to the iron braces of the tower, which, besides, were made solid with this purpose in view. The western end fitted into the ground between two of the marble balustrades which surrounded the Belvedere. From one end to the other, no supports, no reinforcements, no arches, no piles; and not even a suspension wire! The audacity and the grace of such a feat had enraptured even Miss Mac-Head Vohr, who as a rule did not admire anything that was not antique. The engineers—there were two of them, two brothers or rather half-brothers, the Ferratis; Andrea and Pietro—had found in this work the starting point of a career which for both of them could have been brilliant and which, for one of them at least, had actually been so.[1]

By leaning forward a little, Miss MacHead Vohr could see through the transparent floor as if from the cabin of an airplane, all the Eastern zone of the Artificial Island, all of the Eighth Mouth, and a long strip of the Natural Island, which grew larger and larger in proportion as the barouche approached the Iron Tower. That was the name they had given the old antennae, eighteen hundred feet high, although it was naturally not of iron, but of steel; of one of those chromic steels which, in the days before Martium had been discovered, represented the last word and the supreme arcanum of ancient metallurgy.

On the side towards the Eighth Mouth, the Artificial Hill ended in deep slopes, followed by a narrow valley which had been built to make a place for the dock: the Eighth Mouth, from the juncture to the farthest outlet, flowed between two magnificent embankments of orange-colored earth, each one planted with a quadruple row of big trees.

At last, the barouche passed over the current of the water, at an altitude of four hundred yards. And,

[1] In this case the author has been constrained to "anticipate" a probability. For improbable as a footbridge like this would be today, in the estimation of engineers in 1920, it is more than certain that it will be realized long before the year 199—. There is nothing more logical than to admit the discovery of a metal which we call *Martium,* a few traces of which will double the resistance of steel. In the same way nothing is more probable than the invention of a glass in which veins of gold projected by a kind of radio-electrolysis would give a solidity inconceivable in the present day and generation. Finally, in the opinion of the author it is so certain that at Strasbourg or at Nancy experiments will take place resulting in the establishment of a new science, radio technic, that he himself has begun to proceed with it.

at a sign from the master, the carriage stopped short, so that Miss MacHead Vohr could get a breath of fresh air from the river as she had desired. Agile as a young man in spite of his sixty-six years, MacHead Vohr jumped to the ground before the coachman could bring his horses to a standstill, and hurrying around the carriage from right to left was in time to give his hand to Miss MacHead Vohr, who in her turn descended on the left.

Now, one elbow on the glass rail of the parapet, her chin in her hand, and her eyes motionless under frowning brows, Miss MacHead Vohr was searching—searching with really extraordinary attention all this territory of the Siturgic spread out, twelve hundred feet below her, like a gigantic map.

The footbridge had been thrown across from east to west. Whoever leaned on the parapet therefore faced either north or south: southward towards the shore and the Mexican plain; northward towards the great plain which, as part of the delta and of its hundred islands, reached out limitlessly in every direction —to the right as far as the Alleghanies and the Atlantic, to the left as far as the Rocky Mountains and to Alaska; straight ahead, to the Great Lakes and the snowy Hudson Bay, to the Polar Circle and the icebergs.

But Miss MacHead Vohr was not looking towards the south. She would not have seen anything in that direction but the greenish line of the shore about fifteen miles away, with only alluvium in front of it. The

Eighth Mouth, pushing out and extending from year to year the double advance of its two banks like two dikes of the outer port, just flecked with a speck of yellow this horizon which was the color of mud and seaweed. But, towards the North, the property of the Siturgic appeared less monotonous and more variegated. New Orleans was over there to the north east. But there was no sign of the city, because the shops of the Siturgic, this side of it, made a screen which hid anything else from view. Besides they were quite enough to see. And Miss MacHead Vohr was so busy looking at the Shops that she did not see anything else.

The Eighth Mouth, from the footbridge to the juncture of the rivers, was nothing but a single lane of water as straight as a die, from two to three hundred yards wide and from forty to fifty miles long. There was an important turn in the course of the river at this point. The water flowed, deep and swift, between the quays; each quay lined a good third of its length with an unbroken string of heavy cargo boats, loading or emptying their holds. Looking from the footbridge upstream, only the first ten or twelve miles appeared quiet and half deserted. After that, the harbor began; and stretched out indefinitely as far as one could see. A few scattered houses, separated one from the other, dotted the landscape here and there. These were the homes of engineers or of vice-presidents; all the staff of that industrial army—the labor employed in running this gigantic factory—lived in fact in this neighborhood. The Governor—he alone had founded all this, and continued to govern all with absolute power—had in this way foreseen, downstream, below the factory and the workshops, homes for his subordinates and for himself; and homes for labor, for the workmen—in short for all that was arm or muscles, not brain—upstream. Between the Limbs and Gaster, to quote the ancient fable, arose therefore, in the midst of *No Man's Land*, this rampart of iron, bronze and steel: the city of machines, the tool-city. And this was the city, with its port, that stood out prominently from all the rest of the countryside, rising suddenly on both banks up there beyond the tenth or twelfth mile upstream, and stretching and spreading out in two steel rectangles, each one fourteen miles long by four miles wide, intersected by thirty-two railways lengthwise and fifty-six crosswise; this was the city, which belched forth such mountains of black smoke from its three hundred and forty-four factory chimneys that, in the center of each half of the city, and even in the middle of the broad stream separating them, no one could remember ever having had a glimpse of blue sky, nor of the sun.[1]

The Siturgic furnished the entire American continent with bread, pie crust, biscuits, cakes, grits and flour. Therefore there was nothing surprising in the unparalleled immensity of this huge factory, which

---

[1] In order to translate into French measures the dimensions of the industrial town of the American Siturgic Monopoly, each one of the two rectangles of which it is comprised measures twenty-two kilometers by about eight; and all these factories thus grouped together cover a surface of two hundred and sixty-four square kilometers.

had sole charge of feeding some four hundred million human beings.[1]

Distributed in these two rectangular twin cities, each one of which was subdivided by four lines of solid buildings separated one from the other by eight avenues, each one numbered, running parallel to the river and intersected by eleven hundred perpendicular streets likewise numbered, there were fourteen thousand three hundred and thirty-six shops, each one covering an acre—fourteen thousand three hundred and thirty-six shops, supplying the thirteen hundred and forty-four furnaces belching forth black smoke, not one of which was ever idle, except on visiting days, inspection days and for repair.

Leaning her elbow on the parapet, chin in her hand, Miss MacHead Vohr was staring very intently towards the northern horizon. And, by chance, the rosy smile so becoming to her chalk-white complexion—too white perhaps—disappeared little by little from her lips. At this unusual sign an expression of great anxiety suddenly came over the father's face, a countenance ordinarily so immobile that it might well have been of stone rather than of flesh. And all at once the Governor put his hand on his daughter's shoulder:

"Eva, what are you looking at down there among the shops? Come, tell your father, my dear!"

Miss MacHead Vohr lifted her head and tilted her chin vaguely towards the juncture of the two streams.

---

[1] In 1790, America had less than forty million inhabitants. In 1890, these forty million had become almost one hundred and fifty. In 199—, the count will assuredly have gone well past four hundred million.

"I am looking down there, Governor—towards the docks."

"Towards the docks? At what, more precisely?"

MacHead Vohr had never been put off by an evasive answer. Three seconds had not passed before he insisted.

"Just what were you really looking at? The cargo boats?"

Miss MacHead Vohr let go of the rampart and drew herself up; then, turning to the Governor and looking him straight in the eyes she finished her reply, —in the most indifferent tone in the world besides:

"No, Governor, not at the boats. I am looking further, beyond that: I am looking at the Blocks."

"Oh!" exclaimed MacHead Vohr very much surprised. "What's that? At those ugly things? The Blocks, eh?—You are looking at the Blocks, really?"

"Yes, really."

And, as she spoke, Miss MacHead Vohr began to smile again. But the Governor, disturbed, had turned away from his daughter and instinctively followed the direction of her gaze.

They were very far away—away beyond all the enormous city of machines; beyond the fourteen miles of iron, of bronze and of steel; away off at the horizon, and barely visible; only here and there the thin watery outline of the Mouth, and when you reached the juncture, several irregular piles of white points that resembled villages. This is what the Blocks looked like, the city of workers, the home of labor necessary, in those days, to keep the wheat machines running.

For there were still laborers in the year 199—, indeed there were still a great many—noticeably as many as there had been sixty or eighty years earlier, in the year 193— or the year 19—. That is, as many and more than the planet had ever had since the origin and beginning of our era of industrial civilization up to the invention and general use of the machine-hands which first became known in the world in 199—, —machine-hands which, little by little replacing muscular strength everywhere with mechanical power, finally freed the human race from any labor other than that of the brain. The man of today thinks and creates, he was still sweating and suffering in 199—, and only to make bread.

Having in his turn glanced at those far off specks, the Blocks, the Governor turned back to Miss Mac-Head Vohr:

"Really, now," he said—"I would like to know, Eva, why you waste a glance or a thought on those Blocks which you can scarcely see from here?"

Miss MacHead Vohr shrugged her shoulders gently, as if doubting whether she herself really knew:

"As a matter of fact," she answered, "I think it is simply chance. And yet, Governor, I am curious— tell me, what are those Blocks?"

MacHead Vohr raised his eyebrows.

"The Blocks?" he repeated in astonishment, "why, you certainly know that! They are the quarters I provide for these human arms, for the labor employed in my shops. Come, Eva, you know that, don't you?"

"Yes."

Miss MacHead Vohr had that strength which is the possession of only a few women and even fewer men: that of looking the person she was talking to straight in the eyes, without wavering. She repeated:

"Yes, I know."

And did not explain until after a little while had passed.

"Yes, Governor, I know—but, like you, I would like to know more. First of all, this name:—Blocks —why?"

At her look of insistence which emphasized the question, MacHead Vohr was more surprised than ever:

"Why? Well, but that's very simple: it's the right name. What could be better? Block means cube. Just look carefully, my dear. That's exactly what they are: cubes; blocks; a huge game of dominoes spread out on the ground at haphazard would look just like that,—down there, near the juncture of the two streams."

Miss MacHead Vohr raised her lorgnette which hung at her waist.

"So it is, yes"—she said—"a game of very, very large dominoes—very small seen from here, however!"

"The nearest are thirty miles away, don't forget."

"So far! Then they must be more than large, enormous! I suppose there is a multitude of people living in each one, isn't there?"

"Certainly."

"And how many inhabitants in all the Blocks put together?"

"Oh! I don't know! Perhaps three, perhaps four hundred thousand souls. They take the census only once every four years; and I don't remember the last count."

Miss MacHead Vohr shook her head.

"Three or four hundred thousand living souls, in there! . . . . Do you really need so many arms for the work?"

MacHead Vohr pursed out his lips, then drew them in a straight line, making a sharp mouth, hollowed underneath, a grooved mouth something like the concave blades of Arab swords.

"So many?" he repeated. "Oh, no. Not so many at all. On the contrary. I have many arms, it is true. But I only need a few of them. Very few I assure you."

"Why is that?"

The Governor lifted one of his hands to his face, then let it fall, heavily.

"Ah! Eva, my dear, now there you touch on a problem, more than that, *the* problem of our modern social system. And this problem, my darling child, this problem is all the more complex, confused even, because it appears so clear and simple. Well then, I have many workmen because I only need a few. Why is that? Because, not so very long ago, my shops needed many machinists, firemen, mechanics, electricians, chemists, adjustors, and many others, to run the

machines. At present they need fewer men, and soon
will need even less. In spite of which I continue to
employ, and virtually to make use of, and actually to
feed and to pay as many workers today as yesterday;
worse than that; I shall continue to have them and
to submit to having them tomorrow as well as today,
because these workmen, sons of the workmen, who, in
former days, lived by the work of their arms, of their
muscles after all, and nothing but their muscles—of
their muscles, understand, and not of their brains—
would continue to live today as their fathers lived
yesterday, and to work as their fathers worked—in
spite of the fact that this work may have become fruitless and an illusion; because they do it and because
society tolerates it, resigns itself to it, and abdicates
its rights if not its duties, by permitting things to remain as they are."

Neither blame, nor approbation. And not a spark
of irony. The master's immobile countenance registered
the statement of this formidable problem, impassively.

And impassively, too, Miss MacHead Vohr had
listened. She was still smiling. Miss MacHead Vohr's
smile was too becoming to her grave and pale face; it
lent her too visible a charm and seduction to be always
quite spontaneous. . .

The horses pawed the ground impatiently. The
glass floor, vibrating at intervals, gave out sounds like
the long wail of an aerial.

As Miss MacHead Vohr was getting into the carriage again, she stopped suddenly, one foot on the

step, and, looking back once more towards the Blocks, now almost invisible behind the evening mist which had begun to rise from the plain, said:

"By the way, Governor, these workmen, sons of their fathers,—your workmen of today—who would continue to live and to work as people lived and worked yesterday—perhaps they can't do anything else, can they? The man who has never done anything but manual labor is poorly prepared for mental work."

The Governor, nodding his head like a ruler, approved:

"My dear, you are right. It is quite possible that these workers of mine may be incapable of using their brains, dulled and atrophied through atavism and lack of education. Quite possible, to be sure!"

She had seated herself. He got into the carriage in his turn, then touched the coachman's back with the tip of his cane. The latter suddenly gave the horses their heads.

"However," finished the Governor, "it doesn't matter in the least whether or not it is the fault of these men. Society, permitting them to live as they do live, like parasites, and to eat, although they produce nothing, society is wrong because it goes against the natural law discovered by the great Darwin:

" '*Whoever, race or individual, does not adapt himself to the conditions of existence resulting from time and place, from era and climate, is condemned to death by the irrevocable law termed selection.*'

"Eva, dearest, my precious little one, that is the way

it is, inevitably. Oh, what is the matter? Are you cold?"

Her face had grown quite white and her lips, red with life a minute before, had lost color. MacHead Vohr, distracted a moment by his own words, noticed this with sudden anxiety. But Miss MacHead Vohr hastened to protest:

"Not a bit cold, Governor. But I am always taken by surprise when the barouche goes under the Tower gate"—

The carriage had in fact come to the end of the footbridge. Through the gate of which Miss MacHead Vohr spoke it was entering the forest of steel pillars, the foundations of the eighteen hundred foot tower. Horses and carriage had already come to a standstill in the cage of one of the elevators which, a few seconds later, deposited them right on the macadam highway which traversed the whole Natural Island, from South to North. . .

CHAPTER III

THE BOARD OF CHIEF-ENGINEERS

IN THE belfry of the Moorish courtyard the clock struck seven. The double row of footmen in full regalia ranged themselves on the steps before the Gothic door; the buglers flourished their silver trumpets embannered with azure; and, in the silence which gradually settled down, a faint noise arose in the distance, regular as the iron hammers of the jacks in the belfry: the rolling of a swift carriage and the sharp trot of a pair of dashing horses. The pibroch rang out, the antique barouche swept from the avenue of sycamores into the horseshoe of the courtyard and, just as he had done two hours earlier, the tall figure of the Master, his left hand resting on the shoulder of Miss MacHead Vohr who walked beside him, passed beneath the ancient Gothic arches whose oaken portals were swung wide.

Inside the Gothic door, the High Palace presented a succession of vast *salons* in the Arabian style of the Alhambra. The entire entrance floor had been conceived in the same style, except the façade opposite the horseshoe in the Moorish court, which was an exact reproduction of the façade in the royal castle of Versailles. The French *salons* in this wing communicated directly with the Granadan chambers of the horseshoe, which really served as ante-chambers to the former. Ten elevators, comfortably furnished, connected the entire ground floor, which comprised all the apartments for daily use and for informal receptions, with the first floor where the private apartments were, and with the state apartments, theatre and ballrooms which occupied the greater part of the second floor.

On his return, the Governor went up with his daughter to the first floor, and spent a few minutes with her before coming down again. And, once more with his clock-like punctuality, he pushed open the door of the Council Chamber at the precise moment when the clock in the belfry was striking quarter after seven, the hour appointed for the opening of the meeting of the Board of Chief Engineers.

The guard at the door announced pompously:

"His Excellency, the Governor."

And one hundred and fifty men, seated in a semi-circle—the chief engineers, each one commanding a hundred or more shops, with more than a thousand workmen, foremen and engineers under them—all rose to their feet in visible sign of respect.

Without pausing, MacHead Vohr went straight to the armchair in the center of the circle and sat down. To right and to left of him were ranged about twenty other armchairs not so high as his, but higher than the seats of the rest of the assembly; the bench— this was the official term—of the vice-presidents and councilors. There were fifteen vice-presidents and only four councilors.. The staff of the Siturgic was ruled like the general staff of an army. And discipline reigned here even more despotically, if possible, than in any army of the Prussian kings.

Absolute silence greeted the Master's appearance. MacHead Vohr had entered wearing his hat, which he did not remove until after he was seated. At last he spoke, and his voice sounded sharper and more imperious even than it had a little while before when on the drive he had, in his daughter's presence, given orders to the coachman.

"Gentlemen, the meeting will come to order. The Secretary of the Board will read us the semi-monthly report on manufactured products, imports and exports."

A tall, lean and bony young man, seated at a side table behind several voluminous documents, stretched out his hand silently towards the group of four stenographers (his own secretaries), took several prepared sheets which they handed him, and, without preamble, began to read the semi-monthly report, a paper of remarkable conciseness, empty of phrases but packed with figures. So many cargo boats had come in displacing so much gross tonnage and carrying so many hundredweight of cereals, of which so and so much was old wheat, so and so much young wheat, rye, barley, oats, maize and sesame. So many cargo boats had gone out, carrying to such and such destinations such and such quantities of different kinds of flour, grits, dough and pastries, over and above bread, the distribution of which was minutely detailed. In this way the amount of exports and imports was closely balanced. Other figures fixed exactly the importance of the production—transformations of wheat into grits or flour, of grits into nourishing pastries, of flour into bread, cakes, biscuits and other eatables made of cereals. The entire industrial activity of the Shops was clearly set forth in a few arithmetical equations. And to finish, a table of contents, with the quotas distributed among the American States, was placed side by side with the respective demands of each of these States—demands which, naturally, had not all met with the same reception. The Government at Washington dictated the policy of the Siturgic Government. And the Governor, MacHead Vohr, sometimes added his own particular policies which he did not submit to the Board of Chief Engineers, nor, for that matter, to any of the other boards that he had established to aid him in the weighty government of this gigantic Siturgic.

The Board of Chief Engineers was not in truth the only assembly that could be convened at the High Palace. The Governor, should the case arise, had recourse to the advice of two assemblies which were more restricted (therefore more important) by their functions no less than by the qualifications of the dignitaries who composed them. The first of these assemblies was the Board of Vice-Presidents, composed, as its name indicates, of fifteen vice-presidents and had au-

thority over the one hundred and fifty chief engineers,
over ten or twelve thousand foremen, and, finally, over
one hundred and thirty or forty thousand workmen
of the Siturgic. And the second, called the Grand
Council, comprised only the four councilors who were
superior to the vice-presidents, as these in turn were
superior to the chief engineers. These were the councilor of the Intelligence Department, the councilor on
Public Works; the executive councilor and the councilor
for Home and Foreign Affairs, called familiarly the
privy councilor. All of them, for that matter, members of the Grand Council and members of the Vice-
Presidents' Board alike, attended punctually, like the
Governor himself, the meetings of the Board of Chief
Engineers; all, except one, that is—a Frenchman, a
strange man, very old, who lived in an isolated tower
outside the grounds of the High Palace and beyond
the Residences, and who was scarcely ever seen in public. The Governor overlooked numerous eccentricities
in this man, as much because of his age as on account
of his technical ability, which was unparalleled. This
man, who bore the title of Councilor of the Laboratories, was George Torral.

The secretary finished his report. Behind him the
stenographers were still busy setting up an illuminated
bulletin board on which a keyboard kept writing out
the figures and equations of the report. As soon as
the report was finished, the light on the bulletin board
was extinguished. And MacHead Vohr who had listened
attentively, his head thrust forward, chin out, nodded

with a gesture as sharp as the stroke of a guillotine.
Absolute silence reigned again. From the moment the
Governor seemed to give his approval, no one dared
to comment, even by a word, on the account just rendered of the fortnight's operations.

Meanwhile the Governor had raised his head and
was scrutinizing the faces of the assembly. The lamps
threw into bold relief his face with its sunken cheek-
bones, its heavy square jawbone, surmounting the
pointed chin, as in times past the enormous poop of a
battleship surmounted the sharp pointed curve of the
stern-post. Having looked slowly, searchingly, at
everyone in turn with a glance which seemed to each
man to pierce through him personally, the Governor
turned towards one of the men who had been seated
nearest to him—a pink and white old gentleman whose
short moustache and carefully combed sideboards,
white as snow, adorned the face of a worldly priest:
Ralph Athole, the councilor for Home and Foreign
Affairs, called the privy councilor.

"Athole, you spoke to me this morning of several
matters, among others one of special importance. I
consider that these gentlemen ought to be informed."

The privy councilor made an involuntary grimace.
Those who were well acquainted with this man so
wonderfully constituted for diplomacy, and who had
remarked that this pucker of his mouth and of the
dimples of his chin were the only signs betraying any
emotion whatever on his face, could not help suspecting

that he had let his sideboards and moustache grow in order to dissimulate as much as he could the slightest outward reflections of his inward emotions.

"Governor," said he in a placid, smooth tone which was his usual voice, and which no one had ever heard raised or lowered, "Governor, these gentlemen are surely informed by now. Otherwise, they would be naïve—indeed, a little more than the regular operation of the Siturgic warrants. No matter, we can be more definite. The simplest way is for us to take a look at the latest report of my good friend Just Bellecour, our executive councilor. Bellecour, old man, if you please?"

He had risen and stepped forward, from behind Mac-Head Vohr's chair, towards the executive councilor, who was seated near the group of stenographers and their chief, the secretary of the Council. A Frenchman by birth, from Lyons—nine out of ten Frenchmen that one meets outside of France are born in the ancient capital of the Roman Gauls, in Lugdunum, native land of Claude, the Emperor—Just Bellecour, the executive councilor was as much like Ralph Athole, the privy councilor, as a bulldog from Bordeaux is like a collie. The Scotchman, Athole (his name did not belie his nationality), was a native of County Argyle. Imprinted on his whole face and figure, Athole showed finesse, wise caution and statesmanship; whereas the man from Lyons, in his countenance at once sensual

and thoughtful, expressed nothing but energy, energy
and again energy, with that addition of dogged patience
which gives success to energy.   Athole, therefore, went
up to Bellecour, and leaned on the table with the keyboard.   The secretaries had already loosened the minutes of the report requested.   But Bellecour, taking
a note book out of his pocket, held it out to the privy
councilor, who turned to the typed pages in the note-
book and went back to his seat, thumbing the leaves
of the book and smiling as if to mask with this smile
the tell-tale grimace he did not want to show.

"Well?" insisted the Master, curtly.

"Well!" said Athole, "I would be surprised if these
gentlemen have not all remarked during the past fortnight, and each in his own department, a proportion
of mishaps, accidents and damages—I am speaking of
material, operation and production, I am not speaking of injuries, illnesses or deaths of men—a proportion I say, of divers misadventures sensibly higher
than any in the worst fortnights I can find record of.
This is not guesswork, it is a question of facts.   Each
one of these gentlemen controls a hundred shops or
more; in other words twelve or fifteen engineers, one
hundred and thirty or forty foremen or supervisors
and some thousand or twelve hundred workmen.   This
is enough to eliminate any elements of chance from
our calculation.   If a single one of the one hundred
and fifty chief engineers present has found any evidence contrary to mine in his group, I beg him kindly
to report it immediately to the Governor.   One excep-

tion, for that matter, would confirm the rule. But I'm
afraid that there may not even be an exception."

And there was none. A dull rumble of proposals
exchanged in low voices had suddenly replaced the
silence until now unbroken. The fact stated by the
privy councilor had evidently struck everyone. And
the sudden revelation that it was a general fact, nay
even without exception, without *one* exception, aroused
a natural and extreme agitation.

Imaginations worked overtime.

With a single question, however, MacHead Vohr
cut short this buzzing and suddenly reestablished
silence:

"The cause, Athole? Give me your opinion."

Athole bowed his head, and his voice, always perfectly placid, became doubly suave:

"The cause, you say, Governor? It is plain to be
seen and lies in the three words: discontent, conspiracy,
sabotage."

At this, the silence was broken. But instead of
the gentle hubbub that, a few minutes ago, had greeted
the privy councilor's first words, there was a barely
audible murmur that rippled from one end to the other
of the vast room. It seemed as if a mysterious
anxiety had swooped down on the assembly, like an
enormous bird with flapping wings.

"Discontent?" MacHead Vohr repeated slowly after
a pause, allowing time for the assembly to become
calm and attentive. "Discontent? Who is discontented?"

Athole shrugged his shoulders lightly:

"Naturally," he said, "those who have reason not to be—the workmen."

"Ah!" was MacHead Vohr's reply.

The Wheat King was not accustomed to hesitate in any matter whatever, and his whole life was a proof of this. The reply his privy councilor had just given him was not, on the other hand, a surprise to him, but he had purposely lead Athole to make it; for there was nothing impromptu about the scene which was taking place at this moment in the heart of the meeting; its details had even been formulated in advance between the Governor, his councilors and several supernumeraries. Was it the very simplicity of Athole's· words? Nevertheless it seemed that having said "Ah!" MacHead Vohr hesitated a fairly long time before continuing. And while he was hesitating, some one who until then had not uttered a word, took the floor unexpectedly.

"Governor, will you allow me, on the occasion of the facts in point, to renew here the regret I have already had the honor of expressing to you? I do not think that anyone can reasonably have anything to say against the opinion which the councilor on Home and Foreign Affairs has just advanced. It is only the more regrettable to find that a cause as puerile as the discontent, without rhyme or reason, of several workmen, can react on the production output of the sole factory in the world charged by fifteen or twenty nations with assuring their subsistence. And that too, when the muscular power of these workmen could be so easily replaced by the more tractable and equally pliant energy of several of those recently invented machines of slavery which are called machine-hands."

Complete silence gave approval to this speech. Mac-Head Vohr, more cordial than he had been yet, looked at the speaker. He was a handsome young man, with an elegant dark moustache, who could easily be recognized as an Italian from Tuscany. His name was Andrea Ferrati and he was one of the half-brothers who had formerly built the footbridge over the Eighth Mouth. Andrea was the younger. The elder, Pietro, born of another marriage, had not been a member of the Siturgic for quite a long time. Andrea, scarcely twenty-five years old, had just been promoted chief engineer by special favor of MacHead Vohr, who had had his eye on the boy since the construction of the footbridge. He showed his interest in his brief reply.

"Right, Ferrati, you have already told me that. But you are wrong in thinking that your words have fallen on deaf ears."

He broke off, looked slowly around the meeting, coming back to the young chief engineer. "It is not the time yet, Ferrati. But that day will come. Until then, useless to speak of it. Don't be premature."

And brusquely, addressing the entire board:

"Gentlemen," he continued, "it is of very little importance to know who is discontented and why, and how; it is not even important to know whether or not anyone is. Or, at least, it is not important for you.

On the other hand, it is important for all of us to reduce to a normal figure the number of accidents or irregularities, which may be reported to me in the course of the fortnight to come. You are warned. I don't actually bring up the question of responsibility. It will be brought up at the next meeting if necessary. I wish that it may not be. It goes without saying that, if it is necessary, it will be done in all justice; never blindly. A leader is responsible only when the culprits he commands have escaped his vigilance. I have spoken. Gentlemen; the meeting is adjourned."

He rose first, and immediately the entire assembly followed suit.

Standing, he motioned ten or so of his assistants to remain; the four councilors, several of the directors, and the chief engineer who had spoken, Andrea Ferrati.

The crowd withdrew, however, without any noise other than the moving of chairs. Empty, the room seemed more enormous than ever. It was a reproduction, but on a triple scale, of the celebrated Hall of the Ambassadors in the Alhambra. Fountains, springing from basins at the side, which had been turned off during the council, suddenly began to play, spraying strong and invigorating perfumes, which permeated the room and drove out the stifling heat left behind by this crowd of one hundred and fifty men who had scarcely departed.

The doors were hardly closed when the Governor pointed his finger at the privy councilor.

"Ralph Athole," he said without preamble, "you did not say all you wanted to say."

The Scotchman with a nod of his head, agreed.

"Certainly not, Governor. Do you want a serious secret to become public property? The way to do it would be to confide in the one hundred and fifty good men who have just gone out of here. Do you think there are less than one hundred imbeciles among them, perfectly ready to gossip when it is vital to keep silent?"

MacHead Vohr agreed with him.

"That may be," said he, "but, at present, I think there are no more gossips here, certainly no imbeciles. So then, if you please, Athole, finish."

Ralph T. Athole brought the tips of his fingers together in a gesture habitual to him.

"Gladly, Governor," he said. "I spoke of discontent and you were incredulous. Not that discontent is unknown among your workmen. They are children and nothing else. The peculiarity of children is to get annoyed at the wrong things. But, until today, the output of the shops has never suffered as a result. And the actual change may surprise you, and with some reason. It is clear that we find ourselves confronted today with a new and unaccustomed situation. For one hundred and fifty executive departments numbering each one hundred shops, all to suffer the reaction of an access of bad temper, which has really no definite cause—this, I say, is unusual. It took one word of command and the intervention of an organization. This is what I am sure of. That is why I used the word conspiracy. I cannot give you details or exact information, but I am proceeding with an investigation which will throw some light on it for me. From this moment I am convinced that the key to the mystery lies in the Blocks."

"You don't think it's possible that there could be a general wearing out of the machinery?" asked the executive councilor.

It was Andrea Ferrati who interrupted him:

"In a few years, at the most," said he: and he did not hesitate to shrug his shoulders; "still," he added, "to reach that point it would be necessary for the technical service to have been worse than negligent in successive repairs."

"The councilor of the laboratories could give his opinion on that point," replied Just Bellecour, looking at the Governor.

"The councilor of the laboratories asked to be excused," said MacHead Vohr shortly, "but it is easy to telephone him."

The secretaries had withdrawn with the bulk of the assembly. The Governor unhooked the loud speaker himself. One of these hung on each of the cedar pillars encrusted with mother of pearl and ivory.

"Hello! The Tower?"

The reply came, audible to every ear:

"Hello! Who is speaking?"

Then followed a brief dialogue:

"I, MacHead Vohr. Is that you, George Torral?"

"Yes, Governor. I am working. Please pardon my absence."

"That is all right. I want to ask you a technical question."

"All right, go ahead."

"We have noticed, during the present fortnight, a perceptible increase in the number of accidents and irregularities that have occurred in operating the shops. Do you consider that there could be a technical cause for this?"

"No, I don't think so."

"Material wearing out?"

"No. The material is too new. Besides, mathematically, a new effect demands a new cause, Governor. A cause of a technical order would be an old cause. Useless then to look in that direction!"

"Then in what other direction?"

"That is not my business, Governor. Your material is not at fault. Take that as a fact. I am a technical councilor, I am not an executive councilor, nor a councilor on Home and Foreign Affairs."

The sound of a bell punctuated the sentence. George Torral had hung up his loud speaker. MacHead Vohr, deep in thought, followed suit.

"Well, Governor?"

The privy councilor had evidently interpreted the words of the technical councilor as a personal confirmation.

MacHead Vohr stood up and pulled his watch out of his vest pocket:

"Well!" he repeated, "it is eight o'clock—then, you are all free! Athole, make your investigations. Good evening, gentlemen."

A respectful silence was the only reply.

CHAPTER IV

Miss MacHead Vohr

THE moment she had returned from the drive, Miss MacHead Vohr had gone to her own apartments. The Governor's daughter occupied the Oriental wing of the first floor in the High Palace. There she had the equivalent of a princely mansion: dressing rooms, drawing-rooms, rooms for a great variety of purposes, all disguised in the fashion of half a dozen departed centuries. The bedroom, to give only one example, was Assyrian, and four winged bulls, of a splendid antique green, supported the bronze bed which was reached by mounting four steps. Besides, this was not the room, naturally a little bit fantastic, which the very expert and genuinely learned antiquary liked best of all. Miss MacHead Vohr preferred, and rightly so, her library, distinct from the official library of the High Palace, and a finer collection, although not so large. The Governor had collected thirty thousand volumes for his own use. Miss MacHead Vohr did not possess half that number. But the bibliophiles of New Orleans, even those of Boston, spoke with admiration of what all America and even Europe had called the Eva collection. The room which served as a shrine for all this library, was considerably more vast than was necessary, so that the books, admirably framed in a mediaeval setting—"period"—gave the appearance of wealthy chatelaines who transform their castles into museums. Besides the volumes that were dear to her, and not a few of which had been annotated in her handwriting, Miss MacHead Vohr had assembled in her library the elements of an old picture gallery that was not without merit. A well-directed light fell from high Gothic casement windows, and the corbelling of carved oak which formed a gallery from one end to the other of the immense bow with the rose window, was repeated outside in a double granite balcony, with a covered arcade. This balcony was an extension of the library, forming a kind of outdoor annex. Huge boxes of flowers and greens, placed everywhere, transformed it into a hanging garden. There Miss MacHead Vohr had seated herself before taking off her coat. Besides, perhaps this twilight of a newborn spring—it was still in the last days of March—was cool enough to necessitate a bit of covering if she were going to sit there, motionless, exposed to the chill of the evening mist.

The sun had set half an hour ago. In the west, the sky, reddened by the afterglow, was covered with a veil of mist that threw a smoky shadow over its purple. In the east the coming night was mounting the plain—a clear line of demarcation, divided, in the middle of the sky, the western splendor of mixed blue and emerald that was invading the eastern heavens.

A great calm had settled down over the earth, and the silence of evening reigned supreme.

As she passed along the bookshelves of old oak where her books slept so luxuriously, Miss MacHead Vohr had picked out a volume at random. Now, seated on her granite balcony, facing the magic of the heavens, half day, half night, she opened the volume haphazardly. It was a work written in French. And at the bottom of the page numbered 293, Miss MacHead Vohr read these singular lines:

Letter No. XXV, 1774,
Every moment of my life,
My dear, I suffer, I love you and I await you.

When she read this the Governor's daughter gave a start of evident surprise and put down the book. Then she went and leaned on the granite railing, facing the coming night, and, for a very long time, dreamed.

Undoubtedly the text she had read had accorded strangely with some one of her secret thoughts. In fact, what young girl will ever read three words of love without suddenly finding their echo within her own heart?

And it was doubtless this echo Miss MacHead Vohr had heard, and which had surprised her—unless a more secret or more particular coincidence might have provoked it. . . .

A light step on the mosaic parquetry. The very respectful voice of the chambermaid:

"Mademoiselle knows that it is quarter to eight? Which gown will Mademoiselle wear for dinner?"

"The ivory *crêpe de Chine*."

The reply had come promptly. The voice was not that of a woman in a dream. And yet, perhaps Miss MacHead Vohr had been dreaming—perhaps she was still dreaming. But she was a true daughter of the Wheat King. Her maids were not in the habit of knowing her private affairs, and she herself had never felt the need of confiding in a servant.

In the dressing room, vast as a diplomatic salon, four maids—two standing, one kneeling, one stooping —were folding and draping the material, the color of new straw, around her body.

Half undressed—gowns in 199—were still being worn very low, front and back, the shoulder and the right arm entirely free, while the fashion of skirts slit on the left was already coming into vogue—Miss Mac-Head Vohr looked unexpectedly different. An hour before, in her street gown, she had been a sportswoman, slender but muscular. At present, a woman of the world appeared, and the unbroken line of her pure arm was so harmonious that one dreaded a movement which might spoil it. Miss MacHead Vohr was tall and slender, lithe and supple. Though her face was as white as chalk, the skin at her breasts was like snow.

Nevertheless, as pale as Miss MacHead Vohr was, she did not appear any paler than she wanted to. Besides, although unmarried, she knew how to make up, but she only did it, with perfect taste, in the electric light which is less pitiless to subterfuges than the rays of the sun. Daughters of kings do not wait to be married before making use of the privileges of married women. And certainly MacHead Vohr ruled over too many people not to be more powerful than several kings.

Through the door of the dressing-room came the sound of a gong.

"Twenty-five minutes past eight?" asked Miss Mac-Head Vohr.

She was ready. The mirrors gave back a reflection which seemed to satisfy her.

"Twenty-five minutes past eight," confirmed the first chambermaid.

Ready to go down, Miss MacHead Vohr hesitated a second, half turned about, went back into her library, took up again the volume which she had opened the hour before, reopened it, reread one line of it—the same perhaps; then, without speaking or showing the slightest emotion, she left the room.

CHAPTER V

MacHead Vohr, Governor

MAC HEAD VOHR was waiting for his daughter in the small drawing-room. Two guests were with him; Ralph Athole, the councilor on Home and Foreign Affairs, and Andrea Ferrati, the chief engineer.

They were both talking, the one very stolidly, the other with some animation. And the Governor, silent, listened to them both.

It was Ralph Athole who spoke now, or rather who replied:

"No, my dear fellow, I have nothing yet. As simple, as elementary as an investigation like this may be, still you must have time to go, to see and to understand. Caesar himself took this time: *Veni, vidi*—I will know what goes on at the Blocks when my agents come back from there. The matter seems serious enough to me to exclude *a fortiori* telegraphs and telephones."

"Oh! Indeed?"

"That's very evident. Just think it over, Ferrati! You were indignant a little while ago, on account of the stupidity of the workmen and our helplessness against the increase of ill will which has just arisen, like an epidemic. Except for the indignation, a superfluous phenomenon, you were not wrong; we are impotent at this moment, that is a fact. Don't let us add the mistake of being imprudent; the result might prove very embarrassing."

"You don't think it is now?"

"No. Not yet. Don't you agree with me, Governor?"

Deferentially the Scotchman had turned toward MacHead Vohr. The latter silently nodded his head. In his turn, Ferrati turned towards him.

"Governor, it is the first time, however, that such a thing has happened, such a very extraordinary affair! The output of the fourteen hundred departments, of the entire fourteen hundred departments, dwindles all at once, in a single fortnight—the same day, you might as well say! This must be impossible, unless done by order! And this order itself would be such a senseless act!"

Athole smiled.

"Senseless from your point of view. From mine too, for that matter. But that is not the question. Evidently, we are in the presence of something new———"

MacHead Vohr lighted a cigarette. He nodded approval again. As he moved, the cigarette described a ring of blue smoke which rose slowly, horizontally.

Athole repeated:

"Of something new. That is a fact, too. But, personally, I have never found novelties annoying. Nevertheless, as far as this is concerned, let us hope that they stick to the first edition."

"That is your business. We can do nothing against the unexpected. But the moment the unexpected ceases to exist——"

"It *has* ceased," cut in MacHead Vohr, speaking for the first time.

The conversation became general.

"What seems to me the worst phase," Ferrati began again, "is the cause of the workmen's discontent—supposing that you are right, Mr. Athole, and that there is discontent. Not that I do not admit the hypothesis, since you admit it yourself! But I can't see the reason for this business at all——"

"Not at all?" repeated the Scotchman. "What I can't see at all is the reason for your incomprehension. Look, Ferrati, you are young, excuse me for reminding you of this in front of the Governor, but you already have three stars——"

Stars, embroidered on the black uniforms of the officers of the Siturgic, marked the difference in rank and position. The heads of the shops wore one star, the engineers two, the chief engineers three, the vice-presidents four and the councilors five. Only the Governor did not bear the mark of any insignia.

Ralph Athole continued:

"The reason for the discontent?"

He took three steps toward the opened arches. The small drawing-room, adjacent to the private dining-room, communicated with it by this arch.

"Ferrati, my dear fellow, just look over here. Come! a glance—just one—at that!"

His extended arm pointed to the table set for dinner.

The table was oval-shaped and small, set in the center of the immense octagonal room; a rectangle with rounded corners, thirty yards long, by twenty wide. Twelve openings, closed by as many plate-glass windows which went up or down by pressing one finger in their granite grooves, let in all the milky mystery of a night of full moon; the twilight had fled suddenly, as tropical twilights do. In order not to lose any of this exquisite half-light which flooded the room, not a chandelier, not a side bracket had been lighted; only the lamps on the table shone brightly: eighty-four branched candle-sticks, placed two by two to right and to left of each of the four dinner guests; thirty-two electric candles, shedding the full power of their golden light on the cloth alone, from under as many yellow silk shades embroidered in black and red Chinese characters. Not another light in the room. The table, all glittering with napery, glass, silver, bronze and gold, stood out from the semi-obscurity of the room as outside the moon from the almost starless firmament.

Andrea Ferrati had stepped forward.

"Well?" said he after looking at the table. "What am I supposed to see there?"

"By Jove! This and nothing else."

Stepping forward to the table, regardless of etiquette, Ralph Athole stretched out his forefinger and touched one of the four pyramids of fruit that decorated the cover.

They were two plates of melons, one green, the other

pink, and two plates of strawberries, the one white, the other crimson.

It must be remembered that, since 199-, fruit hothouses, although not yet so highly perfected as they are today,[1] had already made great strides toward much of our modern progress. In taste and beauty, the fruit of those days was nearly equal to ours. The melons offered on the table of the Governor, MacHead Vohr, were almost as small as in ancient times green gages or wild cherries; and the cultivators of fine fruits had been able to give them in perfume what they had taken from them in size. As for the strawberries, even in those days they were larger than the most enormous pineapples and only their skins, slightly toughened— in 199-, hothouse strawberries still had to be peeled— differentiated them from the strawberries that we eat at present.

Notice that, in 199-, hothouse fruits required much more care than was necessary afterwards. Choice soil, special manure, intricate hothouses heated by radium power—none of these things could be neglected in those days without running the risk of serious reverses.

Since then we have improved, that is to say, simplified the process. But, at that period, a giant strawberry or two dozen dwarf melons sold at a higher price than we could imagine now, after a century and a half has passed.

"This? You mean, this?" the chief engineer, Andrea Ferrati, had repeated, echoing the words of the privy councilor, Ralph Athole.

---

[1] "Useless Hands" is supposed to be written in the year 2130 or thereabouts.

His Italian eyes, alert and curious, widened as he looked at the fruit.

"This, of course," answered Athole. "This fruit—these melons, these strawberries—do you think they grow like this in the next best garden of any old workman? Do you think they eat melons like that at the Blocks? Do you think that, for the cost of the work of producing these, they could not have produced hundreds and hundreds of common fruits, coarse melons, wild strawberries? And do you think that a wily agitator could not make the people feel that we, their masters, eat melons that are too small and strawberries that are too large, while they, our subordinates, have not enough common strawberries and common melons to eat? The *'reason why'* of the discontentment, you ask? The *'reasons why'* you should rather have said! Well, there you have one of them, the first that comes to mind. If you like I can find you ten more. But, as for me, I don't bother about that: I don't care much about the *'reasons why'*! Only the *'how'* interests me—for I have just spoken of an agitator and as yet there is nothing which gives me the right to use that word. No matter, he who lives will see. To come back to your curiosity of a little while ago, never forget this then, my dear fellow; that a workman—manual laborer, understand!—don't forget that such a man is a child. Everything that flatters the child will flatter the workman. And in the same way that a child frankly envies everything he observes in the hands of grown-ups, the workman will envy, even more frankly, everything he will observe in the hands of his masters. I say everything, for the one as for the other: the child wants needles, pointed scissors and matches: the workman wants our wealth, our luxury, our authority and especially our leisure—that is to say, the leisure he imagines is ours: for, incapable of doing the things that I do and that you do, incapable even of understanding them, nay even of imagining them, the workman persuades himself that you and I do nothing."

"When it is he who does nothing," MacHead Vohr suddenly broke in with his harsh, cutting voice.

He had rejoined them. His tall figure stood out in bold relief against the brightly lighted frame of the opening.

He did not add a word of explanation. And it was Athole who vindicated the assertion.

"Without doubt, nothing; since what he does, a machine could do in his place, both better than he, more quickly, and more economically! By the way, Ferrati, what do you call those new machines you were talking about a while ago at the council?"

"Machine-hands."

"Well? I wager they don't eat any strawberries at all, neither big ones nor little ones, eh?"

Athole was laughing. Ferrati began to laugh too.

"By the way," continued Athole, "these machine-hands, just what are they?"

"A toy," replied Ferrati, "a toy destined to replace the human hand, to do all the manual labor of the men, and even to command, to start running, to regulate and to stop all the other machines actually in use. That's what they are for!"

"Pretty!" said Athole.

Ferrati explained:

"Imagine a clock-work mechanism controlling a transformation-starter. The apparatus once regulated perfects a certain movement, a certain act, to be more exact, a certain hammer blow, or this pressure, or that attachment, or this rotation during so and so long a period. Then a certain other act during another certain length of time, and so on in succession; in short, exactly the work of a human hand. There is nothing new in that. What is new, is the addition of a second mechanism called *reflexes;* and the result of this addition is the following: no matter what damage, no matter what disturbance may occur in the course of the work, the machine-hand receives a shock that the dynamometers measure, as much in strength as in direction and even in kind—other parts intervene then, and transform the shock received into restored effort—I will explain: an exaggerated resistance, for example, does not have the same effect as the blow of an unexpected shock. But each of them changes either the circulation, or the direction, or even the order of the successive durations of effort furnished by the machine. Briefly, the machine adds to its brute force a real intelligence. . . ."

"The intelligence"—approved the Scotchman—"of the man who invented it. And this is the machine-hand?"

"The machine-hand. It is not badly named."

"Quite right.   Recent invention?"

"Not so recent.   I saw the first one fully four or five years ago."

"However, it is not generally utilized that I know of, is it?"

"No, and I don't know why."

"But I know," said MacHead Vohr.

The other two looked at him.   He explained briefly:

"The machine-hands are not used because if they made use of them, no more workers would be used. One thing or the other: the two would be incompatible. I myself do not make use of my machine-hands because I have orders from Washington to utilize my workmen.   It is the same other places, evidently."

"But why such orders?" questioned Ferrati.

He was genuinely astonished.   Athole, smiling, considered him; and as MacHead Vohr did not reply, answered for the Governor:

"Because the workers are men, Ferrati, and because men must eat to live.   Therefore society is obliged to feed those who would not be able to feed themselves by their own efforts.   In feeding them, society hopes to obtain from them, in exchange, something that resembles work."

"That resembles it maybe, but that is not; since this pretended work is both burdensome and badly done— very badly done—a striking enough proof of that was given today!—and since several machines, which have already been invented, would do the same work better and at less cost; one hundred machine-hands would not be as expensive to feed as a single workman; and a single machine-hand, working, twenty-four hours a day in place of eight, would cut down the work of the laborers——"

"You forget the inevitable repairs——"

"No, for I do not forget illness either."

"And the initial cost of the machines?"

"A small matter. Besides, what about the initial cost of the laborer? To make a man, you must have, besides another man, the father, who does not count economically, a woman, who does count; the mother —this woman whether she works or not, must be fed until the day she gives birth to her child, and the son must be fed in his turn, free of charge, until he is grown up. Sum total: two useless mouths to be fed, one for twenty years, the other for sixteen. If my machine-hand were made of gold instead of steel, it would not be as expensive. And I don't have to provide it with a retired pension from the day it is no longer good for anything, up until the day it is pleased to die."

Athole, who was slightly shortsighted, adjusted his monocle in his eye to consider the chief engineer more attentively.

"Exact," he concluded after a while, "but harsh."

"Harsh?" exclaimed Ferrati in surprise.

Everything about the man evidenced his sincerity. He showed this somewhat naïvely:

"I don't see the harshness in all that. Are you thinking of the workmen? But I do them a service by proving that their hands have become useless in the present day and generation! They have brains, haven't they? Let them use them! I don't wish them any harm when I want them to adapt themselves to the age they live in!"

"And what if they cannot?"

"If they will not, you mean?"

"No. I mean what I say. What if they cannot?"

"They could do it, if they wanted to."

"Hm—you are young, forgive me for repeating this over and over. I believe on the contrary that if they could, they would do it. And they don't seem to want to——"

"Ah," said the Italian, disconcerted by the force of his reply—"Oh, well! Obviously, if they cannot——"

MacHead Vohr, Governor, turned towards the door at the rear; the soft rustle of a gown announced the presence of a woman—his daughter. However, he turned back to Athole and Ferrati:

"Gentlemen, if the laborers of today cannot adapt themselves to their era, it is so much the worse for them, but we ourselves can do nothing about it; above us as well as above them hovers the law of selection, and neither they nor we can avoid being ruled by it. Whoever does not adapt himself to his era is condemned by his era to die."

The words fell as sharp and incisive as the blade of a knife.

"In case of necessity," added the Governor after a pause, "the law would even compel us to carry out the sentence from which we would have neither the right nor the power to escape. So much the worse for those who are condemned; so much the worse also for the executioners; it is the fault neither of the one, nor of the other!"

The door opened.

"Besides, here is my daughter," finished MacHead Vohr—"my daughter to whom a little while ago I was telling a story in the same vein, as we were crossing the footbridge over the Eighth Mouth, this afternoon before the meeting of the Council. Good evening, my darling!"

Immediately the butler appeared in the doorway opposite the one by which Miss MacHead Vohr had entered. He announced dinner—in French, the official language—as the solemn booming of the dinner gong resounded through the house.

CHAPTER VI

HIGH PALACE, LOW PALACE

IT WAS a clear night in spring. The moon, almost at the full, rose in the eastern sky putting out the stars by its brilliance. And the night wind had not yet come up. The cool breeze of dusk had raised a soft, diaphanous mist from the ground which mingled, a milky cloud, with the lapis lazuli of the sky above.

The dark bulk of the High Palace stood out sharply against the sky. Below the turret—in which swung the belfry hammers—was the triple layer of high stories placed one on top of the other; the lower, Moorish at the rear—facing east—old French in front —facing west; the middle layer, Corinthian on one side, Ionic on the other; the top floor, wall flush on the court-yard, hypostyle Egyptian gallery overlooking the gardens and, on the two sides, a double sequence of Gothic arches. And this harlequinade, which by day was saved only by its sumptuous richness and its imposing size, appeared, in the moonlight, less extravagant and almost harmonious. It seemed to be nothing more than an immense palace—any palace at all—whose two hundred and fifty windows, all brilliantly illuminated, shed their radiance far into the night.

Now, whoever, turning his back on the High Palace,
on the Artificial Island, on the Residences, on the
Shops, and on the Blocks, had looked over toward the
Natural Island, beyond the watery boundary of the
Eighth Mouth, could not have failed to perceive, at
about ten miles more or less, and outlined clearly
against the milky horizon in the east, another mass,
almost as gigantic, the mass of another palace, this
one surmounted, not by a single turret, but by two
spired towers: the huge bulk of the Low Palace which
had formerly been the Governor's residence in the first
days of the Siturgic, and which, for ten years, had
been no more than a formidable pile of stones, utterly
deserted, waiting until Time, which plays swift havoc
with our modern architecture, should reduce this pile
of stone to a ruin majestic among the most majestic.
The Low Palace was square instead of being, like the
High Palace, shaped like a horseshoe; and all in the
Gothic style instead of being a mixture of all styles.
A third as vast as the other palace: and as the nineteenth century often is compared to the twentieth, more
mediocre, less barbarous. But at this hour there was
not a light in the place, in contrast to the brilliant
illumination of the High Palace. For, except for a
caretaker, an old man who always went to sleep at
nightfall, no one lived any more in the old dwelling
which had fallen into disfavor. And Miss MacHead
Vohr herself—carjng, it is true, about antiques, but
less recent antiques—scarcely ever deigned, so they
said, to honor the Low Palace with a visit.

Between the two Palaces, but nearer the living than the dead, a third building appeared, just as visible in the night, even if there had been no moon; an isolated tower called simply The Tower. For that matter it had nothing to do with the antennæ of the T. S. F. at whose base emerged the footbridge thrown across from the Belvedere on the Natural Bank. This other tower, of free-stones heavily cemented, seemed more like a building of bygone days than a modern construction. In those days the builders must have built more solidly than is the custom now; the isolated tower had been made with the purpose of sheltering the experimental and test laboratories of the Siturgic. And the chimneys of the councilor George Torral, the old Frenchman in charge of the laboratories, never stopped rumbling weekdays or Sundays; and the four round windows which opened higher than the highest loopholes, and from which George Torral's own apartment received light and air, outlined sharply their four well-lighted circles every night and all night long, from dusk to dawn. George Torral never slept at hours when everyone else sleeps. Therefore without any annoyance to him they had been able to place, high up in his Tower, a searchlight with a steady gleam, which made it easier for the cargo boats with wheat or the boats carrying bread to go out and come into the port at night or outside the limits of the Siturgic harbor.

Half past nine. The Governor and his two guests had just risen from the table. Before the wine of the Island was served, Miss MacHead Vohr, had, according to custom, preceded them to the drawing-room.

Before rejoining her, MacHead Vohr, Athole and Ferrati, cigars or cigarettes lighted, drew near one of the windows opening on the park. At the touch of the Governor's finger, the plate glass which enclosed this opening was lowered.

"A fine night, Governor!" said the privy councilor, taking a deep breath.

Intelligent in the extreme, therefore delicately voluptuous, Ralph Athole delighted in the deep nocturnal odors of the trees and flowers with which the High Palace was entirely surrounded, indeed, almost buried under, since the balconies and terraces were covered with hanging gardens.

"A fine night," agreed MacHead Vohr.

This man whose vital force dominated his whole intellect, tasted only the animal delight of purifying his lungs in the invigorating air of nearby shrubbery.

"A good night for an investigation!" declared Ferrati, speaking in his turn. "If it had rained, the human beasts down there would have crowded into their thirty story dens and your agents, Mr. Athole, would have had more difficulty in bringing you news in a little while——"

Athole considered him, as he often did, indulgently and ironically.

"You are very curious about that news, my dear fellow."

"I should say so!" exclaimed the other sincerely.

The Scotchman smiled.

"Come, come! patience—but at least you certainly don't pose as a man bored with the things of this world!"

His cigarette was half burnt out. He threw it away.

"Governor," he began after having looked towards the east for a while, "just see what a queer night it is— foggy, isn't it? And, yet, you can see so far!—Look, look down there—that is the Low Palace, those two black towers—down there, to the left of the tall cedars——"

A light dress had just appeared on the terrace.

Tired perhaps of waiting in the drawing-room, Miss MacHead Vohr had come out on the terrace, followed by two lackeys carrying a table, with coffee and liqueurs.

The men had their backs to her. No one had heard her enter.

They started as she spoke.

"Oh!" said she in surprise, lifting her lorgnettes, "oh! are you sure, Mr. Athole? The Low Palace, you say, that little dark speck down there?"

She took a cup of coffee from the table and offered it to the councilor.

"You will have this, won't you? Coffee?—And you really think that is the Low Palace?"

Athole took his cup and bowed.

"Yes, Miss MacHead Vohr, really. I'll wager it is quite a long time since you have been to the Low Palace!"

"Oh! I don't know when!" she replied carelessly.

CHAPTER VII

THE TOWER

"AND what is that?" continued Miss MacHead Vohr when she had served her father and their two guests, "that tall sinister thing, so black, that looks at us with its two red eyes?"

"That?" queried MacHead Vohr, replying in place of Athole. "Why, Eva, dearest, don't you know that is The Tower? That is where our laboratories are, and George Torral is there too, the councilor you used to be afraid of when you were a little girl. Those two red eyes in The Tower are George Torral's round windows."

"George Torral," laughed Miss MacHead Vohr, "still frightens me even now that I am big!"

And Ferrati spoke as if involuntarily:

"I feel almost like you, Miss MacHead Vohr! Councilor Torral frightens me too—certainly not because of his long white beard and his eye, redder, my word, than the eyes of his Tower, but because of his knowledge, which is really superhuman and supernatural. Never, never, never, was there such an engineer, I believe. At times, it seems quite clear to me that if George Torral had been born a hundred years earlier,

69

the science of mechanics, the science of all machines would have evolved a hundred years more quickly. And today we would be, not as we are, in 199-,—but as the world will be, about 209- ——."

Athole, who was lighting a second cigarette, turned towards Ferrati:

"Look here, tell me, Ferrati! How do you know him as well as that? He sees no one, no one ever sees him and the Governor has even given him permission to absent himself, one might say, permanently, from all the meetings of the Council——"

"Yes, I have," confirmed MacHead Vohr.

Ferrati shook his head.

"I know him, but I don't know him 'as well as that,' Mr. Athole. Our relations have always been on a business basis—never anything else. I saw him for the first time when I was working with my brother Pietro on the footbridge over the Mouth. We wanted to use selenium steel. As councilor of the laboratories Torral compelled us to use Martium steel. And, moreover, he was right. Since then I have seen him five or six times, not more."

"You thanked him, I suppose?"

Ferrati made a wry face:

"He does not like to be thanked, and he has a way of cutting short any amenities. This man seems to live in despair because the minutes in the day are too short. His watch never leaves his table. In his presence you don't feel like wasting words."

"After all," concluded Athole, "what is he working on day in and day out, all day long?"

MacHead Vohr furnished the reply:

"Useful matters of which no one but him ever dreams!"

At the top of The Tower George Torral's two red eyes gave out intermittent sparks.

CHAPTER VIII

Ten o'Clock at Night

DARKNESS hid from sight the clockhammers in the belfry! But, in the heavy silence, the strokes of the clock striking ten, iron against bronze, rang out louder and more vibrant than the hours ever sound in broad daylight.

MacHead Vohr retired early. Rarely did he stay up after ten o'clock. He was one of those fortunate men who fall asleep immediately and who never. feel more fit than at the moment of waking. The forms and ceremonials of the High Palace had been regulated accordingly. The Governor worked alone in the morning, with his own secretaries, from breakfast to tiffin; with his councils and commissions from tiffin until dinner. And, dinner over, the Governor did not do any more work, except in urgent or unforeseen cases.

To tell the truth, the present situation was unforeseen and might become urgent. Neither Athole nor Ferrati were surprised therefore when, the last stroke of ten having sounded, MacHead Vohr bade them good-night. They had drawn near together, ready to take their leave of the master. But the latter, with a sign, detained them, at the same time designating Miss

MacHead Vohr with a look that imposed silence. Miss MacHead Vohr, too, had drawn near; and she was surprised, not being in the secret.

However, it was not unusual for the Governor to detain one of his councilors beyond the usual hour, indeed even one of his vice-presidents, to talk shop with them. Therefore it was only Ferrati at whom Miss MacHead Vohr looked in surprise. Ferrati seemed to her a little young to take his part already in the state secrets of the Siturgic. And, if he had the honor to be invited to dine sometimes, rather frequently even, at the Governor's table, Miss MacHead Vohr had several reasons for believing that it was rather on her account and not for any ordinary reasons.

To speak plainly, Andrea Ferrati had never appeared insensible to the rare beauty of Eva MacHead Vohr. And the very discreet courtship which the young man had entered upon had not seemed to displease the Governor, who was too keenly alive to anything that concerned his daughter, not to have seen it all, thought the matter all over, and considered it from all sides.

The fact was that, in spite of her father's billions, Miss MacHead Vohr was nearly twenty-four years old and was not engaged. And her father did not want her to grow up an old maid. Andrea Ferrati was only chief engineer, and there were one hundred and fifty chief engineers in the Siturgic. But so much for the man, so much for the place. Andrea Ferrati was well under thirty, scarcely twenty-seven, and as a rule the third star was never won before a man reached forty. In addition he was the builder, one of the two builders at least, of the footbridge over the Eighth Mouth. MacHead Vohr considered him therefore a man with a marvelous future. And he had not been at all displeased to see this man look at Miss MacHead Vohr with evidently infatuated eyes.

Miss MacHead Vohr, about to retire, looked at Andrea Ferrati and Andrea Ferrati looked at Miss MacHead Vohr.

"I am going in," declared the young girl suddenly. "The night is cold. Do you live far from here, Mr. Ferrati? Wouldn't you like a car? It would be very easy."

Two limousines were in readiness in the courtyard, as was customary at the High Palace, every time the Governor entertained at dinner.

But Andrea, thanking her, declined the offer.

"I live quite near, Miss Eva!—And I would not miss walking home on such a clear night as this!"

"That is true, it is clear!" said the young girl as if to herself.

She turned her head towards the north. A breeze was rising, but as yet was barely perceptible. However, it had already cooled off the air, and Miss Mac-Head Vohr was the first to notice it. Ferrati, who was still looking at her, was astonished to see her frown slightly, as if this rising breeze had come to annoy or disturb her, although there seemed no reason why it should.

"You don't like wind, Miss Eva!" He could not prevent himself from thinking aloud.

She gave him a swift glance, which surprised him even more: what he had said could not have offended her, no matter what she might think. But no, she was already replying, very gaily:

"Oh! of course, I don't like the wind, especially when it blows in the faces of my friends, who have to go back to their cottages all alone, on such a wretched, chilly night——"

"All alone?" replied the young man, laughing in his turn. "And why, all alone? It is up to you, Miss Eva, if you wish to accompany these friends you pity!"

She laughed louder than he:

"And who would come back with me, in my turn?"

"Why, your auto which would follow you!"

"Well!" she said after a moment's hesitation—but so slight that he could scarcely notice it—"Oh, well! I do not say no! and the first time you come to dinner I shall promise to take you back to your door—not today, by the way, I am too tired to gad about——"

A feeling of keen joy stirred Andrea's heart. To speak frankly he was not actually in love with Miss MacHead Vohr, but he found her infinitely pretty and seductive, and the slightest attention from her delicately flattered his vanity as man and as male. More than that, he thought of her often, too often perhaps to be wise. So much the more so because he had never received a definite impression of pleasing her. The words she had just given him—and in a more than friendly tone, even affectionate perhaps—therefore marked a progress as definite as it was unexpected. A fatuous man might even have taken it for a promise. In the States, to be sure, a girl calls on a man and no one thinks anything of it; but not two hours before midnight and not when the girl is the daughter of the President or of the Governor of the Siturgic!

Delighted, but taken unawares and vaguely embarrassed how to answer, Andrea Ferrati kept silent, then quite seriously held out both his hands to Miss Mac-Head Vohr, who, without the slightest hesitation, this time, put both her hands in his:

"A promise signed and sealed!" she said, still laughing.

Ferrati looked at her with an emotion which he had not stimulated.

"You are good and kind!" he said.

She shook their four hands linked together:

"You are good and kind, too, Andrea!—and then, you do not love me and I am glad of that—because then I can like you very much, frankly and unreservedly——"

In themselves words like "you do not love me, I am glad," are not words to satisfy a lover. But what woman says anything else, even when she does not believe it? Andrea Ferrati was of pure Italian blood. His ancestors' greatest deeds of prowess had been to court woman, to force her refusal, to conquer her modesty, to outplay her ruses and to understand yes every time

she said no. Blood will tell. Andrea Ferrati, having
decided only a minute earlier to try his luck with Eva
MacHead Vohr, smiled at what he could only take as
the first feint of an adversary with whom one has
crossed swords.

He was overconfident in the same way, so much the
less sincere, at present, because he had been all the
more so a little while ago.

"Unreservedly, of course!" he affirmed. "But you
are quite right: the promise is registered and the door
of my cottage awaits your coming."

"Agreed!" said Miss MacHead Vohr.

She lifted her face to the Governor for a kiss, then
gave her hand to Ralph Athole. After that, coming
back to Andrea:

"Good night to you too, Andrea! But oh! yes! that's
so! you are going to cross with me, aren't you!"

To leave the High Palace it was necessary to cross
the full length of the building; the only night gate
opened opposite the great courtyards.

"No," replied Ferrati, embarrassed. "I'm not going
over yet——"

She was surprised.

"Is the Governor keeping you in a secret session?"

He hesitated; then judging that it was better to tell
a lie than to betray the secret about which, besides, he
had not been advised.

"In secret session, no," said he, "but, however, he
is keeping Mr. Athole and me——"

"Long?"

"A quarter of an hour or two at the most, I imagine. We are expecting some news."

"Some news?"

"Oh! nothing interesting, just some news from down there, from the Blocks——"

"From the Blocks?"

Miss MacHead Vohr gave a slight start.

She gained control of herself immediately, and said, very lazily:

"Not very interesting indeed, your news! I will leave you now. I am sleepy. Good night, Mr. Ferrati!"

She went away, walking slowly.

CHAPTER IX

Eleven o'Clock

IN THE dressing-room were waiting, in addition to the four maid servants, the lady's maid and the reader.

Miss MacHead Vohr, at that end of the twentieth century, retired almost as regally as the royal princesses of Louis XIV at the end of the seventeenth century.

When she entr red the room, all the "attendants" gathered about her.

"Mademoiselle is tired," said the lady's maid with a keen glance.

She alone allowed herself liberties, respectful ones for that matter: but as her mistress did not reply, she did not insist and departed into the bathroom to prepare the evening ablutions, while the maid servants followed Miss MacHead Vohr into the Assyrian room.

The reader followed also. But, passing before the bookshelves, she stopped:

"What does Mademoiselle wish to read? I noticed that Mademoiselle had picked up the *Lettres de Lespinasse* a little while ago—what will Mademoiselle have?"

"Nothing. You may go to bed right away, Sophie."

Sophie protested. She was a Parisian and openly proud of it, but her English showed scarcely any traces of French accent. Moreover she read with expression and taste.

"I am not the least bit tired, Mademoiselle! And I can stay, in case Mademoiselle might change her mind——"

But Miss MacHead Vohr seldom changed her mind and did not like to repeat her sentences. She cut her off, dryly:

"You may stay, of course, since that is among your duties. But you must not, since I wish the contrary. Leave me now. That will do."

Without a word the reader disappeared.

"The bath is ready," announced the lady's maid.

Miss MacHead Vohr stepped out of her dress, which had fallen to the floor around her feet, then shook off her antelope slippers, and stretched out her foot towards her mules gilded with little pincers. This style had just been resurrected after some twenty-five centuries; they had not gilded shoes, in the fashion in which they gild books, since the passing of the elegance of Egypt and Phrygia; neither the Rome of Augustus Caesar nor the France of Louis IX had known this art.

The chemise fell, as the dress had fallen, not without some difficulty: Miss MacHead Vohr, undressed, was no longer a very fashionable woman of the world, nor a muscular scrawny tennis player, but a beautiful antique body perfectly modeled, and typically feminine;

the rounding thighs were much heavier than the shoulders which were more sloping than square. The general appearance was very delicate, but very feminine; more woman perhaps than girl; in any case, infinitely young.

The first maid servant held out the negligée, a Moroccan bournous of a stuff more transparent than any linen. Enveloped from head to heels like a nun, Miss MacHead Vohr went towards the large fountain from Languedoc, which was her bathtub and in which the rose and blue tints seemed to float under the mobile transparency of the water.

Having bathed, dried, reclothed in a black and gold Chinese robe, Miss MacHead Vohr returned to the Assyrian bedroom and, on the threshold, dismissed her attendants. One, the lady's maid, went in ahead of her mistress, to see if the bed covering was properly arranged, if the curtains had been closed, the windows opened. Miss MacHead Vohr always slept with her windows opened wide.

She sat down in an easy chair while the lady's maid was bustling about, silent and alert. The skins on the hardwood floor deadened the sound of her steps.

When she had finished the nocturnal rite, the servant came to her mistress and dropped a curtsey:

"Mademoiselle does not wish anything more? She does not want any one?"

"No."

"I wish Mademoiselle a good night."

"Good night."

And the lady's maid went out.

A long time passed. Miss MacHead Vohr had not gone to bed. She still sat motionless, huddled deep in her easy chair, lazily stretched out.

In front of her, a little clock standing on the night table was beating a light tick-tock, second after second. And it seemed that Miss MacHead Vohr had eyes for nothing else but this little clock, as if the day had not come to an end, as if there remained still some little thing to do before going to bed and to sleep.

It was long past eleven. On the platinum dial the hands of yellow gold and steel blue were moving very slowly.

Suddenly the clock struck, solemnly, and as if from a great distance; the silver hammer beat against a bronze spring in the form of a spiral. Eleven, first, then, in a different tone, three double blows: quarter to twelve.

Then Miss MacHead Vohr arose from her easy chair.

But, instead of going towards her bed, she went towards one of the Assyrian pillars which supported the intercrossed cornices of the ceiling, and from a telephone low speaker which hung there, unhooked the two receivers.

CHAPTER X

MIDNIGHT

MISS MacHEAD VOHR spoke softly into the telephone. And the telephone made so little noise that one would have had to hold one of the receivers in order to hear the replies that came over the wire. But Miss MacHead Vohr held both of them herself.

And this is what she was saying:

"Is this Boris at the phone?"

— — —

"Ah! I recognize your voice now. Ready?"

— — —

"Where is the car?"

— — —

"No, not necessary."

— — —

"Yes. Don't go away, wait for me."

She had hung up the receivers. She went straight to one of the neighboring pillars, ran her hand along until she felt a spring, which she pressed and the pillar opened.

It was nothing but a secret wardrobe. Miss Mac-Head Vohr took from it something surprising for the lateness of the hour and the type of woman she was;

a gown of brown cloth held in at the ankles; a heavy woolen coat lined with fur, a kind of fur bonnet too, but fur outside ⸴ which fastened under the chin with two straps of heavy knotted silk.

Having closed the wardrobe Miss MacHead Vohr, without the help of her lady's maid and her assistants, put on the clothes she had taken out.

She dressed quickly, more quickly than her maids had dressed her earlier in the evening. In place of the gilded slippers she wore low-heeled, laced shoes, and her little hands disappeared in great gauntlets.

When finally ready, she went first to the two doors of her bedroom which she locked one after the other carefully. For that matter, no one could tell, not even the Governor himself, that his daughter was not at home, sleeping soundly.

Then Miss MacHead Vohr walked towards a pillar symmetrical with the pillar containing the secret wardrobe, hunted again and pressed a spring similar to the other. As before, the pillar swung open, discovering this time, not a wardrobe, but a spiral staircase which led to the ground floor of the Palace.

Just as she was about to go down, the girl hesitated suddenly, as if struck unexpectedly by a thought. She had her foot already on the first step of the spiral staircase. She changed her mind, turned half about and, returning to one of the windows, opened behind closed blinds, she slipped behind it, passing noiselessly from the bedroom to the outside balcony which over-

looked the park: the Assyrian room opened on the rear
façade of the High Palace.

The moon, almost at the full, lighted up this façade
quite plainly. Miss MacHead Vohr seemed annoyed at
this. Undecidedly, she looked around her. The left
corner of the balcony offered a square of shadow, narrow but grateful just the same to anyone who did not
want to be seen from outside. But certainly, the
daughter of the Governor of the Siturgic had no reason
for concealing herself. And yet, it was in this obscure
corner that Miss MacHead Vohr hid herself after having stooped lower than the stone railing, to pass from
right to left on the balcony. Straightening up and
leaning on her elbow over the railing as if suspended
in the silent night, she neither moved nor breathed for
some time.

She gazed at the park spread out under her eyes,
and visible for quite a distance, for the High Palace
justified its name in more than one sense, and the balconies of the first floor looked down upon the highest
shrubbery round about. The great marble terrace lay
bathed in moonlight, white as milk; white too the mirror
of the great fountains, whose jets of water, lessened
every evening, wept gently without disturbing the immobility of the clear sheet where the reflection of the
trees was sharply outlined in grotesque shadows!

A cat could not have crossed the greensward, almost
as white as the fountains, without being seen for a
quarter of a mile. But there was neither cat nor man

in sight. The park was deserted. Miss MacHead
Vohr stood up, ready to leave the balcony.

At this moment the sound of a voice speaking fairly
low rose from the ground to the balcony, a voice was
murmuring:

"Mr. Athole, your airman doesn't come back from
the Blocks very often."

And Miss MacHead Vohr recognized the voice of
Andrea Ferrati.

MacHead Vohr, Athole and Ferrati had not gone in.
The Governor had sent for some overcoats. All three,
muffled up to the ears, comfortably braved the night
cold and the wind, which was beginning to blow up
briskly. They were seated in front of the very windows of the dining-room, but near enough to the Palace
to be sheltered by it, although the moonlight shone
above them. Miss MacHead Vohr had at first thought
that the chairs were empty.

She listened now, invisible and secretive as a spy.

Athole was answering Ferrati:

"My dear fellow, you don't appreciate how difficult
it is for an agent forced to be extremely cautious—
if he is to avoid being caught—to have in five minutes,
I don't say some bit of information or other, but even
what you expect from him: and I am not talking about
information easy to obtain, like the announcement or
the explanation of a very simple fact, which is common
property; but the key to a mystery, which you yourself have qualified as extraordinary, and which indi-

cates more than probably, on the side of the adversary, a strong and mysterious organization, with a carefully guarded secret. Not only am I not surprised that we have no news yet, at this hour, but when the news comes, I do not expect to receive very full or detailed information."

A silence followed.

A few minutes later, Miss MacHead Vohr, suddenly rousing from her immobility, raised her head sharply and appeared to be listening to something other than the voices below her.

A sound had just arisen, imperceptible, already musical, however, and too well known for anyone to be mistaken about it; the sound of an airplane about to land and descending from higher altitudes towards the earth.

Airplanes were not frequent in the landing places of the Siturgic. Ten or twelve made up the very mediocre fleet belonging to the Governor, who, like the majority of men of his age, only used aerial vehicles for his trips of some distance and habitually preferred his motor cars or his yachts. Miss MacHead Vohr was too fond of horses to enjoy gasoline motors, although she was an adept at flying like all the girls of her age and of her class. And following the lead of the Governor and his daughter, few of the engineers of the Siturgic took much interest in aviation. The work in the shops naturally did not require any kind of aerial transportation. The terrace of the High Palace had not even been arranged as a flying field and landing place. As a result the few airplanes forced to land in this neighborhood had no other choice than to come down on one of the greenswards that joined the palace with the park.

That was therefore what the airplane, which was approaching, was going to do, if it was really the one Miss MacHead Vohr supposed it to be—the one which her father, with Athole and Ferrati, was waiting for. And that is just what it did. For, at the same moment, the whirring noise grew rapidly louder, and Miss MacHead Vohr perceived distinctly the three pilot lights of the apparatus; a white glow-worm, between two colored glow-worms; the green on the left, the red on the right. It was clear that the airplane was coming straight ahead, pointing downwards. The noise of the propellers ceased abruptly when it stopped about two miles away: the pilot was driving ruthlessly like a man in great haste. Miss MacHead Vohr was better aware of this when she heard the furious throbbing of the motors, suddenly reversed and running backwards at full speed. She had just time to throw herself back; the aviator had turned on his searchlight. The dangerous proximity of the Palace, against which the airplane had crashed, at the same time prevented pilot and passengers—two men occupied the cabin cockpit—from catching sight of the young girl huddled down on her balcony.

The projector went out all of a sudden. The airplane landed thirty feet from the terrace, more or less. In the darkness, blacker after the dazzling searchlight,

Miss MacHead Vohr could scarcely make out a brown shadow; one of the arrivals who jumped out of the carline, and three other shadows, the Governor and his guests who had come to meet the man who had jumped.

All four having met, stood still an instant, conversed in low tones, then came back towards the Palace, went in and disappeared from sight.

As they came up the great steps, Miss MacHead Vohr heard the voice of the newcomer, though the words were of little importance:

"Yes, Governor," this man was saying, "it is exactly as Mr. Athole thought; a man who remains in hiding and who is in command——"

The secret door was closed again, and the hollow pillar assumed its appearance of solidity. Miss Mac-Head Vohr had left the Assyrian room. And no one in the palace would ever have guessed where she was.

She was going down the winding staircase—a comfortable staircase thickly carpeted; velvet from Scutari on the walls; a luminous banister to light the steps, which were steep . . .

At the foot lay an octagonal room, narrow but comfortable, with two doors facing each other and several peep holes well distributed; the staircase ended in the massive part of one of the corner pillars, which separated the Moorish *salons* from the French drawing-rooms on the ground floor.

At the moment, reception rooms and halls were deserted. Miss MacHead Vohr nevertheless put out all the light in the staircase before opening the doors at the foot. She shut them, then went away, walking boldly but without making a noise, and omitting no precautions to avoid leaving any traces of her strange nocturnal journey. The door of the staircase, at the foot as well as at the top, had been carefully concealed. Not a slit appeared and the peep-holes, tucked away in the cornices of the capital, were very inconspicuous.

Miss MacHead Vohr crossed the Moorish room which, copied from the room in the Alhambra called the *salle des Ambassadeurs*, gave directly, without any windowpane or door, on the arcaded cloister which was raised above the great court. The porphyry pavement glistened in the moonlight. Miss MacHead Vohr was careful not to cross it; instead she followed the arcades to the end of the horseshoe and to the North angle of the Palace.

One of the two limousines in readiness for the guests had just drawn up at this corner opposite the half circle of the steps. There was no sign of a chauffeur near, which surprised her. Then suddenly remembering something, she put her hands to her forehead.

"That's true!" she murmured.

A telephone box stood at each corner of the palace. Miss MacHead Vohr went to the northern box. A man was waiting there, the receiver to his ear. Miss MacHead Vohr called him:

"Boris!"

The man jumped, and turned.

"Oh! Miss?—you told me not to leave——"

"I had forgotten all about it. Come, let us be off, quick! Come on now!"

"At your orders, Miss!"

"Don't make any noise!"

"No noise, certainly not."

Already the wheels were turning——

"Low Palace, Miss?"

"Low Palace."

The ten miles separating the two palaces were covered in four minutes. The road was in a direct line. The auto shot along it like a cannonball.

Scarcely had they come to a stop when Miss Mac-Head Vohr jumped to the ground. She took hardly time to call back her orders over her shoulder.

"Go back! And be here again in four hours——"

"I know!" said the man, who was already turning his car. He added, as he shifted gears: "Miss Eva knows she can count on Boris."

"She knows that."

It was clear, from the tone in which this was said, that Miss MacHead Vohr was very sure indeed that she could count on Boris.

The motor car started off and was swallowed up in the night. On the threshold of the old, deserted palace, Miss MacHead Vohr was left alone!

Seen from close by, the Low Palace took on the aspect of a cathedral. It was Gothic from top to bottom and two wings lengthened its two tall towers.

From one wing to the other, and from the foundations to the roof, the palace was a mass of arches, rose windows, gargoyled buttresses! The black obscurity of all this, where not a stump of a candle sputtered, added to the ecclesiastical illusion.

The lodge of the solitary caretaker was close by the main entrance. It was not in front of that entrance, a monumental gate with triple arch, that Boris's car had deposited Miss MacHead Vohr, but rather at one of the side postern gates, giving access formerly to the serving-quarters of the palace. Miss MacHead Vohr had the key to this gate, a modern key about as big as a pin, which contrasted amusingly with the mediaeval hasp, of massive oak, and all studded with nails. Such a door as this seemed to have been closed for centuries. But it turned on its hinges without the slightest creak.

Arrived in the courtyard, the visitor was satisfied to find her way by means of a pocket-light, which she fearfully lighted only at intervals as a soldier would who was risking his life in the blackness of a trench or in a suspected ambush. The way was fairly long, however, and very complicated. Room after room, staircase after staircase Miss MacHead Vohr walked and climbed for at least five minutes, before coming out in the open air, on the very broad platform which connected the North Tower with the South Tower at the level of the roofs.

There, well-sheltered as much from wind as from prying eyes—except for the birds no one could see the platform hidden on all sides by its balustrades as high as walls—an airplane without a pilot was waiting.

A small airplane it was; a monoplane, an eleven-foot-six wing spread, a single seat, four hundred horse-power; the unpolished steel wings did not give out a reflection. Even the glass of the cabin, annealed and tempered, scarcely shone. A bashful, retiring little airplane, if there ever was one.

It was in good running order. Miss MacHead Vohr knew this. Expert aviatrix, she made quick work of finding out whether there was enough gas and whether the engine was hitting on all cylinders. And, suddenly, without superfluous preparation, she got into the cock-pit, fastened the hood, tried out the controls, tested the engine, gave it gas, adjusted the spark, threw the clutch in.

With a single bound the machine crossed the entire platform, leaped into space, soared and rose, heading north.

A heavy gale shook it in full flight, rocking it in a long roll. The aerial currents were getting stronger. The wind from the north was blowing up, colder every minute.

PART II

The Arms

CHAPTER I

The Other Side

O F THE twenty stories in Block 216, nineteen were sleeping, all windows dark.

The City of Workmen was composed of six hundred and twenty blocks divided into two sections, a fair distance from each other, for the Eighth Mouth, which was quite broad near the juncture, flowed between them. Only three tunnels—the shortest at least two miles long—separated the East Blocks from the West Blocks. And in spite of the fact that the government had established a free tram car service between the two banks, the workmen from the East seldom mingled with the workmen from the West, and vice versa. For that matter each of the two sections was a regular city in itself: the East Blocks—on the Natural Island—numbered in the neighborhood of one hundred and ten thousand inhabitants, men, women, old people and children; and the West Blocks—on the Artificial Island—almost two hundred and fifty thousand. This entire population of three hundred and sixty thousand human beings included nearly one hundred and sixty thousand women, but only forty thousand children. Americans are not at all prolific; and, although legitimacy

was obligatory among the Siturgic laborers,—concubin-
age was forbidden by law, and unmarried women in-
variably classed under the category of prostitutes—
those households officially blessed by priests or pastors
were rarely so, in the Biblical sense, by the Lord.

Six hundred and twenty blocks, three hundred and
sixty thousand souls! Nearly six hundred inhabitants
to a twenty-story house—thirty to the "square" to
use the slang term in vogue in the Blocks.

And these thirty inhabitants represented a dozen
households, or ten flats, five in a row on either side of
the corridor. Ten flats, all identically alike: each one
having three rooms—sitting-room, bedroom, kitchen;
four windows; steam heat, electricity, passenger elevators, freight elevators; in short, necessities and com-
fort, without luxury. The walls were uniformly covered with tiles. The administration had tried to min-
gle the maximum of hygiene with an attempt at elegance. But the workmen, rebellious as ever to any
innovation whatever that their rulers offered, did not
think very much of these bright, clean walls, to which
they attributed all the bronchitis and colds in the head
that Winter brought to the Blocks, and they generally
re-covered the walls either with calcimine or with cheap
cotton cloth, both nests for microbes and germs. The
floors, too, made of reinforced quartz, spotless, easy
to keep clean and agreeably warm to the feet—for
vapor-heating pipes ran between ceilings and floors—
were generally despised and laughed at; and there was

not a workman who would not have felt disgraced if he had not squandered his salary buying horrible moquette carpets or linoleum that promptly went to pieces, for the climate of the Delta had never erred on the side of too much dryness. All things considered, the laborers' flats, as in almost all laborers' quarters everywhere, for that matter, should have seemed really quite pretty and pleasing to their prospective tenants. But constraint always engenders revolt. Because they were obliged to live in them, the workmen did not like the flats: because forced on them, tiles and quartz were detested. And because the "boss" had wanted cleanliness, simplicity and good taste, throughout the city a spirit of rebellion arose, bent on establishing pretentious ugliness and cheap, imitation wealth.

This is the way men are—all men! And the moralist who waxes indignant over this state of affairs and the Utopian who tries to ameliorate the trials of humanity are, to be quite frank, nothing but two foolish children.

The luminous hands on the electric clocks at the squares pointed to eleven. The moving picture houses had closed an hour ago—as the law decreed. The bars, also.[1] Only the houses of ill-fame were still open. For there were some, in spite of the police, and although the minions of the law were very severe. Needless to say these houses were hidden away well out of sight.

---

[1] The author is of the opinion that before 199- the prohibition laws in the United States of America will have been repealed.

They did not add to the life of the town, which at this hour was almost dead.   Eleven o'clock at the Blocks was bedtime hour.

And the occupants of nineteen of the twenty stories in Block 216 were asleep; consequently all lights were out.

Block 216 was one of the West Blocks, located at the corner of Fourteenth and Third Streets.   Third Street did not extend beyond this corner, and Fourteenth Street, farther on, ended in a dock on account of a bend in the river; so that Block 216 faced on the river front.   There were only four windows of this front which still showed bright spots in the midst of the enormous sooty rectangle, standing out straight against a slate and pastel-colored sky.   Four windows, one flat—only one!   Four spots of light high up in the air, four windows on the twentieth floor!   The twentieth floor in the Blocks had the use of terraces which took the place of roofs throughout the entire city.   These terraces, converted into gardens, in imitation of the terraces at the High Palace, and at the greater number of the engineers' and foremen's homes, should have been charming places to frequent in good weather. But they were the common property of the ten tenants on the twentieth floor of each building, and not one of the ten ever took the trouble to work them, nor to spend any money on them, with the result that not one of the six hundred and twenty blocks was shaded by a single tree.   Scorched by the sun or frozen by an icy wind, the six hundred and twenty terraces were like so many desert wastes, and except in very rare cases, a workman never even went up on them to enjoy a breath of purer air.

These terraces were simply concrete platforms, twelve yards wide by twenty long. Their parapets were nothing but iron hand rails which could easily be taken down to transform the terrace into a landing place for airplanes. So far no one had bothered to do this, for airplanes were much scarcer at the Blocks than at the Palace or at the Residences.

Four lighted windows! A flat—living-room, bedroom and kitchen! In the kitchen, a samovar was boiling on the gas heater. In the living-room three men around a white wooden table were writing silently. And through the half-opened door the bedroom could be seen, attractively arranged and more sumptuous than laborers' bedrooms usually are. An embroidered silk shawl covered the low, wide bed; some water-colors decorated the walls, bouquets of roses were stuck in large Chinese vases, modern in style, but very beautiful: and last of all the moquette carpet—there was a carpet, as the fashion among the workingmen called for— was hidden under large Oriental rugs with bright, soft colorings of gaily flowered meadows. The living room, on the other hand, made not the slightest pretention to elegance. The single red Turkish shawl—worn, spotted and greasy—that covered the wall from ceiling to floor, showed a carelessness so noticeable that it appeared deliberate. To give just one detail—it really seemed as if the green cloth on the pine table was put there only to show off its holes, broad and all run together so that no one could help seeing them. The man who kept such a cloth would never be content with being a workman—supposing that he really were one; he was making an effort to appear one; more than that he wanted everyone to know that he was one.

This man, the owner of the flat, of the entire flat in which he lived alone, was there in the room. The two other men who were seated beside him writing were only his guests—his secretaries, to be exact; secretaries appointed and paid: for this man who pretended to be, who proclaimed himself a workman, and who boasted of being one, was nevertheless a kind of boss who employed a personnel and engaged men on salaries. And this man, in love with liberty, nay even with license, in love with equality, nay even with Utopia, because it was necessary, because the end justified the means— this man deprived other men of their liberty by dominating their wills, and violated equality by ruling other men as harshly as master ever ruled slaves. And all this was done besides in good faith and with a great and generous intention. For this man was neither a charlatan, nor a fool, nor a rogue. On the contrary: what an intelligence, and a vast if not a sound one; a heart, and a warm one, although fantastic. Besides, what warm heart could ever withstand the eternal seduction of chimeras? And last of all, a will, headlong and brutal, but powerful! Moreover, he was a scientist who had already made a name for himself, before he had found "his road to Damascus," before he had changed his social class, and had passed from ruling to being one of those whom others try to rule, willy nilly, in short, before leaving his career of engineer for that of a laborer. That was three years before. At that time this man, scarcely out of college, had built, with the help of a younger brother (a man not so clever as he), the footbridge over the Eighth Mouth. For this man was Pietro Ferrati; and although they had not had the same mother, he and Andrea Ferrati had had the same father.

Now it was he, of all men, Pietro Ferrati, less a workman than an agitator of workmen, who had begun, fifteen or twenty days before, secretly stirring up the entire force of the Siturgic. And it was he, Pietro Ferrati—hidden power ranged silently against the open power of Governor MacHead Vohr, with his work and his billions—it was he, Pietro Ferrati, who, declaring war against the Wheat King and the social world he represented, had, with his first hostile gesture, lowered the production of the fourteen thousand three hundred and thirty-six flour, grist, dough, biscuit and pastry factories—of all these fourteen thousand three hundred and thirty-six shops charged with kneading and baking the bread for all the three Americas, for the entire American continent.

CHAPTER II

SPARTACUS

SEATED at his white wooden table covered with what was more a green rag than a cloth, in the middle of his living-room which he had deliberately made ugly and sordid, he was busy writing—and dictating as he wrote—dictating to right and to left. He was tremendously vain—a little childishly so—of this unusual faculty he had of applying his intelligence and his attention to three different objects at one time. There was much of the child in him. Of the savage, too. After all it was a primitive trick to try and flatter the people he was leading by a show of poverty and coarseness equal to the most abject poverty and the grossest coarseness among the real people. But it was a trick, for that matter, which succeeded admirably. To conquer the proletariat it is not a good thing—it is even harmful—to be too much of a psychologist and too clever a one. With them, open artifices are the most successful. Pietro Ferrati was so convinced of this that he did not trouble to shut his bedroom door, disdainfully allowing his secretaries to mark the contrast between the dainty luxury with which he liked to surround himself and the vulgar ugliness he affected

104

to prefer for this room which was his public office, his reception room and his study all in one.

At this moment he was hurrying through his work, restless and nervous. The secretary on the right was taking down in shorthand an outline for a popular speech, sketched rather than prepared; enough to provide a theme for some second-rate orator, clever at reeling off words, but incapable, without help, of putting ideas behind the words. All orators have this defect, or at least almost all. They are like the people themselves—strong when it comes to overthrowing the social edifice with verbal blows, but weak afterwards, when it is a question of having ideas and deeds to build up anew on the site of the old order they have destroyed. The secretary on the left was taking down another speech, but this one was different, and remarkably concrete. Had they heard it, MacHead Vohr, Athole and Ferrati would undoubtedly have understood better that these men had not carried out the secret processes which can infallibly weaken the output of an old-fashioned type of factory, where, lacking mechanical hands, human hands still had charge of the principal machines, motors or generators.

Finally, Pietro Ferrati himself was comparing the piles of loose leaves with the account lists. The heads of the Siturgic would also have profited by looking over these lists. And the secret information of Ralph T. Athole, councilor on Home and Foreign Affairs (Home chiefly) was scanty compared with that which had been inscribed here in these big notebooks bound in brown

cloth. Pietro Ferrati took them one after the other,
filled them out, annotated them with notes taken from
a huge pile of penciled slips of paper spread out in
front of him. There were fourteen lists, each one
representing a department of ten groupings, or one
hundred groups, or about one thousand shops, or ten
or twelve thousand workmen. There was a long list
of names, the majority with a mark after them. Ralph
Athole, privy councilor; Just Bellecour, executive councilor, and above all, MacHead Vohr, Governor, were
justified in believing that they knew their personnel.
But the fact was they knew much less about it than
Pietro Ferrati, delegate from the Council of the Order
of Anarchy to the working people of the Siturgic, and
leader of and ruler over all these men more or less
affiliated with the gigantic organization of systematic
disorders with a view to getting revenge for the people's claims; master of their wills voluntarily yielded
up, leader of their probable and approaching rebellions,
invested with full power over them, and charged to
lead them from peace to war, and from war to victory!

To victory——!

In ancient times there was a man named Spartacus
—a great man. In those days, just as today, there
were rulers and slaves. And perhaps there was less
reason than at present for such a condition to exist.
The rulers, of course, oppressed the slaves, tyrannized
over them, even tortured and killed them, at their
pleasure. Now one day Spartacus appeared. He
broke the slaves' chains, armed them, disciplined them

and flung their army, he himself marching at their head, against the army of rulers. Since that time the name of Spartacus has been immortal among all men in the world who are slaves or who think they are, and who aspire to liberty for themselves and slavery for others. Spartacus, however, was defeated, and all those who had followed him tortured.

"Stop!" ordered Pietro Ferrati.

The two secretaries remained motionless, pens in hand, their eyes raised.

Pietro Ferrati spoke to the man on the left.

"Did you understand? Do you think you will make yourself clear? I can't repeat the explanation, nor the demonstration for everybody myself. You must try, therefore, to follow me as carefully as possible, and repeat it afterwards, everywhere, as well as you can. We have begun with the easiest, the strike of non-resistance. That was all right for a time, for a fortnight: the minute this public demonstration was known, it was stopped! From now on, if we want to force an issue, we must make them fear us; and, to make them fear us, we must show our power by lessening the production as it pleases us, whatever the officials may think, say or do. But if we want to do that, we must get our wits to working. We have the advantage of a start over the enemy. It is not an advantage, however, if we misuse it. Therefore, at least once every two weeks we must change tactics and, to achieve our aim, use a new and different method. A physiolog-

ical method, mechanical, or some other; that will depend upon conditions. For the moment I have chosen
a system of slight accidents, which will occur during
a period of two weeks and will hinder the running of
an essential part of the pie machines: the grinder. A
little while ago I dictated to you four exact methods
for four different types of accidents, each one involv-
ing the stoppage of a grit crusher for eight or ten
hours. And the same method applies to the pies. For
flour, I have also dictated to you the methods of other
accidents similar in result, and very good for interrupting the action of the upper millstones for the same
length of time. What we must do at present—between
now and tomorrow evening—is to inform and instruct
our thirty thousand adherents sworn to direct action.
Teach them how to go about it, in other words! I cannot, I repeat, instruct thirty thousand men myself. I
instruct you, that will have to do. You in turn will
instruct the fifteen or twenty delegates whom the division of the Council of the Order will send you the first
thing tomorrow. Each delegate, in his turn, will look
after his subdivision and so on. You say you need
demonstrating machines? All right. I have had four
of them set up in the cellars of Blocks 151, 196. . . ."

He hunted for a list:

". . . 151, 196, 312 and 504. Of course, we will
change quarters every two weeks to throw any spies
off the track. It is all the easier since new demonstrating machines will be needed for studying further dam-

ages; they will therefore be set up somewhere else—
you have an objection to make?"

The secretary had made a gesture of the hand, which
he checked:

"Yes," said he quite timidly (Pietro Ferrati, imperious and self-contained, easily upset his subordinates)
"if I have understood correctly, all the damages and
all the accidents to be anticipated in the next fortnight
will affect the same part of all the machines? It seems
to me the management of the Siturgic can scarcely help
noticing that this is a carefully planned scheme, a con-
certed movement"——

"Well—what of it?"

"Well . . ."

"Ah, indeed? You would rather not have the management notice it? Rather have them attribute all that
has already happened, all that is going to happen, to
chance? Why, you are crazy, my dear fellow! If we
do these things, it is precisely so that they may know
we are the ones who are doing them, so that they may
be sure of it, so that no one can have any doubt about
it! What is the use of it all otherwise? Do you
imagine we have any interest whatever in disturbing
the work of the Shops, in tying up the production, in
limiting the output at the risk of starving America?
America, that is to say four hundred million human
beings, of which three hundred and fifty million are
laborers and farmers, therefore three hundred and fifty
million comrades? Never in the world, my dear fel-

low! We are interested in proving our power, in forcing our employers to fear us and to yield to our demands, to consider us, and to treat with us as equal to
equal, or as inferior to superior, if possible! And it
will be possible if our discipline and our energy do not
fail. As far as our organization, our plans, our means,
our methods are concerned, we must keep strict sec-
recy; but concerning our existence, our purpose, and
the forces at our disposal? Never in the world!"

He shrugged his shoulders. The secretaries acquiesced abjectly. MacHead Vohr, giving orders to
his councilors or to his vice-presidents was not more
imperious, nor more silently obeyed— In days of
old, Spartacus, commanding the slaves who had revolted against Rome, was, for that matter, more brutal
than any consul and any imperator——

CHAPTER III

THE SLAVES

"YOU may go now!"

Thus dismissed, the two secretaries who were already standing, bowed much lower than it is customary among companions.

"Be here tomorrow morning, from six o'clock, eh?"

To hear was to obey, as in the Orient. Pietro Ferrati was left alone.

Freed from a constraint which, however, had not weighed upon him at all, his first gesture was to reach for his watch which he consulted anxiously. It was not yet half past eleven! Pietro Ferrati seemed glad of it, as if relieved. For a while he walked back and forth in the room, undecided rather than hesitant. Suddenly, he realized that the place was very dirty. There was no use trying to remedy it! Though Hercules alone had been able to clean out the Augean stables, Pietro Ferrati did not attempt it and contented himself with putting out the lamps and closing the door. There were separate entrances to the flat through the living-room and through the bedroom. When the latter was closed off, the flat, reduced to half its size, became a habitable dwelling, clean, at-

111

tractive, dainty. And the man who, a moment before, seemed satisfied in this setting of vulgarity and pretentious ugliness, busied himself for several minutes in changing the water in the large Chinese vases filled with fresh roses.

He did more than that: into an old bronze Chinese vase of the eighteenth century he poured alcohol, lighted it, and threw two handfuls of benzoin into this improvised incense burner. The warm, sensual odor spread through the room; and for a long time Pietro Ferrati, strike agitator, stood watching the gray spirals of the perfume rise above the blue flame.

Then, going out of the flat, he locked the door; and went off, climbing the steps of the twenty-first floor —of the roof—to breathe the night air on the terrace.

The wind had already risen and was blowing strongly. One felt it more at the Blocks than at the High Palace; the Palace, in fact, was sheltered by the lower slopes of the Artificial Hill. The Blocks, on the other hand, astride the juncture of the two rivers, were surrounded only by bare plains; and the whole valley of the Mississippi stretched out to the north of the juncture, as far as one could see, and then beyond. The wind, especially the wind from the north, raged there wildly. Pietro Ferrati, emerging from the narrow staircase into the open air, was knocked breathless by a tremendous gale. He swayed, before putting his back against one of the chimneys of the Block. It was only the weakness of a moment. He straightened up immediately, and having glanced around to make sure that he was alone on the terrace—besides, it would have been very surprising if he were not—Pietro Ferrati immediately busied himself with a strange task: one after the other he took down the bars of the railing that enclosed the flat roof; for this railing, by a probably unique exception, could be removed. It was quickly done; each bar was only an iron rod stuck in a socket, and the top rail a simple round bar clamped onto the supports. The whole thing came apart as if ready to fall. And Pietro Ferrati went back to his chimney to take shelter from the gusts of wind, which, from minute to minute, were growing stronger and more frequent.

The chimney was of brick, fairly low, and surmounted by a row of sheet-iron pipes. Pietro Ferrati was a head taller than the level of the bricks. He leaned his elbow on the chimney, while waiting for something— who knows what? His eyes wandered by chance over the circle of the horizon bounded everywhere by hard ridges, crossed at right angles, by those heavy buildings of the town, the Blocks—

To the north, except for the flat water and bare land, there was nothing in sight, for Block 216 bordered on the Mississippi. The Mouth, wide as an arm of the sea, gleamed faintly beneath a moon too high in the sky. And beyond, the plain stretched away, black as a pit. To the east, to the south, to the west, the Blocks surrounded the flat roof like an army of tall stones, sharp as hatchets. And this army of sharp points bristled with chimney flues that wore a threatening air. Finally, not a light anywhere now, midnight was going to strike, the Blocks apparently were all asleep.

"Except perhaps," thought Pietro Ferrati, "except perhaps those where the cellars do not sleep—151, for example—and 196, and 312, and 504—"

He drew himself up. His chest swelled with pride. "They sleep—if I permit!"

After a while his head drooped on his shoulder. An expression of strange tenderness passed over his Italian features, severe and finely cut like the intaglio of a medallion. Pietro Ferrati looked like his brother. But Andrea's mouth, ordinarily less impetuous and less arrogant, would not, however, have been able to smile with so much sweetness and almost with tenderness:

"They sleep, if I permit," repeated Pietro. "If I wish; but some day they will sleep better than they are sleeping today and will dream more beautiful dreams; because I shall have wished. . ."

He let his gaze wander slowly from the east to the west, before finishing impressively:

". . . Some day: the day that I shall have made of all these brute slaves rulers, first of all, and men afterwards!"

They were, indeed, brute slaves, these poor, scarcely human, creatures, who lived in the Blocks.

Can we imagine today, with the progress of Time, the life led by these human arms without brains, whose

purely mechanical task was, such a short time afterward, performed by mere machines?

Like other men they got up in the morning after
having slept some eight hours or so. Their ablutions
were brief and summary; their breakfast plentiful, but
coarse. They had risen late, as late as possible: for,
in their minds, destitute of malice, to get up late was
synonymous with being rich, that is to say, with being
free. They got up late to give themselves the illusion
of not being so poor; and they lacked time for dressing and for their morning meal; time, and, to tell the
truth, money too: for their salaries were not munificent.

Electric cars carried them to work, in great crowds.
At the beginning of the innumerable streets that divided the Shops, engineers and foremen waited for
these cars. The human cargo distributed itself of its
own accord between the departments, the groupings
and the groups. Each shop snapped up its group of
ten men, and the daily labor began. For it began
every morning and finished every evening, after only
eight hours of production. And during the sixteen remaining hours, the machines, silenced by the men's idle-
ness, remained idle themselves. The uninterrupted
production of our modern factories had not even been
dreamed of in 199— . . . That would have necessitated
three shifts of men; and so many men were still needed
to run any of the motor or the generator machines of
that day that three shifts of workmen would have
been no solution of the problem. The heads of the

Siturgic preferred to lose two hours out of three and not to have, instead of one hundred and fifty thousand, four hundred and fifty thousand adult mouths to feed.

. . . And the daily work began.

It lasted eight hours: from seven in the morning until eleven o'clock; from one until five o'clock in the afternoon. From eleven o'clock to one o'clock, the men ate their lunch in the group canteens. Easy work it was, all mechanical, but whilst it did not tire, it brutalized. A man of broad intelligence would have retrogressed at this game. An artisan would have become a day laborer again. A day laborer would have been very quickly changed into an animal.

. . . Open or shut a regulator; lift a watergate or lower it; start a grinder running; slow it up, accelerate it, stop it; regulate the rotation of a screw, modify the circulation of a multiplier; thicken, by a turn of the wheel, the dough of a trough; thin it out with a backward turn, check or let out again the motion of the chopping knife; fill or empty the valve of a boiler according to its manometer, and every six minutes feed a furnace basin that has to be stoked every eighteen minutes. This was the work done by human hands in the Shops.

Five o'clock in the evening: groupings, groups, shops, streets, all were emptied—the entire factory! The trams took aboard their dusty, tired cargoes again. And once more the Blocks received their inhabitants. One hundred and forty thousand men jumped off trams too tightly packed, and stormed the elevators, to find their young and their females again in their burrows. One hundrèd and forty thousand? No—a good third of this crowd was not in such a hurry to get back to their own places and to isolate themselves between four walls—the bachelors, first of all; the unhappily married next; and last of all the drunkards, and these were legion. The bars absorbed all this inevitable clientèle. And there the biggest salaries were squandered, salaries sufficient in themselves, but only if the men practised economy. And economy has never frequented the tavern. Two, three, four hours later the bars threw out the mob which had filled them, and threw out with them misery, decadence, and sometimes hunger.

This condition was not noticeable at first sight. The crowds at the Blocks did not present the miserable aspect that the degraded multitudes of the poor quarters of Europe and of America frequently offer. The contrast of luxury in close juxtaposition, which the rich quarters of London or of New York display, was lacking. At the Blocks there was no opulent city in close proximity. The Residences were only a large village; fifteen or eighteen thousand inhabitants, engineers, and chief engineers, foremen and contractors —a large village, besides, all built in the woods, therefore half invisible, and situated beyond the immense screen of the Shops, that is to say, out of sight of the Blocks. Many of the laborers had never been there in their lives.

No, the Blocks might be fairly gloomy to live in; but they did not give that appearance. The bars created an artificial but noisy gaiety. The moving picture houses, the dance halls had increased in number. A fever of pleasure frequently galvanized the two cities, each on its bank of the Eighth Mouth. At such times the sound of music, the din of songs, the tumult of shouts and of laughter filled the air for miles around. And the engineers and the foremen, and all the free race of the Residences, hearing this noise where the slaves of the Blocks seemed to be amusing themselves, willingly imagined that happiness dwelt on the other side of the factory town, as well as, perhaps even more so, than on the side of the leaders and of the rulers—on the side of liberty—

Happiness? . . .

They might have known it just the same—who knows?—these men, the slaves of the Siturgic. But, if they had, it would not have been necessary for other men, like this man here, who at that very moment was leaning on his elbow on the brick chimney of Block 216, to come and remind them that their ancestors had been freer than they were now themselves—and that rebellion could give them back their lost liberty. . .

CHAPTER IV

Eva

STILL leaning against the brick chimney, Pietro Ferrati had little by little bowed his forehead, perhaps under the weight of his thoughts. One does not undertake to rouse men by the hundreds of thousands without finding the responsibility he assumes a heavy one. Below him, Pietro Ferrati could see the luminous dial of one of the pneumatic clocks on the square. The two hands, one on top of the other, pointed now to midnight.

An immense silence rose from the sleeping city. The nocturnal silence of places which all day long have been full of crowds, tumult and noise, is not like any other silence. It is more despotic, doubtless because it has subdued and dominated all those noises whose place it has usurped. It is more solemn and more expressive. No one dreams of breaking it. Pietro Ferrati, yielding unconsciously to this oppression, had walked on tiptoe a little while ago, then talked to himself through closed lips. Now he did not stir. And to make him lift his head, it took, from far, far away and very high up the air, between the sharp moans of the wind, which was already blowing strong, a sound musical and vibrant: the sound of an airplane coming from the south and headed towards the ground, as if it were going to land on the Blocks themselves. . .

Immediately, Pietro Ferrati stooped and picked up an object lying at the base of the chimney: a large electric lamp with curved reflectors and annularly concentric lens; a veritable pocket searchlight which he promptly placed on the chimney, at the top of the highest of the sheet iron pipes, then lighted. And it was a beacon of good luck which he had thus improvised, a beacon whose rectilinear shafts of light went darting towards the south, at an altitude of forty-five degrees. The airplane, if it really intended to land, had the best kind of a beacon at its disposal; so much the more so as the wind had not yet entirely cleared away the light mist that had floated about the first part of the evening. In this mist, so light as to be almost imperceptible, the luminous shafts of light traced a visible stream of fog, white, dazzling. And the airplane, having seen it, veered, immediately heading straight towards it.

Ten seconds later the plane landed and Pietro Ferrati recognized it as the one he had been expecting: a small airplane, monoplane; an eleven-foot-six wingspread; a single seater; four hundred horse-power; and not a gleam on its dull steel wings, nor on the annealed and tempered glass of the cabin. . .

The airplane, guided by the hand of a master, had landed exactly in the center of the terrace. The pilot jumped out of the cockpit;—a woman! There was not another soul on board.

This woman, without a word, came straight to Pietro Ferrati, and throwing herself in his arms, embraced him passionately, savagely, as only mistresses embrace their lovers.

And as he returned embrace for embrace and kiss for kiss, she threw back her head, half swooning, and the moon shone full on her face—the face of Eva Mac-Head Vohr, of the daughter of MacHead Vohr, Governor of the Siturgic!

How had these two, Eva MacHead Vohr and Pietro Ferrati, discovered each other in this vast world? How had they found each other, chosen, taken each other? She, from the race of the ruler of rulers, he, the leader of slaves in revolt? Just as lovers, all lovers, find each other—by chance! He had known her at the time when he was still in the service of the factory and was building the footbridge over the Mouth. He was twenty-five years old; she, nineteen. They had looked at each other; and, both of them at once, had felt themselves mysteriously stirred to the very marrow of their bones. Afterward he had left the Siturgic suddenly, without anyone knowing why, without even informing his brother. And she had suffered secretly because of his departure. They had seen each other again two years later, in New York. It was then that suddenly, by chance, one stormy afternoon, they had yielded to

their love, and had sworn eternal loyalty to one another. And it is then that he had trusted her and
had put himself in her hands, and that he had told
her everything: the reasons for his former departure,
his bewildered conversion to the most violent socialistic
doctrines, and the mission to the workingmen which
from henceforth was going to be his whole life and his
whole reason for living. She, proudly, had received
his confidence and bore it from that moment with the
exaltation with which a woman bears the fruit of her
love. Not that she, like him, was converted. The blood
of MacHead Vohr flowed in her veins, and she had altogether too much aristocratic pride and too much
sense of realities to allow herself to be taken in by
any Utopian theory whatever, especially a Socialistic
theory. But her passion for antiquity, therefore for
history, had at first enflamed her with the thought of
the civil struggles to come, struggles like those of olden
times between patricians and plebeians, between all the
Mariuses and all the Syllas of dead centuries. That
in the last analysis all the Mariuses had always suc-
cumbed, and that every victory of the people had been
succeeded by the disorganization and the decomposi-
tion of the races, then the invasion of the Barbarians
and the return to the most decisive reactions, to the
most absolute despotisms—this she did not doubt for
a second. No matter. She did not even try to convert
her lover to her opinion. Such as he was, she admired
him too much, she loved him too much, and too passionately. Converted to ideas that dwarf, would he

remain for her the same lover? She did not know and preferred not to risk the test; she kept quiet therefore, remaining submissive to him; so very submissive, that, without remorse, she would have been his spy had he wished. But he himself, respecting her, had been careful never to ask anything of her, except herself. Alone and isolated between two irreconcilable camps, they had succeeded in being nothing but two magnificent lovers.

And they were proud of it, immeasurably so. . . . And, not for anything in the world, would they have risked becoming anything else. Married; or companions? That would have been to lessen their love too much.

In their bedroom, now, he had taken her in his arms. And they were talking—lovers' conversation which, nevertheless, held an undercurrent of heavy restlessness, almost of embarrassment. Two hours before she had learned some things that concerned him and that she might have wanted and yet that she did not want to tell him; he felt her confusedly restless, divined the cause of her anxiety and feared that she might give in, and that she might speak! . . .

. . . Then he took her in his arms again. . .

She spoke, however, but later on, and cautiously; and he was satisfied.

She said:

"Pietro, do you know whether my father has been informed of your presence at the Blocks?"

He looked at her before answering:

"No, I do not know."

She insisted, after having reflected:

"If my father heard it, would it be annoying for you? or for your plans? . . ."

He hesitated.

"If he should learn—what?" he asked finally. "That there is someone here? That I am that someone? Or that this person is doing what I am doing?"

She came to the point, bluntly, like an American:

"That there is someone who is doing what you are doing, first of all . . . and finally, that this someone is you?"

She hesitated in her turn, then clasping him to her:

". . . That this someone, dear love, is you?"

With a kiss, he stopped the words hovering on her lips.

"Hush!" he said. "If they know that a man is here to do what I am doing, that is all the same to me; indeed, it is very useful; I don't know whether they know it today; I hope they will know it tomorrow. If they should know that I am the man, it would make little difference to me, if—if you were not there, and especially if you were not you. Don't speak! listen, understand: we cannot control what is. Talking of it does not help matters. I will answer you now:—I hope that, down there, everyone may know of my presence and that no one may know my name. That is all. You know what you wanted to know, and I—I do not want to know anything more."

All that they said to each other, outside of that, is

not subject to put in a book. Those who will read this book will remember perhaps their own love dialogues, if they have once been in love. And those who have not loved, not being able to remember, do not need to be told—they would not believe.

Before four o'clock in the morning, Eva MacHead Vohr came to herself again, alone, in the cockpit of her airplane, as one regains consciousness in bed on waking from a dream. The wind was blowing a gale now. Wild gusts of wind hurled themselves against the airplane, lifting it and dashing it downwards in furious lunges one after the other. From the Blocks to the Low Palace the distance was not thirty miles. Eva took nearly half an hour to cross it, forced as she was to fly high and to make an immense turn to get the wind behind her back before coming down towards her narrow landing place. Little did it matter to her. Crouched in the bottom of her cabin, the brutal gale of the storm whipping her face, she tasted the powerful delight of feeling beneath her closely wrapped furs the amorous moisture of her body, gladdened by caresses, and the sensual perfume which arose from all her flesh to her dilated nostrils. Grappling with the controls, she struggled against the force of the wind, as an hour ago she had struggled—she, the female against the male—and swooned with pleasure at the memory. A gust of wind bent the apparatus vertical. Daringly, she drove the plane headlong towards the ground, with difficulty restraining a groan of pleasure. And having completed the landing she did not jump to the ground at once, but sat there in her seat, rallying one by one all her bruised and weary muscles which had been routed, as it were, by the exertions of her anguished joy.

Boris was waiting with the car at the postern gate of the Low Palace. In the High Palace there was no one in the court of honor, no one in the Council room. At the top of the spiral staircase Eva, become again Miss MacHead Vohr, gained her bedroom, closed and mysterious, and went to sleep in her bed, mysterious herself.

CHAPTER V

A CELLAR

IT LOOKED like a schoolroom. There was nothing lacking, not even the blackboard. Standing near this board, with the chalk in his hand, the professor was explaining to his pupils the figure traced on the board and the pupils were listening, following with their eyes the plan.

It looked like a schoolroom. It looked like a cellar, too, on account of the heavy square pillars of rough stone, and the Roman vaults of brick assembled in an arch of exactly a half-circle. It looked like a cellar and it was a cellar—the cellar of Block 196. The pupils were two hundred workmen, adherents of direct action; the professor, John Faraway, a secretary of Pietro Ferrati's; and the figure traced on the blackboard represented the grinder of a pie machine. John Faraway, patient and precise, was repeating "for those who have not yet understood" the careful demonstration of accident number three, calculated to hinder or prevent the action of the grinder, indeed to put it out of commission and to make it necessary to replace it. "Those who have not already understood" were just stupid; for the procedure was simple and within reach of the most rustic minds.

"I will begin again," Faraway had started to say. "All the work of the grinder consists in grinding the water-soaked grits between its bottom surface, which is smooth and slanting, and the top surface of the bottom of the trough, which is horizontal and ridged. To get the result we want, it is necessary and sufficient for the grinder to drag; that is to say, the bulk at the rear should graze the millstone which forms the bottom of the trough. If the grinder is regulated too high, and does not touch the millstone, the grits slip between grinder and trough without being ground; if the grinder is regulated too low, it strikes the bottom of the trough one blow after another and is damaged— Did you understand this time?—Good!—Well: that is what we want to get at: that the grinder, instead of being regulated as it ought to be, should be regulated too high or too low, or too loosely, and that it should hit—to get this result—first process,—it could not be simpler—make the rolling castors oval. The grinder, instead of turning around on its axis, will go up and down by jerks, damaging itself and the millstone. So go after the castors then! And if you know what you're about six or seven thousand grinders ought to be out of business tomorrow evening !'"

The chalk struck the board forcibly. John Faraway, his demonstration made, came back to the point, underlining heavily the rolling castors which it was important to make oval. Then he came to the details:

"To make a castor oval: unscrew and take apart

its axle, then put it together again after leaving out
one of the three pads—here—like this—"

Leaving the blackboard, he had picked up on the
table, from among twelve or fifteen pieces of machinery,
all prepared, a castor unscrewed in advance and, going
up and down the crowded rows of the auditorium, he
showed with his own hands the right way of taking out
the pad, then putting the castor together, so that the
missing pad could not be too plainly noticed—at least
for the moment.

"Afterwards," declared John Faraway, "that will
not make any difference. The engineers will evidently
not be stupid enough not to discover the mistake, but
the delegate from the Council of the Order told me
himself particularly, that he didn't give a damn if they
did find out, and you needn't give a damn either."

A hesitating murmur ran through the audience.
Someone, speaking in a low tone, took it upon himself to express the general apprehension:

"We needn't give a damn! Well, say! That's all
right—if we don't get caught at it! Because the
delegate from the Council of the Order is all right;
but, just the same, the fellow who gets caught, if he
doesn't already know the way to the house of correction, will march there in double time . . . A
strike—that doesn't hurt anyone; but smashing a piece
of machinery a man is supposed to run—well, the
judges call that petty larceny, and they give a man
the jug for that!"

This was, in truth, the law of the States in 199—.

Caught unawares by this objection—Pietro Ferrati had not thought to foresee it—John Faraway swore energetically to give himself time to think. Neither time nor reflection brought him a plausible answer. But while he was vainly racking his brains, another voice than his answered in his place, with swift, impulsive, burning eloquence.

"Jug or no jug, what the hell difference does that make? Those who are afraid of losing their earthly paradise in the Blocks had better clear out right away and go back to their palaces of tile and concrete which their rulers in their munificence have granted them! The Council of the Order of Anarchy didn't send me here as delegate for the sake of slaves who are content to remain slaves: they sent me to help slaves who are determined, at no matter what cost, to be free men again! Whoever is not with me is against me! About face, cowards! Get out of here! And watch out as you go! I warn you—the cellar stairs are full of spies!"

Pietro Ferrati, scoffing and terrible, had suddenly appeared in the midst of the wavering workmen.

Not one of them budged. The tirade had nailed them to the spot, all of them; already ashamed of their weakness, all of them at heart were more afraid of Pietro Ferrati than of MacHead Vohr himself. At the same time, several men instinctively looked towards the stairs which Ferrati had said were full of spies. And they trembled as they saw that there actually was a man there: only one man, it is true: but a man they did not know, but whom they looked at distrustfully before reflecting that, without any doubt, he could only be a secretary or a friend of the delegate from the Council of the Order. (Not one of the workmen of the Siturgic could have called Pietro Ferrati by name.)

The delegate from the Council of the Order, too, instinctively followed the gaze of those who were looking towards the staircase. And he saw the man who had just come. For a moment, he stopped short. A look of surprise passed over his face. But in the same moment he resumed his expression of indifference, and, as if he had not seen the man, or as if, having recognized him, he did not bother any more about him, he continued his harangue boldly:

"Hullo, what's this? So there aren't any cowards here after all since you are all staying? All right! So much the better! Get busy there and keep a stiff upper lip! And if the enemy dares to send any man to the house of correction, I swear to God I'll get him out myself!"

Every man in the place believed him.

The man, who was still on the steps of the staircase, was listening.

CHAPTER VI

PETER AND JOHN

BY SIX o'clock the cellar was empty. The cars carried back to the Shops all the male population of the Blocks. Pietro Ferrati had sent Faraway off on some other business. He himself was the last to leave. The man who had followed the entire meeting and the demonstration of direct action, without anyone's knowing exactly whether he had the right or not to be there, had left with the crowd, but had not gone very far away. And the first person Pietro Ferrati saw, as he in his turn came out of cellar 196, was this man. This time, Pietro Ferrati did not show any surprise; the man did not show any either. They both looked at each other steadily, then they walked straight up to each other and, with the same impulse, rushed into each other's arms. The man was Andrea Ferrati, the brother of Pietro,—his half-brother, to be exact. But they had always loved each other as if they had had the same mother and had been nourished at the same breast.

"You! It is you, Andrea!" Pietro had cried. "Oh! I recognized you the moment I laid eyes on you, a little while ago! You poor reckless fool! Why, by

132

all the gods, if those wild beasts in there had even
suspected who you are, I myself wouldn't have been able
to stop them from tearing you to pieces on the spot
as they do spies. Spies—oh! Andrea! Andrea! It can't
be so! You aren't a spy, are you? Tell me, you aren't
that? I wouldn't believe it even if you admitted it,
even if you swore it!—"

Nevertheless Andrea Ferrati had all the appearance
of being a spy, and unmistakably one. A false beard
covered his cheeks; his black hair was dyed gray;
painted wrinkles corrugated his forehead. Pietro Ferrati would never have recognized him at first sight,
as he had said, had it not been first of all, for a deep
fraternal instinct, and secondly for Andrea's Italian
eyes, which gleamed like two black diamonds—eyes
that neither paint nor dye could keep from shining.

To his elder brother's cry of tenderness, the younger
man only replied at first by hugging him a little tighter.

"Don't worry!" he cried warmly, without taking his
arms away. "Me, a spy? Yes, when you become one!
Never before! *Caro, caro, carissimo!* My nurse gave
me milk, you, honor! Don't be afraid, *Pietro mio,*
but make fun of my false beard, if you like! Not too
much however, brother: it is on your account that I am
wearing it, and on your account that I am here—"

"On my account?"

"Yes, yours! to get to you more quickly and more
quickly to cry to you, Fool, thrice fool! Thrice dearly
beloved fool! there is still time: quick, quick, stop and
turn back on your abominable path—it is a matter

of life and death, Pietro! Of your own, first of all,
and perhaps, probably—no, most certainly—of the
lives of many others—of all the others rather, of all
those you drag after you on this path which only
ends in an abyss!"

While he was talking the obviousness of the state-
ments he was making rushed to his brain, to that Italian
brain prone to intoxication, like all the brains of lands
too temperate and too burnt by the sun. Suddenly,
he yielded to his southern emotion violently; and, still
clinging to his brother, he burst into tears.

True, they had always loved each other dearly,
Pietro and Andrea. But, strange as it may seem, from
the day that their political differences had separated
them, in body as well as in spirit, they had loved each
other more dearly. Living, one in New York, Chicago,
St. Louis, wherever the Anarchist Party needed his
presence; the other, from necessity, at the Siturgic,
where he was chained by his daily task of bread-maker,
entrusted with feeding four hundred million human beings, and to do this every single day of the three hundred and sixty-five days in the year (for one single
day of rest, one single day of suspension of work, of
strike or of vacation would have meant a day of famine
for the Three Americas!)—living thus, separated one
from the other, with nothing left of their old fraternal
past except a double regret, and not even able to hope
for a return to this past so dear to each, they had
both redoubled their tenderness, they had multiplied
it by all this regret, by all this gentle bitterness that

they suffered in recalling their lost paradise. For they had been wonderfully happy before, in all that time they had lived together at the Siturgic, one household, one task, and sharing with each other all their cares, their pleasures, and even their dreams. They were both orphans and had no other relatives. Two brothers left alone in the world, and replacing father and mother for each other from childhood, they knew a tenderness so delicate and so pure that even two lovers, madly in love with each other, could not begin to conceive the sweetness of it.

Alas! this sweetness was suddenly changed to gall on the day that Pietro Ferrati, like the apostle of old, and no less suddenly, had found his road to Damascus. A mathematician, therefore a mystic, the moral and intellectual misery of the manual laborers, had, as soon as he had noticed it, pierced his heart like a sword. That men could be hungry he had known for a long time and had been very little moved by it: he himself, and Andrea as well, had often gone without their meals to add one hour more to the daily hours of work. That these men, gnawed by hunger, were in addition crushed with work and bent double each evening under the burden of their weariness, was another puzzle! What was the work of these men compared to that on which he spent himself, and even his dearly-loved brother? A straw compared to a beam! What, in truth, is weariness of muscles compared to weariness of brain! Nothing, all that! Less than nothing! But that men might not know how to read; worse, to know how and not to

know anything more; to confine themselves, in consequence, to spelling out the moving picture announce-
ments of the five-cent papers; that they might live
in ignorance of those human intoxications called physi-
ology, chemistry, mechanics, and analysis; that men
might be content to be like this; it was that which
Pietro Ferrati vowed to blot out of the world. And
immediately, with might and main, he threw himself
into the pursuit of this Utopia: to set free servile
humanity in order to enlighten it; and to enlighten
it in order to make it worthy of being free; Utopia
the maddest of the mad, the most imposing also, and
the most generous. . . .

And the two brothers had not been together half an
hour, reunited for the first time after two long years of
separation equally hard for both of them, when already
Pietro had once more passionately gone over all these
points and pleaded their cause with Andrea. But
Andrea did not answer, not even by a gesture, except
to shake his head, then lower it, as if it were too full
of thoughts, too heavy to hold up.

In the end, however, when Pietro stopped talking,
Andrea spoke:

"Brother mine," said he—and instinctively, he had
chosen their mother tongue, that Italian so soft that
Charles the Fifth of Spain would never speak any
other language to seduce his mistresses—"Brother
mine, brother dear, most dear to me, do you know why
I am here, in disguise, grotesque as a clown? Do you
know why I am making a travesty of myself as a spy,

at the risk, you yourself said so, of being discovered, and taken for one, and as one torn to pieces and shreds, which isn't a great matter in itself, but on top of that, dishonored, which is worse? Do you know why I had to lie a while ago to get in there,"—he pointed to Block 196—"and to say that you were expecting me, and that I had an urgent report to make to you?—Do you know why already I have lied to get away from up there, to leave the High Palace without suspicion, as soon as I guessed that you were the man delegated by Anarchy to overthrow the Siturgic—Do you know the reason for all this, all these dangers, all these lies? Brother, for your sake! to warn you—listen, Pietro, listen—to warn you that the Governor has just learned that you are here, and why you are here, and what you have already done and what you are going to do— everything! Pietro, everything! He has learned all and there is not one of your secrets he does not know! Had you forgotten, *caro mio*, that the Siturgic has eyes everywhere? Did you think, do you think you can make a move, say a word, in the Blocks, in MacHead Vohr's Blocks, without MacHead Vohr, an hour later, not being warned of it? Pietro, brother mine, dear brother! then you don't know this man, the Wheat King, the man of terror! Have you forgotten—?"

He was getting excited again. Pietro, cooler, stopped him with an abrupt question:

"Andrea, what did you say? They know who I am? They know my name?"

There was a note of anxiety in his voice. Andrea

caught it and attributed it to the affection of brother for brother. Pietro feared for him, Andrea, that the name of Ferrati had become known. Andrea hastened to reassure him.

"No! not your name, not your name—or, at least not yet—they only know that a man arrived twenty-two days ago—is that it?—and that this man is a delegate from the Council of the Order . . ."

He did not have a chance to say any more: Pietro learning more than he ought to learn from such lips, and anxious for his brother's honor, had stopped him with a finger on his lips.

The street, around them, was empty, but at the windows heads of women, of old people, of children, were appearing. These people, curious and only vaguely informed, pointed out these two men to each other, the delegate from "Those down there," so the murmur ran from ear to ear; and the other man "a queer cove" who was talking to him, and who had embraced him so violently.

Pietro, a little tardily, became aware of this curiosity all around them.

"Come," said he, taking his brother by the arm.

Andrea demurred.

"Not to your place," he begged; "I don't want to know where you are hiding!"

Pietro began to laugh.

"Nonsense!" said he, "have you discovered the way to tell one of these prisons from the other?" He pointed to the Blocks, disdainfully, even spitefully. He burst out laughing. "If so, the Siturgic must have progressed since the day I handed in my resignation!"

And he finished passionately:

"Ah! brother, my dear brother! You with so great a soul and so upright a heart, how can you serve in the camp of the oppressors?"

Andrea pressed both his hands, strongly.

"Brother, dear brother! Because my eyes are too clear, and my heart too full of pity for the oppressed —Ah! if you knew my horror when I hear this word you have just said: 'camp'—you see, they park cattle in camps, too, before sending them to the slaughter-house. . . ."

CHAPTER VII

Two—and One—

"I HAVE seen you, I have warned you, I have pleaded with you!—I can do nothing more, and, never in my life have I felt more helpless or more terrified! Brother dear, forgive me . . ."

About to leave, Andrea was embracing his brother again.

In their gestures, as in their speech, there was a little of the Italian exaggeration which does not detract at all from sincerity, whatever strangers may think, often disconcerted as they are by this exaggeration, which only mathematicians know how to reduce, by dividing the exaggerated force of each expression by the coefficient of the climate.

"Don't go yet," begged the elder brother. "Stay and tell me about yourself—I don't know anything about you!—What have you been doing all this time? What has happened to you?"

Andrea shrugged his shoulders.

"Nothing, my dear fellow, what do you expect? You know my life. How do you expect it to change?—"

A smile lighted the other's face:

"It will change inevitably one of these days, *bambino!* You don't know yet that something exists in the world called love?"

140

Impulsively, Andrea had grasped Pietro by the shoulders.

"Do you know it yourself, old man?"

A mysterious silence weighed on them. Each was on the point of giving his confidence, and each withheld it, darkly.

"Do I know it?" was all the elder brother said. "Brother—have you looked in my eyes?"

Andrea looked in them, and without being able to tell why, he grew serious. A strange fatality was guiding the conversation, unknown to the speakers.

"In love?" Andrea had asked.

Pietro bowed his head. A great pride filled him as he thought of her whom he loved, and had just held in his arms. Andrea looked at him with a kind of apprehension:

"You are in love," he continued after a pause; "you are happy, it radiates from every feature—and, instead of living out your love and intoxicating yourself with it, you continue your existence of a wandering convict, you persist in this hopeless mission?"

Pietro stopped him with a cry.

"Do you think that she would love me, this woman who loves me, if I were a lover like all lovers, neither greater, nor more noble?"

"A proud woman, eh? So that is what you love, as if all the misfortunes you are seeking already as a kind of diversion, were not enough for you?"

Pietro Ferrati threw back his head proudly:

"Do not speak of her!"

"She is yours, brother; so don't be afraid: how could

I not respect her? But also, how could you keep me from seeing her as she is, as she cannot help being: a victim grieved, wounded, revolted by the inevitable social injustice, to the point of becoming more unjust herself than even all this injustice, than all the injustice in the world?"

Pietro Ferrati, silent, had begun to smile again. Beneath the corners of his tightly pressed mouth a trace of irony appeared. Andrea astonished, looked at him. At this moment, he felt a sudden constraint and a strange chill within him. But already, Pietro had checked him.

"Leave her alone, brother, leave her as she is. One must not bother about the loves of an outlaw unless one would be sad—and then, it is about you, only about you, that I am worried. So you are not in love yet. Who knows, however? It seems that in any case you are not far from falling in love!"

In spite of himself Andrea had blushed. He tried to joke:

"If I were in love," said he, "it would be from last evening"—

"Why not?" said the other quite gravely: "One never knows when the lightning will strike!"

He frowned suddenly and stared piercingly into Andrea's eyes:

"Last night?" he repeated, as if disturbed.

When they parted, each went his own way. And each man was silent for several moments, thinking deeply . . .

PART III

Mechanism vs. Organism

CHAPTER I

Shop No. 6666

THAT same morning, as the electric clock of Shop No. 6666 pointed to seventeen minutes past ten, two of the eight grinders of the shop, those with pie troughs number 5 and number 7, "cracked" the bottom of their troughs almost simultaneously. The two millstones exploded and fell apart. Grinder number 5, completely "mangled," was put out of order; and grinder number 7, harder hit, fell to pieces. A fragment of pig-iron, or of stone, struck a workman on the hip and cut him seriously, while another fragment, striking the foreman of the shop, broke his thigh. An extraordinary tumult followed: it was all the worse because, as the boss of the shop was lying unconscious beside some machines that were out of commission, there was no one else there to impose silence and re-establish even an appearance of order.

The accident was finally reported by the foreman of the neighboring shop, No. 6668. Informed by telephone, the department concerned, after having referred the case to the main office, sent for one of the chief engineers on duty. The injured workman, register number 116,083, was Hamish Andrews; the other injured man, the foreman of the shop, George Wilson; and the chief engineer sent for was Andrea Ferrati.

The two broken machines were still in the condition they had been in at the moment they made their last revolution, both axles now motionless, the one, bent. Andrea Ferrati, chief engineer, charged with the investigation, did not even glance at the machine.

"Unscrew the axles first," he ordered, "then the flywheel, then the main part of the grinder and the rolling castors. And lay aside—here wait!—lay aside each rolling castor, as you take it apart. The castors all together, eh, just as they are—without touching their pads. Whoever touches one of the pads without my order, will be arrested on the spot. The police are here, aren't they?"

This was addressed to the secretary, who was following the chief engineer.

The two injured men took part in the investigation: the foreman lay stretched out on the ground, a bundle of clothes under his head in place of a pillow; and the workman was seated in a corner. Ferrati, glancing at this man, saw him suddenly look very uncomfortable, as if embarrassed. He went up to him.

"Are you in pain?"

The man swallowed hard.

"No, sir—I can stand it—"

"How were you hurt?"

"The foreman had gotten up on the trough of number 5, because there was already something wrong there—"

"Never mind about the foreman. I'm talking about you. Where were you when the grinder broke?"

"I was oiling the rolling castors when—"

"All right, that will do. We'll have a look at those castors. The grinder was already beginning to get out of order when you were oiling the castors, you say?"

"Trough number 5 wasn't working right."

"I'm talking to you about trough number 7. Were you oiling the castors of trough number 7?"

"Yes, sir."

"Well, was there anything wrong with number 7?"

"Er—I don't remember now."

From his improvised bed, the foreman supplied the answer:

"No, Mr. Ferrati: number 7 wasn't working right, and I had got up there to have a look at it. But number 5 wasn't moving, nor the other grinders either. Andrews took the oil-can to be on the safe side. And I was going to give the order to oil up everywhere, when 7 began to knock louder. At the same time, without any warning, 5 gave one loud bang, and smashed."

"Andrews—is that his name, Andrews?—Andrews had been oiling it for some time, eh?"

The question was directed at the foreman. It was the workman who answered:

"No, sir! I had only just begun."

The foreman shot him a look of amazement, which Ferrati caught!

"He had only just begun, eh?" he repeated, in his rôle of questioner, fixing the foreman with a keen glance.

The stretcher bearers had just come in to carry the latter off.

"Well, sir, he'd only been at it a little while," said the foreman evasively.

Andrea Ferrati went up to the trough which was being taken apart, and examined it.

"For a little while, eh!" he said ironically. "Well, he had had time to oil all these castors! The oil is still running over everywhere!"

A silence followed. The man who was most seriously hurt had been carried off. After a few minutes had passed, Andrews, the injured workman, came up to Ferrati:

"Mr. Ferrati, I can go to the infirmary too, can't I, sir?"

Ferrati looked at him attentively.

"What is there to prevent you?" he asked, affecting surprise.

The man stepped back a pace.

"Oh! see here! just a moment, please!" continued Andrea carelessly. "Wait, I don't know yet which infirmary—"

He stopped abruptly. The last castor had just been put down in front of him.

Andrea Ferrati, with the tip of his foot, turned over all the castors one by one. Whereupon, without saying a word, he swung about towards the secretary who accompanied him, made a sign to him, and thrust both his hands in his pockets, with an air of complete indifference.

Four policemen—two from the State of Louisiana, two from the Federal Government—had just entered. With a tilt of his chin, Chief Engineer Ferrati motioned towards the injured workman, Andrews;

"That fellow over there! Take him to the prison infirmary!"

"I arrest you in the name of the law!" pronounced one of the policemen.

"Me!" protested the workman.

"Yes, you!" affirmed Andrea Ferrati, mockingly. "Idiot! You don't yet understand that, for the last half hour, you have not opened your mouth without putting your foot in it, without giving yourself away!"

Terrified, the man did not say a word. Ferrati turned his back on him in contempt. They went away together—the victim between the four policemen, the victor followed by his secretary, who carried two of the rolling castors, one from grinder No. 5, one from grinder No. 7.

CHAPTER II

THE BROKEN GRINDER

"TO SUM it all up," concluded Governor Mac Head Vohr, "the grinder was smashed to pieces, because your man Andrews is an imbecile."

"That's it exactly, sir," said Andrea Ferrati, chief engineer. "The idiot, instead of carrying out the letter of the instructions he had received—I mean, that he must have received—tried to be smart, and thought he could improve on the method. He should have done to grinder number 7 what had been done—and very cleverly for that matter—to number 5; that is, take out of one of the rolling castors one of the three pads which support the castor on its axle, enough to make the cast-iron grinder "bump" against the millstone of the trough, and damage the whole machine pretty seriously, without any risk to the men. But people are either clever or not: and Andrews, who believed that he was, took two pads out of his castor instead of one. Result: a hard concussion instead of a knock; and this concussion split the cast-iron of the grinder to pieces and hit two men, one of whom was the culprit. That is all there is to it. Now you know all I know about it, Governor!"

As he talked, Andręa Ferrati had been manipulating
the two castors, the cause of both of the accidents, and
had taken them apart and demonstrated the two cases.
There could be nothing more convincing. MacHead
Vohr was silent.

Ralph Athole, the privy councilor, and Just Bellecour, the executive councilor, were the only ones present at the hearing which Ferrati had requested the
moment he came out of Shop No. 6666. As soon as
Ferrati had finished making his report and the demonstration, Ralph Athole took the floor.

"If I have followed you correctly," he said to
Andrea, "one of these two injuries to the machines was
well done—from the point of view of our adversaries
—and the other poorly?"

"That is right!" agreed the chief engineer.

"In that case, they are very probably not done by
the same hand, are they? Almost certainly not!"

Athole turned towards Bellecour.

"My dear fellow, that means that out of every ten
workmen in one of our shops, there are two adherents
of direct action. What do you think about it?"

"I think that the situation is not lacking in gravity."

Just Bellecour, from Lyons, had the qualities and
the defects of his race, one of the strongest and the
most tenacious in the world. He took few things
tragically, but everything seriously.

MacHead Vohr had not yet spoken.

"It is evident," continued Athole, "that we are

up against an organization, and that this organization is very strong."

"Organization for methodical destruction?" objected Bellecour, do btfully.

"No, to obtain the claims put forth by the workingman. The destruction is only incidental. They will destroy if we do not yield. They have destroyed to prove to us that it is easy to destroy, therefore to starve. They are powerful, and they want us first to get some idea of this power. After that, when we have had a chance to weigh the risks and inconveniences of war, they will offer to make peace with us, that is clear."

"Is that the way you sum it up? Why?"

"Because a strong organization presupposes a brain behind it, and because a brain does not destroy without rhyme or reason. Now this I grant you, looks like a fairly good reason, and this reason rhymes with the facts. Therefore, I think it is very probable. After that, if you have another explanation to propose, we will examine it and I will laugh at myself willingly."

"No, I am the one the laugh will be on," answered Bellecour, almost persuaded that the other man was right.

MacHead Vohr had lifted his head. He looked keenly at the three men who were watching him. Then:

"We will pass over that," he said briefly. "It is of no interest, since we have nothing to do with this proposal as long as the brain, which Athole imagines to be there, has not delivered its ultimatum. That is

what you mean when you say they will offer us peace,
I suppose?"

Athole bowed.

"Good!" continued MacHead Vohr. "We agree,
that is enough; and I repeat, let us pass over that.
When we come to the bridge, we will cross it. Let
us look to the present, not the future. Andrea Ferrati, you have had this Andrews arrested. Guilt
certain?"

"Certain," affirmed the chief engineer. "If he had
confessed, his case could not be clearer."

"It would be better if he did confess for the moral
effect."

"I will do what I can to make him."

"Do everything except promise him pardon. Not
that, because, on the contrary, he must be punished
and very severely too: he is the first man taken and we
have had forty accidents to the grinders on the running mills this morning!"

"Forty-seven," corrected Bellecour.

Athole and Ferrati, who did not know this, exchanged
glances. Athole, admiringly; Ferrati, aghast, shivered.

"God!" he murmured in spite of himself, "but what
do they want, what do they want?"

"By Jove!" exclaimed Athole, also speaking low.
"I told you that last evening! They want strawberries
and melons, little melons and big strawberries!"

Overlooking this aside, MacHead Vohr continued.

"Briefly, Andrews will get the maximum. How
much, Bellecour?"

"Twenty years on account of the injury to the fore-man."

"Providential injury! Then the man will get twenty years. Athole, telephone to the presiding judge and tell him to await my orders this evening. I will talk to him myself. But you with Ferrati, however, see this Andrews and let him know that his twenty years are coming to him, without repeal: that he cannot escape the verdict but that he can, by his own choice, either work out his time from the first day to the last, or be let off at the end of twelve months or so and receive in addition a check of ten or fifteen thousand dollars, if he knows how to earn it, and, at the same time, a ticket for Liverpool or London. See that you make him understand this, eh?"

Athole looked at Ferrati. The latter nodded his head.

"He will understand, sir—or I am much mistaken; that kind of a man is not difficult to handle!"

"I will depend upon you two gentlemen."

Just Bellecour, frowning slightly, scrutinized the Governor's impenetrable face.

"Governor," he asked suddenly. "May I ask one question?"

MacHead Vohr looked at him before replying:

"Yes."

The man from Lyons explained.

"This Andrews in question is a well-behaved, good-natured fellow. I am surprised that he has done this thing. In any case he could not have done it unless

forced to it; his very awkwardness is proof of that.
The workmen know this as well as I do. Since you
permit me, I will say that, in my opinion, giving this
man the maximum of the law, besides being an individ-
ually unjust condemnation, will be considered by the
workmen as a mistake on our part, and, consequently,
will fail of the result we want to obtain, which must
be to frighten the people and show our power."

"No," said MacHead Vohr. "That is not my
object."

He thought a moment. Then, instead of replying
to Just Bellecour, he turned to Athole.

"You were speaking of a brain," said he. "I think
that you are right. If you are right, this brain is the
only thing that matters. And to expose the worst consequences of his distardly work before his eyes, is to
hit him harder than ever. If he is not corrupt, if he
is a sincere man—like that tremendous imbecile of tremendous good faith in the Nineteenth Century in
France, that absolutely empty orator, Jean Jaurès!—
if, therefore, our man is like that, he will be very much
upset to see a practically innocent man crushed immediately on account of the damage to the machine
he runs. As for individual injustice, it is not important; it is excellent for one man to die, if needs be,
for the happiness of a multitude—wrote the great
Rudyard Kipling.[1] Good-bye, gentlemen."

---

[1] "On the Wall of the City."

CHAPTER III

The Attack on the Mill

"SO THEY gave him twenty years, eh?" asked one of the policemen, as the armored train cleared the Shops and began to pick up speed on the road.

"Yes sirree, twenty years!" said the sergeant.

"But he confessed, didn't he?"

"Oh, as to that, he confessed all they wanted him to and probably more than he knew. But that didn't make any difference to the judges. They wanted to give him the sack and they did. Just the same, it's not a wasted confession for him. It's my idea they'll pardon him."

"What a business it is anyway! A regular organization, if you please, and those lessons on how to destroy the machines, that they give in the cellars of the Blocks. . . ."

"A leader. . . ."

"That's the pippin of the lot, that leader. . . . A delegate from the Council of the Order of Anarchy! That's not to be sneezed at, I can tell you! And they haven't been able to get his name, eh?"

"No. It's a sure thing Andrews doesn't know it,

156

for, at the point he's reached, one betrayal more or less . . ."

"Don't believe the big bosses are feeling so well satisfied!"

"That's sure, all right! The Governor has taken pretty strong precautions!"

Andrews, condemned the night before to twenty years of hard labor in the house of correction, had just left the detention camp in an armored train, and guarded by fifteen agents of the Federal police—negroes for the most part—more trustworthy than the police of Louisiana. From this camp, situated in the midst of the Shops themselves, to the house of correction at the southeast extremity of the Natural Island, is not more than forty miles. The single track was three hundred feet from the power house which had formerly supplied the wireless of the old Iron Tower with electricity. And this power house, in times past hydraulic —a creek flowed nearby—was called the Mill!

The Natural Island, certainly less picturesque and less irregular than the Artificial Island, also less thickly wooded, was not, however, absolutely flat and barren. The strong wind from the delta, which dried out and stirred up the sand from the floods, had little by little made an oval-shaped hill about ten miles or so wide, about twenty long, and one hundred yards high at its summit.

The railroad from the house of correction encircled this hill on the west, consequently in sight of the Eighth Mouth, but not in sight of the Shops, nor of the Resi-

dences, nor of either of the Palaces: for, as soon as
the hill was rounded, the road swerved towards the
east and disappeared behind the southern slopes. The
Mill was precisely at this point of the line where the
trains disappeared from sight of everyone, except from
the ships coming from the sea towards the Eighth
Mouth, or returning from the Shops towards the
Florida Canal, Jamaica or Cuba.

The armored train was puffing along asthmatically:
for the old railroad was in a pitiable condition. Aside
from the locomotive, an old steam engine, poorly pro-
tected by side plates and a flattened roof, it comprised
a tender of some sort and the prison car—modern, this
latter, and really steel-plated and armed with four machine guns, one at each corner. Eight policemen
manned the guns; seven others were scattered about
rather carelessly on the locomotive, in the car, and even
on the tender. They all carried carbines, since they
had been ordered to. But the government of the Siturgic had not been able to convince the police that
there was the slightest chance of an attack on the
armored train. To tell the truth, MacHead Vohr was
the only one who had foreseen such an attack, and none
of the men around him, Just Bellecour, no more than
Ralph Athole, could keep from opening their eyes in
surprise when the Governor had ordered that all possible precautions should be taken in transporting the
condemned Andrews from the detention camp to the
house of correction.

"Why these precautions?" the executive councilor
could not help asking his chief.

"Because the enemy organization must logically make an effort to recapture the convicted man from us."

"Oh," murmured Bellecour, openly incredulous. "Do you suppose, Governor, that those people over there are so much interested in freeing this Andrews?"

MacHead Vohr had looked the executive councilor straight in the eye with a singularly ironic expression.

"In freeing him?" he repeated in a strange tone . . . "freeing him—yes, if you like: in freeing him, so be it! I really think that they actually care a great deal about it, and that they will make a serious effort. Well then, let us make a counter-effort to prevent it."

And the order was carried out as he decreed.

At twelve fifteen the armored train had left the Shops. At twelve forty-five it passed the twenty-ninth mile. Fifty-eight miles an hour. Nineteenth century speed! The road, beyond, turned to the left, making a cut in the last spur of the Natural Hill. At least one mile ahead the Mill reared its old walls, worn away by the years. The creek flowed alongside. The ruins of the ancient sluice still held the waters which cleared the obstacle in a long leap—half falls and half rapids —noisy enough to be heard even from the panting train. The two sounds put together made such a racket that the engineer scarcely understood his fireman when the latter, tapping him on the shoulder, cried, pointing towards the window in front.

"What do I see down there on the track?"

The fireman was shortsighted. Although not as common as it has since become, nearsightedness was begin-

ning, in 199——, to ravage the eyes of all civilized
peoples.

The engineer knew that the fireman was nearsighted,
so he shrugged his shoulders and said:

"Ye don't see nothin', old man! and there ain't
nothin' to——"

Suddenly he broke off, swearing furiously and threw
himself on the throttle to reverse the engine. Across
the track, six huge pine trees, neatly sawed, but still
full of branches and leaves, were piled up one on top
of the other, a barricade improvised, it is true, but absolutely impassable.

When the armored train stopped, after skidding
nearly a quarter of a mile, the fender grazed the first
of the pine trees. Then, to the utter amazement of
the entire armored train, the foliage of the pine tree
parted and a man, who had at first been hidden by the
leaves, stepped out. This man very calmly scaled the
bottom of the rubbish bank on the left of the track;
then, in full sight, he hailed the convoy in a voice that,
even when not giving orders, had a commanding tone.

"The train-chief, please!"

It never dawned on the sergeant not to show himself.

"Here I am! What d' you . . .!"

He did not have time to finish.

"You and your men get out of there right away!
Come now! Step lively! Hands up!"

In spite of the clear menace of his words, the man
himself did not present a threatening appearance. Apparently he was unarmed. He stood with his hands on

his hips and talked naturally, without raising his voice.

One of the policemen, who later was a witness at the trial, testified that, from the beginning to the end of the affair, this man was "as calm as a bloody Baptist: calm as Chief Engineer Ferrati when he was bossin' the job; and say, that man looked a lot like the Chief; why, he was the very splittin' image of him!"

At the command "Hands up!" the sergeant, his pride aroused, resisted.

"Are you crazy?" he cried in a rage. Then turning to his men.

"Present arms!" he commanded.

The reply came back as sharp as the click of a pistol when it is cocked.

"You're going to get yourself killed, I warn you!"

At this a shot rang out, immediately followed by four others. And four men fell: the sergeant and the three police on the tender, who stood out against the horizon like three targets.

As the man who had held up the train finished speaking, a policeman from the prison car had had the fatal idea of obeying his chief, without waiting for the command; and, sighting his adversary in the middle of his body, he had fired and missed. In an instant, four guns, hidden, as their leader had been hidden, in the branches of the barricade that barred the track, had answered, probably by instinct too, but with more precision. Four policemen were now stretched out on the ground: and their aggressor, the only one in sight, was still on his feet.

For the second time he spoke.

"Cease firing!" he ordered first, facing in the direction of his own men.

Then, addressing the armored train, where the firing had also stopped after the first shot and had not broken out again.

"You've had enough of that, I guess? Look here! You're not dead, are you? That's good! Wait, I'm going to help you——" This last to the sergeant, who, wounded in the shoulder, had fallen out of the car, and was picking himself up rather painfully.

The man who had held up the train now came to his aid. And he supported in his arms the sergeant, who swayed and looked at him round-eyed, not daring to make any more resistance.

"Who the devil are you, anyway?" he asked at last. "And why did you fire at us? What do you want?"

The man answered in no uncertain terms.

"It's none of your damned business who I am! Just the same, I'm going to tell you, so you won't be bothered about it any more: besides you know damn well who I am. Yes; the man in whose honor your boss, Sir MacHead Vohr, sent you here, you and your guns and your armorplate. The Delegate from the Council of the Order of Anarchy, if you prefer. A man like other men, as you can see for yourself. But that's not the point now. The question now is what I want, and what I want is this. The merchandise you are carrying, your prisoner, the condemned Andrews."

This time the sergeant was not surprised. He had had time to collect himself, to get over his first emotion and he was expecting this conclusion.

"Impossible—very sorry!" he said. "You ought to know that yourself!"

Once more he was interrupted.

"*Very* possible, on the contrary!" replied the delegate from the Council of the Order, convincingly and peremptorily.

He explained, succinctly.

"It is a case of *force majeure*. There were fifteen of you: you are not more than eleven now, before you even start fighting. Remember that you men are open targets and that you can do absolutely nothing without getting the eleven men who are left killed one by one."

In spite of himself, the sergeant betrayed his uneasiness:

"You know how many of us there are?"

The other man shrugged his shoulders.

"I even know your name, you are Mulready. Well?"

The sergeant, dumb with surprise, hesitated. Then resolutely:

"Well," said he, pulling himself together, "well! get out of here then: I don't want to play you a dirty trick, but I'm going to open fire!"

"Good!" said the adversary, "fire away! that won't help you much!"

He walked away in a leisurely manner and disappeared in the foliage of his tree. Painfully the sergeant hoisted himself up on the engine. Immediately, the two guns at the front, fired riddling the foliage. There was no answering fire.

"Watch the flanks!" ordered the sergeant.

In spite of his wound which was hurting him, he did not leave his post. At his command, the engineer had reversed the engine. The throttle, opened wide, suddenly sent the train shooting backward down the track.

"The track must be free in the rear. We've just come over it," the sergeant reckoned.

But he reckoned badly. The train had not backed more than a hundred yards when, suddenly, several fairly large-sized objects appeared together on the top of the cut through which the train was moving. Four objects, tall and long, cylindrical in shape: four hogsheads full of water, which the delegate's men had undoubtedly filled at the creek, then rolled to the edge of this rubbish heap below which the train was passing . . .

The hogsheads, pushed out into space, rolled down the slope with a rumbling noise like thunder, and crashing down on the train wrecked it as easily as a child's balloon falling on a house of cards. The train, derailed, turned over, smashed against the opposite bank. The armorplates split apart and ripped from their supporting plates. The guns flew in all directions and were buried in the sand. The prison car was burst open from end to end, and the engine caught fire. Of the fifteen policemen, only five escaped and they were immediately surrounded by the victors, thirty or forty men from the Blocks, all wearing masks except one, their leader.

There was nothing to do but surrender! The five vanquished survivors gave themselves up. They were not maltreated; they were not even handcuffed. They were only disarmed. And the unmasked leader, the delegate from the Council of the Order of Anarchy, without the slightest resentment congratulated them on having performed their duty creditably.

"No one will hurt you," he declared. "And you are even going to be set free immediately, on the single condition that you will take a letter to your boss, the one you call the Governor. You are at liberty to tell him everything you have seen here. Here is the letter."

It was ready and sealed with the symbolic arms of the Order: an isosceles triangle inscribed in a circle split in three places.

After he had handed over the letter, the delegate paid no more attention to the policemen. Another object claimed his attention. From the *débris* of the wrecked prison car the victors had just extricated a man, another survivor, the sixth. And this man, although unhurt, could not have pulled himself out of the rubbish, because he was in chains.

They broke his chains. They led him before the delegate from the Council of the Order. And the delegate from the Council of the Order looked steadily at this man, who, trembling, turned his head away.

This man was the condemned Andrews who, the night before, in the presence of Governor MacHead Vohr's judges, had betrayed the Party! . . .

CHAPTER IV

In the Name of the Enslaved People

"**B**RIEFLY," concluded Pietro Ferrati, in the most indifferent tone in the world, "you have betrayed the Party, not even for the sake of saving your skin, which is not worth anything, but for the sake of pocketing several dollars, and the promise of future freedom. Not very clever, what you did there, Andrews!"

Opposite Andrews, who was standing, held up by two guards who kept their hands on his shoulders, Pietro Ferrati, seated on the bank of the clearing, was presiding over the improvised tribunal. Two masked men, his secretaries, acted as jurymen. The rest of the troop, some thirty of the adherents, not one of whom had raised his mask, formed a circle around the accused and his judges.

The accused Andrews, condemned the day before, found himself for the second time in the presence of new inquisitors. And these men did not demand an explanation, as the judges summoned by MacHead Vohr had done the day before, of the voluntary breaking of a machine which in bursting had injured two men, one of whom was the guilty man—a man so lacking in character and in courage that, before the Governor's

166

court, he had betrayed the secrets confided to him by the anarchists.

The accused, condemned in advance, and for the second time. And not to twenty years of enforced labor this time!

It was with a similar thought in mind that MacHead Vohr, foreseeing what was going to happen, had answered Just Bellecour by asking him if he believed that the anarchists wanted to recapture Andrews "to set him free."

To set him free? Yes! Anarchy was going to set Andrews free, in truth . . . free from the worst and the last earthly shackles: free from life itself!

The unhappy fellow suspected this . . . a little. And few human rags were ever as limp a rag as this creature was at that hour.

The two men on either side of him appeared to be leaning their hands on his shoulders. In reality they were holding him up. Otherwise he would have fallen from sheer terror.

The scene, besides, by dint of being familiar, became gradually sinister, in proportion as the certitude of an inevitable and fatal verdict showed through Pietro Ferrati's ironical and careless questioning. The day before, in the court of the Siturgic, all the paraphernalia, all the judicial pomp, had surrounded the judges gowned in red robes to solemnize their sentence and to make a stronger appeal to the popular imagination. Here, on the contrary, everything was an excess, an exaggeration of simplicity—nothing that could impress anyone in the least. Nothing except—hovering over this living man, who was being held up so that he would not fall too quickly—the motionless wings of Death.

He had stammered out a few incoherent syllables. He himself would probably not have known how to make them more intelligible. Dryly, Pietro Ferrati cut short his speech.

"So you would like to betray the other side at the expense of this side now, would you? The reverse of yesterday, eh? Very sorry! We don't listen to traitors here. They aren't allowed to speak. Silence!"

And, breaking off short, he bent, first towards one, then towards the other of the two jurymen.

"Death?" he asked in a tone which excluded any possibility of an ambiguous reply.

From right and from left the answer came, clear and decisive.

"Death."

"Death."

"Andrews," said Pietro Ferrati, who removed his hat and did not put it on again until everything was over. "Andrews, you are going to die at once. I am sorry I cannot give you a respite . . . the time is too short . . . and, my God! I don't want to reproach you, but it is a little bit your own fault; we would not be in such a hurry if the enemy were not so well informed about everything. . . ."

There is always something comical in the most ghastly drama. The contrast of these terrible words and the sorrowful voice softened, almost brotherly, in tone, bewildered the condemned man's obtuse intelligence. He believed they were pardoning him. He fell on his knees, stammering out his gratitude. And the judges were almost moved to relent.

But Pietro Ferrati, implacable, turned away towards the hangman:

"The rope!"

They brought out the rope. The knot was around Andrews's neck before the man had recovered from his atrocious mistake. He did not understand until he felt the contact of the hemp. Then he shrieked.

"But you've pardoned me! You told me you were pardoning me!"

Ferrati, composedly, denied this fact with a shake of the head and turned away. The two jurymen withdrew hastily. Andrews saw himself lost. His eyes, white as the eyes of a corpse, rolled between his eyelids, horribly. He struggled with his guards, who tried to lift him up: to beg for grace, he persisted in kneeling. Besides he kept repeating the same words over and over, finding nothing else in his brain, maddened with terror.

"You told me . . . you had . . . pardoned . . . me. . . ."

And, first in hiccoughs alternately strong and weak, then, with spasms and groans, he howled like an animal having its throat cut, then gasped like a dying calf.

"You . . . had . . . told . . . par—don. . . ."

Unable to restrain himself, one of the five policemen rushed towards Ferrati.

"You aren't going to murder him like that, in cold blood! I forbid you to do it!"

Ferrati politely shut him up.

"You had a chance to talk a little while ago with your guns. For that matter, you tried to do your best. But now I am the only one concerned in this business. . . ."

At this moment a terrible thing happened. The condemned man, who seemed paralyzed with fear, suddenly straightened up and, with a desperate jerk, escaped from the two pairs of hands that were holding him— escaped, too, from the hangman who dropped the rope. Free, the plain stretched before the unhappy wretch. He could have sought safety in flight. But he did not dream of it. He had not the energy to flee. He threw himself towards Pietro Ferrati, grovelling at his feet like a slaughtered ox. He tried to embrace his knees. Ferrati, for the first time losing his calm, recoiled as if repulsed by contact with a traitor, and Andrews, stumbling, fell face downwards on the ground, his face touching Ferrati's shoes, which he kissed wildly like a fanatic. But the delegate from the Council of the Order, implacable as Anarchy itself, recoiled one step more. And, as the hangman had grabbed hold of the rope again, a jerk of the loose knot stopped the suppliant and pulled him up on his feet, his cheeks green and his tongue hanging out.

"Go ahead," commanded Pietro Ferrati.

He, alone, did not turn away. The hangman forced himself to keep his eyes on the rope.

He had passed it through a pulley, fastened in advance to the largest branch of a huge pine tree, the last of the clump of trees which had furnished the six trunks of the barricade across the tracks. Everything had been prepared, calculated, organized. Pietro Ferrati had not finished giving the funereal order when the cord, hauled taut with a great jerk, threw the victim and dragged him, backwards and head first, towards the gallows. Another jerk and the man was swinging. His last cry for mercy was strangled in a rattle. And Andrews was dead.

Pietro Ferrati came to the corpse, and he, himself, pinned a ticket on it. A ticket bearing the name of the dead man, his crime . . . high treason . . . and, beneath, the Anarchist signature, the broken circle, the isosceles triangle. This done, Pietro Ferrati turned to the five mute policemen.

"You are free," he said. "I am sorry that your comrades are on the ground, instead of being free like you. We are not assassins over here! And you see that we know how to mete out justice in the name of the Enslaved People, who will become the Ruling People when they have punished all traitors and tyrants!"

Silently, and in fear, the five who had listened withdrew.

CHAPTER V

ULTIMATUM

IN CONCLUSION the claims of the workmen may be summed up as follows:

ONE. *Reduction from eight to six hours work a day.*

TWO. *Increase from one hundred and thirty-six to one hundred and eighty-two thousand of the number of workmen employed. This to be done by exclusive enrollment of the children of workmen or of former workmen. The Siturgic having as its duty to feed, for good or ill, not only its workmen, but the children born to these workmen while employed by the Siturgic, and, to provide freely the work indispensable for feeding them.*

THREE. *Increase of weekly salaries, reckoned from one hundred and twenty to one hundred and eighty dollars, this increase resulting solely from the rise in price of the cost of living, and, having been strictly calculated in proportion to this rise. Those who furnish bread for the whole of America have a right not to lack bread themselves.*

Under these conditions no further disturbance will hinder the regular output of the shops of the Siturgic. The increase of laboring force corresponds accurately to the reduction of working hours. And the financial objection does not hold good, given the dividends which the company of the Monopoly of the State pays its stockholders, dividends evidently exaggerated, inasmuch as they refer to the attacks directed by the Socialist party in Congress against said firm.

On the other hand, should the government of the Siturgic go so far as to reject the workers' claims herein above set forth, the output of the Shops, already reduced during the past fortnight, will be further reduced and will decrease regularly in quantity, until the fourteenth day of the fortnight already in progress. This, in lieu of warning, and, in order to dispel any doubts concerning the certainty of our power to execute our final threat, let us summarize as follows. In case of persistent refusal on the part of the government of the Siturgic, work will stop and a general strike will be declared on the fourteenth day of the present fortnight, at six o'clock in the evening. May the famine that will follow be imputed to those who are rightly responsible!

Done in the name of the Workmen of the Siturgic, all adherents, by us, delegate from the Council of the Order of Anarchy, vice-general of the Order for America.

"No signature?" asked MacHead Vohr.

"No signature," said the secretary who had read the ultimatum.

"Give it here," commanded the Chief.

They handed him the letter, of which the above conclusions were a fairly accurate summary of the text.

They were a little group of friends. The Government had considered it unnecessary to call together, for the reading of the strange ultimatum brought by the five survivors of the affair at the Mill, either the Board of Vice-Presidents, the Grand Council, and even less its board of one hundred and fifty chief engineers. Only Athole and Bellecour had been summoned, with Andrea Ferrati. The Governor, in all serious matters, wished to be notified, informed and furnished with documents, rather than to be advised. Men who offered advice were coldly received at the High Palace, and MacHead Vohr, all his life, had practised his favorite maxim. Divide the work, concentrate authority. Four limbs, one brain!

Besides, it was typical to note that, in order to fight this man, Anarchy was borrowing his own tactics. Pietro Ferrati was invested with a power no less absolute over his men than the Governor over the Siturgic. Singular homage which Disorder rendered in this way, willy-nilly, to Order! To conquer the Wheat King, the best they could do, on the whole, was to imitate him.

MacHead Vohr was too exact in everything, he lived too much in the moment ever to remind others that they had been wrong before, while he himself had been right. He did not even agree with Just Bellecour, who loyally referred to his mistake of the day before.

"You were right, Governor, when you predicted that the leaders would make a serious effort to take that poor devil of an Andrews from us! When I ordered out fifteen policemen, I did not do half of what I should have done!"

"If you had sent double as many, they would have sent triple," replied MacHead Vohr phlegmatically. "We are playing poker, that's all. Only, up until now, they have seen our cards and we haven't seen theirs. Naturally, they have won. And that is up to you, Athole. We must see the cards of this man at the Blocks, of this delegate from their Council of the Order, as he is called. We must see the man, too, and know. I ask you, gentlemen, since the question arises. What do you think this man is like? You first, Ferrati?"

The chief engineer, far from expecting the question, started and turned very pale. MacHead Vohr could not help noticing this pallor.

"Are you ill?" he asked, almost affectionately.

"No, Governor," stammered Andrea, rejecting the helping hand without seeing it. "No, but . . ."

MacHead Vohr considered him for a brief second; his prodigious brain worked quickly, grasped the situation.

"Ah," said he, half dissatisfied, half satisfied: satisfied to learn, dissatisfied at what he was learning. "Ah! I understand, he is your brother!"

And as Andrea, thunderstruck, did not utter a word:

"Oh! Come, Ferrati—don't be ridiculous! You are certainly not responsible for your brother's follies— still less for your half-brother's! For this man is only your half-brother, isn't he? I congratulate you, that makes it better for you. Just the same, I admit that this is probably a painful matter, because of your brotherly affection for him. But nothing more. And be assured that this relationship counts for absolutely nothing in my eyes."

His hand sawed the air with the downward motion which was habitual with him. Then, after a moment's reflection:

"In fact, you have certainly seen him recently! Oh! I am not blaming you for anything; and I do not ask anything of you, except this. Is your brother a man who can be won over? I am afraid not! He is more likely a sincere fanatic, isn't he?"

"Yes," murmured Andrea.

MacHead Vohr tapped his fingers on the arms of his chair.

"Don't look like a man about to be hanged! I tell you again, this thing is not important! But I come back to the fact. Pietro Ferrati—it is Pietro, isn't it?—if my old information about him is exact, is an honest man, turned from the right path by false conceptions which are sincere with him. Those men can never be bought. Besides that takes too much time. But they can be converted occasionally, and that is what I ask you, although I know what your reply will be. Is it possible to win your brother over or not?"

Andrea looked at the Governor.

"Don't you think I have already tried, sir?"

"With poor results, eh? No matter. There again, it takes too much time. Besides, it isn't very important; to us, I mean."

He was silent, reflected a moment, and continued.

"Let us leave Pietro Ferrati, then! And let us go on. All joking aside, there are two things to keep in mind. Let us be exact. Today is the 30th of March: the fortnight began on the 26th, last Monday; it will come to an end Saturday, April 7th. First of all, we are threatened, from now until that date, with an increasing reduction of our output, in lieu of warning. Then, secondly, we are threatened at once with a cessation of work in the form of a strike."

"In lieu of punishment, probably," said Athole.

He was smiling. Bellecour, with his Lyonnais gravity, gave him a look of reproach. The situation, in fact, seemed serious. MacHead Vohr, nevertheless, appeared only slightly affected by it. He concluded.

"In short, all that is at least very clear. I have my reasons for not dreading overmuch the effects of the second threat. The first disturbs me more. Ferrati, you are the youngest of us four. Take this and go find the production councilor. Have him read the ultimatum from our workmen, and have him do everything possible to ward off this deluge of accidents of all kinds which are more than probably going to descend on us. An active surveillance ought to be the very thing to prevent at least the greatest number. That is up to you, Ferrati, and your colleagues. Be on your guard. This business is perhaps more serious for yourselves than for America."

"Then you are not afraid of famine?" asked Athole, logically.

"Not much," replied the Wheat King.

But he did not make any explanation.

CHAPTER VI

A Tentative Proposal

THAT same evening, at six o'clock, as Andrea Ferrati was returning from the Shops where he had just had a long interview with the production councilor, which had followed an even longer visit of inspection to three-quarters of the one hundred and fifty groupings (each grouping combined ten groups of ten shops each, and was controlled by a chief engineer, with ten engineers under him, one per each group of shops). Andrea Ferrati, coming back from this tiresome task, which had absorbed him during the whole afternoon, met Miss MacHead Vohr in the middle of the vast park in which were scattered the residences of the chief engineers, the engineers and the majority of the foremen and bosses. Miss MacHead Vohr was driving in her carriage alone.

By a very rare exception, although there had already been a few examples, the Governor had given up his daily drive today. At five o'clock—sacred hour—not an American citizen who did not know about it—Washington still had the Siturgic and its commanding general on the telephone. The conversation had begun at three o'clock in the afternoon, however. But

178

it did not come to an end until a little before seven o'clock. It is only proper to add that Mexico, Montreal, then Lima, Bogotà, Panama, and, at the end of, the meeting, Santiago, Quito, Buenos Aires and Rio de Janeiro, had taken part in the conference.

Whatever might be the cause, Miss MacHead Vohr had been deprived of her father's company. Nor had the beautiful golden chestnuts taken their mistress towards the summits at the south of one or the other of the two islands: for MacHead Vohr, after the recent affair at the Mill, was loathe to let his daughter run the highroads, infested with adherents of open violence, more or less at the orders of the anarchist delegate. Miss MacHead Vohr, always very considerate of her father's wishes, had taken advantage of this opportunity to pay several visits to the wives and daughters of the principal heads of the Siturgic, a fairly restricted feminine world with little variety, but which she visited very willingly, however, since it constituted, first of all, her little court of a Princess Royal, and, in addition, all the social resources at her disposal when she was not in San Diego, or in New York, or in Europe. Miss MacHead Vohr lived in the High Palace about six months of the year. And, of course, New Orleans was only several hundred miles from the High Palace, at the most—therefore right at hand; but, just for that reason, and because she did not feel either quite at home there, or altogether in a strange place, Miss MacHead Vohr did not like to go out in New Orleans society, although it is one of the most diverting and one of the least vulgar to be found in America.

As the clock struck six, therefore, Miss MacHead Vohr left the house of Mrs. Galbraith, the wife of the councilor on Public Works. Mrs. Galbraith was an outstanding personality among the women at the Residences. Pretty and still young, in spite of the forty-five summers she willing confessed to, knowing that they seemed to be only springs, this lady was witty although learned; and one spent very pleasant hours from five to seven at her house, in spite of the fact that too many poetesses were there in the habit of retailing their weekly wares. The good part of these declamatory crises was that politics had no chance to get a foothold at Mrs. Galbraith's. "Shop" was likewise tabooed. Therefore, during her visit, Miss MacHead Vohr could not have heard about the ultimatum which had been delivered the evening before in the name of the workmen of the Shops and the Blocks, by the delegate from the Council of the Order of Anarchy to the Governor of the Siturgic. And as the Governor of the Siturgic always kept all his own counsel strictly, even from his daughter and in spite of his paternal idolatry, Miss MacHead Vohr knew nothing of the dramatic and unexpected events that were taking place at the Siturgic at the moment. Had she, nevertheless, had a presentiment of this? Had Pietro Ferrati dropped any hints of it? Or rather, had she dug up the suspicion from the bottom of her heart, quickly on the alert, as is the heart of every young girl or woman when the life or the interests of their first lover are in question? Cer-

tain it is that, catching sight of Andrea Ferrati at
the moment she was getting back into the barouche,
Eva MacHead Vohr beckoned him most graciously,
with her parasol, to come to her. And Andrea, who
was passing in his own car, an ordinary cab of two
hundred horse-power, good for general use, stopped
short, and jumped quickly to the ground, caught by
the charm of a more gracious reception than he had
expected.

Whereupon Miss MacHead Vohr went straight to the
heart of the question which troubled her secretly.

"How do you do!" she said. "You are coming from
the Shops, I see . . . what news from down there?"

And Andrea Ferrati, taken off his guard, could not
help betraying himself with the first word:

"What?" he cried. "So you know then?"

After that it was easy for her to laugh, and to make
him tell her all he should not have told, without giving
herself away, nor even letting him think that she already knew all about the attack on the Mill, and about
everything that had followed it.

He had distrusted her vaguely, however, for the last
three days. Besides, as often happens, this dull defiance had been a spur to his dawning interest. Formerly, Miss MacHead Vohr had seemed a desirable
prey to him, but almost out of reach. Afterwards, as
he pulled himself up to her level, he had become accustomed to consider her as a companion whom he might
have the ambition to conquer, and who very likely
would not say "no" to him, from the moment the Gover-

nor would give his consent. But, suddenly, a suspicion came to him: he could not have said what; a suspicion, just the same, which convinced him that, behind the smooth forehead of this highly cultivated girl, there were more thoughts than he had yet discovered, even by looking carefully—more thoughts and worse than thoughts, he supposed. . . .

But, having betrayed himself at first, it was not very easy for him to be cautious. They had not been talking a quarter of an hour when she had already learned what Pietro Ferrati had taken care not to let her even glimpse. The imminence of the struggle which was going to put to the test the Siturgic and its work, the social order and the laborers' claims . . . that is to say, from the point of view of Miss MacHead Vohr, her father and her lover.

True to her inheritance, the Governor's daughter received the news impassively.

"You shock me!" she said in almost the same tone she would have said, "You make me glad!" And she added, without changing her tone again: "At least, it will be very dramatic?"

"Probably too much so," said Andrea, coldly.

He who wants to show much shows little. As indifferent as Miss MacHead Vohr had always been regarding anything that concerned the Siturgic, Andrea thought her calm over this incident exaggerated. From that to finding it feigned was only a step.

"If she is pretending," he thought, "*what* is she pretending? And why? or . . . for whom?"

Arrived at this point in the wandering of his suspicions, he had the particular sensation that one experiences on finding one's self again before a bit of countryside which he has already seen before. He repeated to himself, watching her, with a defiance that was rapidly growing hostile.

"For whom? . . . yes . . . for whom is she pretending?"

He felt ill at ease. She plied him with questions which tumbled over each other so capriciously that Ferrati recalled the proverb which says that woman invented the cock and bull story.

One of these questions struck him, however, because he had already put it to himself, that morning.

"My father must be very much upset even if he pretends not to be, isn't he?"

"Possibly," said he; "but, I, who know him better than if I were his son, I assure you he has never been calmer."

"However," she replied logically, "without even speaking of the care he has taken not to breathe a word of this to me, although he knows that I am not interested in politics, do you think it likely that he would sit tranquilly by and accept the prospect of seeing the Three Americas starving ten days from now?"

Andrea had not been able to hide the tenor of the laborers' ultimatum.

Eva insisted.

"If he is really as calm as you saw him, it is because the danger is less serious than you believe. In both cases, your perspicacity seems to me at fault, dear Mr. Andrea!"

He persisted.

"My dear Miss Eva, far be it from me to boast of my own merits which are slender in truth. But you were forgetting the third case, the most probable."

He himself had just discovered that one existed, in fact.

"What is that?"

"The threat is serious, the Governor is impassive, these are two facts; but a threat is only a threat. It's a long way from the cup to the lip."

"Which means—?"

"That the Governor has undoubtedly the necessary means at hand of bringing the workmen to reason when the time comes."

"I do not see what the Governor can do against a strike—one hundred and forty thousand workmen are not replaced at command. And, unless they are replaced . . . an almost impossible feat, I do not see anything that can save the continent from famine. . . . No! believe me. If my father is so calm, it is because he has already made up his mind . . . he has decided to yield."

"That is not at all like him. To yield, why? . . ."

"To be sure he has not yielded . . . often in his life. But there is a beginning to everything."

And in conclusion she added one word too much.

"The Governor must have an adversary of his own size this time!"

"By Jove!" said Andrea, scrutinizing her. "You
have a high opinion of our enemies! . . ."

A complex feeling disturbed him. He was at the
same time proud of his brother, and jealous. The con-
fidences received down there at the Blocks came to his
mind again. . . . This mysterious woman Pietro loved,
who loved Pietro, could it be . . . perhaps?—Impossible?—And yet. . . .

He looked at her, with such attention as might well
have provoked a smile. She was still seated in her carriage, gay, admirably so, impenetrable as certain
women have a faculty of being to the eyes of no matter
what man. He gave up guessing.

"Shall we walk a little while?" he asked.

She replied.

"Yes, very willingly."

They walked side by side along the road. The
antique barouche followed slowly and, behind the barouche, the cab. One of the lackeys had taken Andrea's
place, and was driving the motor car.

The weather was spring-like, uncertain, but clear and
fresh. The woods, dotted with cottages built close
together, were in bud. Fifteen or sixteen thousand
inhabitants peopled this semi-comfortable, semi-luxuri-
ous village. All the chief engineers and all the engineers, the majority of the foremen, heads of shops and
bosses, artisans, six or seven thousands of whom were
employed in the manufacturing, making, marking, regu-
lating, inspecting and repairing of the machines. Those
who did not live at the Residences lived in a similar vil-

lage, although smaller, situated on the left bank of the Mouth—on the Natural Island. Only the common workmen, the simple day laborers, crowded into the twenty stories of the Blocks.

The woods were graded into valleys. Many roads ran up and down steeply between hillocks. Many cottages, on the other hand, perched above the surrounding trees. The coniferous species was in the majority. Pine needles carpeted the ground everywhere, and the healthy odor of the resin made the Residences perhaps the most salubrious of small towns in Louisiana. The north shores of the Gulf of Mexico are commonly swampy, therefore abounding in fevers. It was no slight achievement to have created, in the midst of this death-like zone, an artificial land where contagious diseases were unknown.

Almost in the middle of the dwelling houses a circular center—somewhat similar to the crossroads of royal forests, like the Michelette of Compiègne in France, marked the highest point of the neighborhood. Two circular rows of big oaks formed a shelter for the benches of moss-covered stone. And from this circular center there was a wonderful panorama of the whole country.

Eva MacHead Vohr, arrived there, chose a bench and sat down on it. Andrea Ferrati remained standing in front of her.

They had been silent for five minutes or so. Suddenly Miss MacHead Vohr stretched out her hand and took Andrea Ferrati by the arm.

"Seriously, do you think there is danger of a real war between the Blocks and the High Palace?"

Andrea noticed that she had put the High Palace after the Blocks.

"Seriously, yes," he said, after thinking a moment; "for I am not like you. I do not believe that the Governor is at all disposed to give ground before his workmen."

"But after all," she continued, "even if the strike breaks out, everything may be very peaceable, may it not?"

"Everything *may* be very peaceable, but everything *will* be very war-like. Don't forget that the strike in question signifies famine for four hundred millions of Americans. . . . A strike like that cannot take place without shooting, because the powers that be cannot authorize a famine."

"But the workmen are strictly within their rights in declaring a strike, however! It is legal! . . ."

"Oh!" said Andrea, sceptically, "it is never legal to make four hundred millions die of hunger."

"You take the matter lightly," criticized the young girl, rather dryly.

"Eh!" thought Andrea, "and you take it, as I do not take it! . . ."

But he had the wisdom to keep this thought to himself.

Then she continued.

"Legal or not, the strike is a fact! And, the workmen having declared a strike, it does not seem to me that there is much chance of bringing them back to work by force. . . . I mean when they are one hundred and fifty thousand strong!"

"It does not seem so to me any more than to you," said he tranquilly.

"Well, then?"—she was astonished at this reply, and was visibly upset because he was so calm—"what is this? Your words are contradictory! On the one hand, the strike once declared, you recognize that they can neither force the workmen to go back to work, nor replace them quickly; on the other hand, you consider that the government has the right, almost the obligation to intervene, and you appear to believe that my father, if he shares your ideas, and if, in consequence, he intervenes, will be able to succeed. . . . I am very curious to know how?"

He shook his head.

"Do not ask me state secrets! First of all, my duty, honor, discretion . . ."

He was laughing. She laughed also.

"After all, you are the Governor's daughter. I need only tell you that the Governor has never confided state secrets to anyone but himself."

"Yes," she said, "there you are right!"

Then, returning to the charge.

"Just the same, put yourself in his place. If you were governor and there should be a strike? What then . . .?"

He interrupted her, his hand raised.

"Oh!" he said, "if I were Governor, there would not have been a strike!"

"How is that?"

"There must be workmen to make a strike! If I were governor, there would not be any workmen."

"No workmen? What would there be in their place then?"

"Machines."

"But we have them already! What do you mean?"

"I mean this! . . . a very simple thing: yes, there are machines, it is true; we are not altogether savages; they number here, one hundred and thirty or forty thousand generating or skilled machines, which need, to keep them running normally, nearly one hundred and fifty thousand workmen. Ah! well! if I were Governor, I would always have one hundred and thirty or forty thousand generators; but instead of having one hundred and fifty thousand workmen, I would have twelve or thirteen thousand machine-hands, to call them by their name! . . . and these twelve or thirteen thousand machine-hands would replace my one hundred and fifty thousand workmen, and to advantage, I guarantee it!"

"Yes?" said the young girl reasonably incredulous. "But, if I understand correctly, these auxiliary machines, these machine——"

"Machine-hands. . . ."

"These machine-hands would direct the principal machines? . . ."

"Exactly."

"But they themselves? Who would direct them?"

"No one. They do not need a workman to guide them. They guide themselves and do their task all alone. Someone to watch over them from a distance is sufficient. And our twelve or fifteen thousand foremen would be enough, and not only to do that but also to look after all the material there would be in the entire Shops."

She looked him up and down, impressed, half defiant, half anxious.

"You are not making fun of me?"

"I swear I am not!" he protested. "Would I dare? You know very well I wouldn't. . . ."

She was silent, convinced. He in his turn looked at her, perplexed, moved also. Neither one of them spoke for some time. The breeze blew freshly around the point. And in spite of that the day was warm.

Then suddenly an idea came to him, an abrupt instinct. Perhaps Eva's hand, pressing his arm, had insinuated into his veins the courage he should have had, and that now came to him.

"Eva," he said boldly, "we are perhaps on the eve of terrible days. In hours like these we truly need to consider ourselves, and to lean on each other, to stand shoulder to shoulder against the common enemy. Whether you believe it or not, the ordeal threatens to be a serious one. Look at me and answer me loyally, without any flattery or mockery, straight out, as American girls know how to answer. . . ."

"I have never known any other way!" she said
haughtily.

"That is why I am talking to you this way," he replied quickly, trying to cover his awkwardness. "Look
at me then, and answer me: do you consider me a
fighter for the struggles that are in store for us? Do
you think me brave, tenacious, bold and wise?"

She considered him.

"Why do you ask?"

He insisted, with a gesture or supplication.

"I will tell you, but first answer me. I beg you!
. . . tell me yes or no? . . ."

She considered him again. It seemed as if she were
comparing him secretly with someone else. At last,
without the slightest hesitation she replied frankly:

"Yes, certainly . . . you are all that, without any
doubt. But, once more, why ask me that?"

He took a deep breath like a man who makes ready
for the plunge.

"Because . . ."

He broke off: the impulse was not great enough to
carry him over the obstacle. Partly through real desire for her, partly to dissipate the confused doubt
that persisted in the back of his mind, he had wanted
to ask her, suddenly, just like that, to be his wife. But
he had stopped himself, certain of not being able to get
to the end of his declaration. She was surprised at his
silence. For she had not divined his thought. Women,
so subtle for this sort of thing as long as their hearts
are free, from the moment they fall in love become in-

comprehensive, even obtuse, and willingly believe themselves, because of their love, beyond the reach of all
foreign desire and inaccessible.   Sacred!

She, Eva, was thinking of Pietro, not of Andrea.
And as Andrea had stopped speaking, she did not insist
upon an explanation.   To be quite honest, it made
absolutely no difference to her.   But as Andrea was
Pietro's brother, she wanted to pay him an indirect
compliment, sincerely.

"Besides, it goes without saying that you are brave,
wise and the rest . . . those are elementary virtues
for a man like you.   Good blood always tells!"

Good blood, his, did she mean?   What did she know
about it?   Never had he breathed a word of his race,
nor of his family.   People pay less attention to that in
America than in Europe.   Therefore she knew nothing
about him, except, perhaps, that he had a brother whom
she had seen formerly in the days when he still belonged
to the Siturgic, at the time they were building the footbridge over the Mouth. . . .

. . . Except his brother?

Andrea Ferrati mentally repeated those three words
twice. . . .

And when the thought had penetrated, he did not
ask for the hand of Eva MacHead Vohr.

CHAPTER VII

GRAND COUNCIL

"THE meeting is opened," announced MacHead Vohr, who was seated in his big armchair.

The Hall of the Ambassadors seemed immense. Instead of the one hundred and fifty chief engineers, who only half filled it, when the Board of Engineers met each week, the only council that had been convened for this very restricted meeting was the Grand Council. And again, instead of five councilors, this time they were only four, as often: the councilor of the laboratories, George Torral, had sent his excuses, according to his custom.

With MacHead Vohr, Governor-President, and Andrea Ferrati, chief engineer, acting as secretary . . . (neither stenographers nor lighted bulletin-board today) there were Ralph Athole, privy councilor, Just Bellecour, executive councilor, James Galbraith, councilor on Public Works, and John Tresham, production councilor. All were listening silently.

"Gentlemen," said MacHead Vohr," you have all known of the kind of ultimatum which I received, the 30th of March last, that is to say, four days ago. This ultimatum which I remind you of for the sake of getting things straight, was addressed to me, in the name of the workmen of the Siturgic, by a certain delegate from the Council of the Order of Anarchy, whose name is Pietro Ferrati. No matter. The importance I attach to this detail is shown you by the fact that it is our young comrade, Andrea Ferrati, whom I have chosen, in spite of his relationship to the delegate in question, as secretary for this strictly secret meeting, to which I judged it useful to call you. Let us pass over that. Gentlemen, to be more explicit, I recall the principal terms of the ultimatum in question; first, a threat (by way of warning) of a regular and progressive lowering of the output of the Shops, from March 26 to April 7; and secondly, on April 7, unless there is a capitulation pure and simple on our part, and the acceptance of extravagant terms which are imposed on us, a general strike. That said, I note the facts that have arisen between Monday, March 26, the first day of the present fortnight, to Friday, March 30, the date of the reception of the ultimatum; and from that day until today, Tuesday, April 3, 199—. It is established —the daily reports of Mr. John Tresham, production councilor, show this: that, in spite of all our efforts, the material damages have increased so greatly during the seven working days from Monday the 26th to Monday the 2nd, inclusive, that the output of the Shops has not ceased to be lowered constantly during this period. Despite whatever we might have foreseen and done, the organization of direct action has clearly turned the tables on us. Our reserve stocks in consequence have had to be called on; the manufacturing is no longer equal to the exportation. To cite only one instance, the transit department exports daily three million hundredweight of bread . . . bread made of wheat, rye, barley and additional mixtures. Now, in these seven days the output was only sixteen million hundredweight, instead of twenty-one: that is a deficit of five millions. All of a sudden the totality of reserves went down, from the normal figure of twenty millions to fourteen. We have not baked any more bread in advance for the American continent than just enough for little more than four days. Never, since the time that the art of preserving fresh bread indefinitely has become general, has America been so close to famine. It is clear that without taking special measures, if the strike really breaks out on the evening of Saturday, April 7, the continent will have no more bread by the morning of Thursday, April 12. Do you agree with me?"

The silence which followed was equivalent to an unanimous acquiescence.

Things had actually come to this pass. The formidable anarchistic organization had once more proved its irresistible power. And nothing perhaps is better calculated to demonstrate the absolute chimera of Labor's claims—claims of muscle against brain—than the continual frustration of all industrial attempts to conquer power, in spite of this formidable anarchistic discipline which supports and sustains them. The historic effort of the Trotskys and the Lenins, so powerfully conceived, so implacably realized, at the beginning of the Twentieth century, only ended in a mournful catastrophe; and yet never did better regulated power struggle desperately against the natural order of things, which says that the nerves command and the muscles obey. The muscles are, however, in this struggle, the strongest and the most obedient. All the chances of victory are therefore on their side. And in spite of that they are always conquered. Because their revolt is a revolt against the universal equilibrium, against gravitation, against the Law . . . that of Newton or that of Darwin . . . the law that knows no exception. Imminent justice is powerless against the square of speed. Or rather, it is the square of speed which is imminent justice in spite of the appearances with which our infirm spirits are deceived.

In the case of the Siturgic, anarchistic discipline had done its work, the only work that it was able to carry out to the end—the work of destruction. All the energy of MacHead Vohr and of his men had broken against the patient and regulated effort of one hundred and thirty thousand adversaries, blindly submissive to the orders of a single leader who dictated his will by the intermediary of twelve or fifteen thousand adherents of direct action, chosen from among the least stupid of the workmen. It was, in fact, easier to lead to industrial combat one hundred and thirty thousand almost completely unintelligent laborers than fifteen thousand foremen, bosses and artisans. These latter, representing as many brains, gave rise to as many thoughts, agreements, and individual wills.

Prussian militarism cannot be forced on other than Prussian soldiers, bodies without heads. In order that Anarchy marvelously adept at annexing militarism, should never have known anything but disasters, it has been proved that it must carry within itself its own germ of death and of oblivion.

Matters had come to this point. In spite of all the measures very skilfully taken by the production councilor, Mr. Tresham, the output of the Shops had not ceased going down, from March 26th to April 3rd. Already the fortnight promised to be much more disastrous than the preceding one had been, and that had been a deficit. Unquestionably when the strike had broken out on the evening of the 7th, the stocks, which had been tampered with, put the Siturgic in a very bad position. The Three Americas, the Government had said with certainty, would not have enough bread to eat.

" . . . Unless special measures are taken," Mac-Head Vohr had added, however.

Ralph Athole, who had listened to the whole discourse, one elbow on the arm of his chair, and the left cheek leaning on his closed fist, lifted his head at these words, and, changing elbows, leaned his right cheek on his wrist.

MacHead Vohr, before continuing, glanced at the privy councilor, then repeated:

"Unless special measures are taken."

Then, having meditated for three seconds:

"Gentlemen, I have called you together to inform you exactly of those measures to which I am resolved to have recourse. Moreover, I need your advice on the means of carrying this out, means which I have not yet chosen. Therefore, kindly give me your attention."

He meditated again. Then:

"Mr. Galbraith," he said, turning towards the councilor on Public Works, "a little information, first, please: you have received the two cargo-boats *Baltimore* and *Cincinnati* from New Orleans today?"

James Galbraith nodded his head silently. An American from Boston, the councilor on Public Works symbolized, in the government of the Siturgic, intellectual America. Boston, from the Eighteenth to the Nineteenth century, was always prouder of its libraries than of its banks. Galbraith, very well informed, and with a fairly general culture, got on marvelously with the executive councilor, Just Bellecour. Each exaggerated his instinctive gravity: the Bostonian to pedantry, the Lyonnais to mysticism.

"Just where are those boats?" asked MacHead Vohr.

"Docked, according to your orders," replied Galbraith; "the *Baltimore* at the west piers, the *Cincinnati* at the east piers, both stern to stern. I cleared the two southernmost piers for them according to your instructions."

"The two boats have been isolated, with police guard, and no one from land has communicated with them?"

"Of course, Governor! Always according to your

orders, which have been carried out as unfailingly as they have always been under my direction."

"Good!" said MacHead Vohr.

He rose, and all followed suit, except Andrea Ferrati, secretary, who remained seated before his typewriter. The Governor went up to him, and put a hand on his shoulder.

"Gentlemen," said he, "this boy here, at the last meeting of the Board of Engineers, you remember, took the liberty of interrupting me to remind me of a fairly good piece of advice which he had previously given me. If, instead of workmen, the Siturgic employed machine-hands, he called our attention to the fact that the Siturgic would not be at the mercy of a social discontent so much the more impossible to foresee as it always happens without rhyme or reason! That is what you said, Ferrati. And I answered you, do you remember? 'Your words have not fallen on deaf ears!' I knew very little on the subject of machine-hands when you spoke to me about them for the first time: but, from that moment, I hastened to inform myself more thoroughly. And, having decided that they were interesting, I took the precaution of ordering twelve thousand from the Pittsburgh factories, to be delivered in New Orleans. I did this without informing Washington, in order to avoid any indiscretion and any possible interdiction. Congress talks too much, and even with us the executive power has often been influenced by the radicals. Neither Parliaments nor ministers being in a state to furnish bread to the continent, if the workingmen were seized with a whim to deprive them of it, I acted on my own authority in order to render this whim powerless should it arise. I hope I have succeeded. Gentlemen, this brings us to the point. The *Baltimore* and the *Cincinnati* are bringing us twelve thousand machine-hands, ordered by me in Pittsburgh and delivered by Pittsburgh to the Siturgic! These machines have been stored for sixteen months, according to my orders, at New Orleans. In this way the secret was kept. It was important for it to be. If it had not been, our workmen, or rather Anarchy, which has substituted its will for theirs would have been driven to some act of violence. Besides, we must foresee that we are going to be exposed to it, as soon as the Blocks perceive the inevitable fiasco of their strike. In order not to give the enemy leisure to prepare his attack, I have taken care to maintain the secret as long as may be possible. It is also to facilitate the defense of the cargo-boats, in case of attack, that I have chosen the two most southerly piers we can dispose of for their mooring. By this means, the boats are nearer us and farther from the Blocks. Besides, the danger really does not commence until the night of the 7th to the 8th. I intend to await the proclamation of the strike before having our twelve thousand machine-hands transported to and installed in the Shops. You will have the moving carried out by the bosses and foremen exclusively—you, Bellecour, with Ferrati under your orders. Ferrati will be your technical advisor. And you will act as chief executive for the governmental delegation. Above all,

do not forget to station police everywhere. The affair
at the Mill ought to be a lesson to you. A surprise
attack by Labor would be a very serious matter at this
juncture. The bread of the Three Americas is in your
keeping."

He paused, and took a deep breath.

"It is more than bread," he continued, speaking
slowly. "It is the success of an industrial operation
which seems to me to bear the greatest and heaviest
consequences of all those which were ever attempted.
The folly of our workmen drives us to a sudden realiza-
tion of the mechanical transformation of our Shops—
transformation which, had it come progressively, would
have taken years and years. A harsh necessity and one
of which we are innocent, forces us to bridge this lapse
of time and to accomplish in a single day what, in the
ordinary course of events, would have taken years.
One hundred and forty thousand men compel us to sup-
press their means of existence. I do not hide this fact
from myself. But these men, in doing this, endanger
the existence of four hundred million other men. The
former, to be sure, have the advantage over the latter."

He stopped a moment, then concluded.

"Galbraith, the guarding of these two cargoes until
Saturday evening is your business. The landing of the
machine-hands is your business too. Bellecour, you
will furnish the men Galbraith needs, and you will direct, as I have just instructed you, the transportation
to the shops, then get them installed. Once the machine-hands are in place, Tresham will immediately test

them out. All that ought to be finished by Sunday, April 8th, before daybreak. At seven o'clock in the morning, Monday the 9th, the shops will begin work again. The machine-hands, here for the first time, will replace the human hands, rendered useless by this act . . . useless forever."

MacHead Vohr finished speaking and sat down again. Ralph Athole, more attentive to the speech then perhaps any of the three other councilors, objected in his suavest tones:

"Will there be no other assurance for the subsistence of the one hundred and forty thousand workmen thrown out of work by this act?"

"I think so," said MacHead Vohr. "Washington will certainly take the matter up."

"That will take some time."

"Not so much, certainly, as the strike would have taken."

The reply had fallen with the sharpness and swiftness of a stroke of the axe.

"Oh!" said Athole, gently, "far be it from me to bring humanitarian arguments into the debate! That is not in my field. But those one hundred and forty thousand men, if they are too hungry, will become formidable. So much the more so since, behind them, two hundred and twenty thousand women, old men and children will suffer their share of famine."

"Every battle gained, industrial or military, entails some dead."

The Governor's voice rang like the sound of steel striking steel.

"Yes," said Athole again. "And if I speak, it is solely with the intention of insisting that we may take all precautions, and that a battle which is certainly going to cost many dead, may be a battle we are sure to win!"

MacHead Vohr let his glance, at once sharp and heavy, rest on all four of his councilors:

"Agreed," said he, "that is your business, Galbraith, from today, Wednesday, to Saturday evening, April 7th and Sunday morning, April 8th, and yours, Tresham, after Sunday morning, April 8th, until further orders. During each of these periods outlined, two policemen are at your absolute command. Athole, you have charge of the Intelligence service. Choose the personnel you need; Bellecour will put it at your disposal. And you will report to me every hour, all of you."

"Wouldn't it be advantageous to reinforce the police now?" insisted Athole again.

MacHead Vohr answered him:

"We have eight hundred federal agents and six hundred policemen from Louisiana at our disposal. Two armored trains will come in tomorrow, Thursday, each one bearing four hundred supplementary police, sent by New Orleans; and, the day after tomorrow, Friday, two other trains will arrive from Washington. In adding a special guard to the *Baltimore* and to the

Cincinnati on Saturday, we will dispose of four trains with two thousand, two hundred and forty guns, in addition to our permanent force, which consists of three trains, fourteen hundred men and twelve machine guns. Sum total therefore . . ."

Ferrati calculated rapidly.

"Three thousand six hundred guns, forty-two machine guns, seven armored trains."

Galbraith and Tresham, together, gave their approval.

"That is enough."

"Let us hope so!" said Athole.

"Yes," said MacHead Vohr, "in the interest of all."

Athole looked at him. But MacHead Vohr did not say anything more.

And nothing unforeseen occurred, from Thursday, April 4th, 199—, until Saturday the 7th, the date on which, at the stroke of seven in the evening, the workmen of the Siturgic, as they had threatened, declared to America, represented by the government of Governor MacHead Vohr, the strike!

CHAPTER VIII

MECHANISM VS. ORGANISM

NIGHT, almost without any intervening twilight, had followed day. Siturgic City, situated at 29 degrees latitude north, is nearly tropical, and every evening the sun drops almost vertically to the horizon.

Pier 84, the last pier on the right bank down stream, was deserted when Andrea Ferrati, directing the first detachment turned over to him by Just Bellecour, reached the gangway of the *Cincinnati*. Moored to a quarter of the length of the enormous pierhead, and even more enormous itself, the *Cincinnati* had a tonnage of sixteen thousand gross and a displacement of about twenty thousand, loaded.

In the dark the ship, almost empty, reared the huge sides of its hull, whose few port-holes, all opening on the promenade deck, were scarcely visible from the level of the pier. A blank wall is always a little like a human being, blind, deaf and dumb. So the ship seemed, motionless, concealing in its hold this formidable secret: six thousand machine-hands, ready for work!

"Forward!" Ferrati commanded. His gang—twelve foremen or bosses, that is to say, twelve heads of shops

or artisans, all naturally non-strikers, all living outside the Blocks, at the Residences—climbed the two
gang-planks. At the top, some policemen stood with
crossed bayonets. The countersign was exchanged.
They were allowed to pass.

And, the first, Andrea Ferrati, at the foot of the
ladder, entered the middle hold, the main hold, and
switched on the electric light. The cargo-boats did
not have the profusion of light that passenger boats
have: three lamps dimly lighted the hold . . . and
its formidable cargo.

Formidable . . . ! The unhappiness of many
men, women and children was enclosed there, between
these walls of sheet-iron, beneath the intersected beams
and warp, among these cast-iron stanchions, innumerable little columns keeping the spacing of the platforms
in place . . .

Andrea Ferrati had been familiar with the machine-
hands for a long time. Nothing could surprise him
in the external appearance nor in the internal action
of the six thousand mechanisms that were crowded
together, in the flanks of this huge ship with multiple
holds. But he pulled up abruptly, on the threshold
of the water-tight door which he had just opened, impressed in spite of himself!

The machine-hands were lined up in serried ranks,
from bow to stern and from port to starboard. They
had been stowed away standing. Each one having
about the shape and the dimensions of a watering
trough; better still, of a little stone slab in a Turkish

cemetery. Thus crowded one against the other, they looked, in the half light, like six thousand steel soldiers, drawn up for combat, and ready to kill. And in fact, these six thousand soldiers were going to kill, they, the men of steel, were going to kill men of flesh and blood. . . .

As yet, inactive, inoffensive, the army of metal seemed to sleep. But the awakening was near at hand, and the battle imminent. Battle or butchery? There could be no doubt, in truth, regarding the outcome. These men of steel would kill the men of flesh and blood. And Andrea Ferrati, too much of an engineer not to admire the steel hands more than the human hands, and too fanatic in his faith in the irresistible progress that sweeps clean, wipes out and forgets all that is left behind, all that does not adapt itself to the overwhelming march of the times—Andrea Ferrati, too sectarian in his belief ever to pity the crushed and the forgotten, nevertheless could not help a feeling of swift anguish in the presence of these six thousand machine-hands, all created and put in the world to help men to live, to make life . . . and which a blind and implacable destiny condemned to make, first of all, death . . .

Ten hours later, at break of day, John Tresham and Andrea Ferrati, the last to leave, came out of a shop—No. 6666, to be exact; the one that had been the theatre of the first serious accident due to direct action, to the disorganization of discontented workmen! Ten men had worked there, just the day before. In their place, one machine-hand had just been set up: only one, and it was at work. By this single machine-hand, ten pie-making machines were guided, propelled, regulated, stopped. The solitary boss of the shop, arms folded, watched over the machine-hand, watched over the pie machines. The one guided the other: he merely looked on. The rye, carefully weighed out, fell from the receptacle: the water, from the water-crate. Then, the trough filled, the ungeared grinder pulverized the grain. The dough, made and kneaded at last, the emptying trough opened and the still liquid mixture ran slowly, thickened from sluice to sluice, as far as the spiral shears, which cut it up, to the driers, which solidified it, to the packers which put in boxes or in neat cartons the vermicelli, the noodles, macaroni, cubes, letters, stars, all the nourishing dough for an entire population, manufactured solely by ten principal machines, ten auxiliary machines, and a single guiding machine. . . Thus, the precious manna flowed like a stream of life towards the exit of the Shops, towards the trains or the cargo-boats which carried it away . . . like a river of life whose tides also concealed, alas! an inevitable foam of Death . . .

PART IV

THE AXE

CHAPTER I.

Folded Arms, Vanquished Arms

A T SEVEN o'clock in the evening, Saturday, April
7, 199—, the same dramatic scene was played
simultaneously in all the fourteen thousand three hundred and thirty-six shops of the Siturgic. Everywhere,
at the prescribed signal, work stopped; everywhere one
of the ten workmen of each shop, sometimes the eldest,
sometimes the youngest, went up to the head of the
shop and told him—courteously enough in the majority
of the shops, in a few, rather arrogantly, even ironically here and there, in a few cases:

"Sir, as the Government has not agreed to our just
claims, the strike is declared; my comrades commission
me to inform you of this."

This sentence delivered, all the men had walked out,
in perfect order and without any disturbance whatever. The strikers had been ordered to furnish the
Government with proof of that absolute calm which is
the evidence of strong discipline and presages powerful victories. *Exceptis excipiendi*, has said the ancient
humorist. Every rule, to be humane, must have many
exceptions.

The night of Saturday, the 7th, to Sunday, April

8th, was, in each of the two workers' cities, a noisy and drunken night. The two banks of the Mouth re-echoed to the sound of joyous revelry, all the more tumultuous as it was a celebration on the eve of an exciting crisis, not the day after. War was declared, the victory had not been won. Inevitable risks, certain suffering, possible disasters, not one of the four hundred thousand inhabitants of the Blocks pictured to himself the least of these afflictions which, nevertheless, hung over their heads. The success of the strike, uncertain as it was, and more precisely because it *was* uncertain, was discounted, on the spot, and the discount was instantaneously spent, squandered. Moving picture houses, saloons, dance halls, taverns, all were packed from night until dawn. There was no curfew. By order of the Governor—a very wise order—the regular police had withdrawn from the Blocks. Anarchistic discipline seemed despotic enough, in truth, to reduce to a minimum the danger of serious excesses, of delinquency and of crime. On the other hand it was important, from all points of view, that there should be no opportunity for conflicts between the strikers and the police. The strikers, first of all, would not have failed to find in such conflicts a pretext or a justification for subsequent violences; and these violences were the thing above all others to avoid. Moreover, Washington, and Montreal, and especially Buenos Aires, were naturally only too much inclined to disclaim any energetic measures that they might be forced to take against the strike. And although MacHead

Vohr smiled at it indifferently, seated, as on a throne, on his eighty billions and the bundle of his titles as property-holder—a good half of the State of Louisiana was his personal domain—he preferred, nevertheless, to avoid as much as possible any conflict between his financial power and that political power which, on the whole, was nominally his master.

On the evening of April 7th the police had therefore quietly evacuated the Blocks. The populace scarcely noticed their absence, all intent on its violent joy in having made the savage gesture which is dearest to our savage humanity—a declaration of war. War, strike: synonyms. Men and women of the Blocks, women especially, imagined they smelt blood. As yet there was nothing. But reality is never anything. Only the dream exists. This wine that flows red, intoxicates quickly. There were no crimes at the Blocks during that night of April 7th. But there were numerous accidents, many of which led to the cemetery.

Toward six o'clock the sun rose and day replaced night with dawn. The sky was heavy. The clouds had gathered little by little, before daybreak. With the first rays of the sun they broke, and rain poured down on the city, drenching it in torrents. Those night revelers who were left in the streets, all rushed madly for shelter to their own homes. And the heavy slumber that follows nights of debauch ended the nocturnal fracas. The downpour had put a gag on both the west and the east Blocks. And whoever had seen the Blocks wrapped in that deep sleep, would certainly have predicted that they would not wake up again before night returned.

Now, it was not yet noon before a dull rumbling began gradually to arouse the city. One by one, windows were opened. Elevators went up and down. At last women, then men still half asleep, appeared on the streets, and stood about in groups, palavering. And all, promptly gathered together at the highest points of the two cities—the Natural and the Artificial —stayed and tarried to gaze in the same direction, towards the south, towards the Shops—all of them, every man, woman and child, and all seized with the same great speechless astonishment . . .

At Rome, when the conclaves meet to elect a Pope, the people of the city crowd the squares around the Vatican every evening, to await the unpublished bulletins of the day's balloting. All eyes turn then to the chimneys of the old papal palace; for, according to whether smoke comes out of the chimneys or not, the cardinals will have or will not have burnt the reports of the day's voting, and the Roman people will know that it has not yet, or that at last it has its Pope.

In the same way the people of the Blocks, silent and bewildered, gathered together to watch, above the thirteen hundred and forty-four factory chimneys that crowned the shops of the Siturgic, some thin plumes of smoke, floating in the morning mist!

Smoke, down there, at the Shops?

And all the workmen still here, at the Blocks!

Smoke, fire, consequently furnaces at work!

Who had lighted these furnaces? The bosses, the foremen? Possibly—evidently! But why? What could they do with lighted furnaces? Who would keep these furnaces going, first of all? Who would stoke? And who would convey the motor power afterwards to the utilizers? And who would run the machines? Who would start them going, who would regulate, who would check, who would stop them? Impossible! And again impossible! There must be workmen to run the machines! And where were the workmen? Here! Here at the Blocks! There were no workmen at the Shops! There could not be any there: where would they have come from? And who would they be who would have dared to brave the formidable veto of the Council of the Order of Anarchy? Not one! Not a single man!

And yet—the chimneys were smoking!

An hour later, a kind of cortège formed, which ran haphazard through the streets of the Blocks. The working people, confusedly restless on account of this sword of Damocles which they sensed without yet feeling, were hunting for each other and for their chiefs, their leaders, those who had drawn them into this *impasse* which instinct already warned them was narrow, short and perhaps fatal. The tumultuous joy of the night before had changed, brutally, into anguish.

At first they could not find their leaders.

Bewildered themselves, the leaders had, first of all, called a meeting of their own and consulted together.

That is to say, the moment he was warned, Pietro Ferrati had called together in a cellar, still unknown to his adherents, his secretaries and the two dozen particularly reliable men he employed in serious cases to inflame or guide the ardor of the revolutionary workers. And there, in the subterranean silence and in the twilight, an anxious council of war was held.

The discussion was summed up in one question, a question of life or death.

What was going on at the Shops?

The disembarkation of the machine-hands and their installation had passed unnoticed. Their presence in the Shops had not been revealed until the chimneys had begun to smoke.

At two o'clock the excitement calmed down. The chimneys of the Shops had stopped smoking. The crowd, sensitive only to immediate impressions, was, if possible, more quickly reassured than it had been frightened. The council of war in the unknown cellar, less quick to forget and less carefree, did not stop holding their sessions. They had despatched all the emissaries they could find towards the Shops to get information. But the police, withdrawn from the Blocks, formed a particularly tight protective cordon around the Shops. The afternoon, then the evening passed, without any information being brought from the Shops to Block 395 . . .

It was not until past midnight that an airplane, coming from the south, from no one knew where, landed secretly on the terrace of another Block, of Block 216.

Pietro Ferrati, leaning on the railing of the terrace, and someone leaning beside him, looked for a long time at the city of workmen, where the excitement had little by little subsided.

The night before, all had been tumult and noise. Now there was nothing but silence; a silence too heavy not to be filled with anguish. And this anguish, little by little, was becoming terror. The mass of people had had too much faith in the infallibility of this childish weapon, the strike, not to be terrified at the first check to its effectualness. What was this! They had folded their arms, and would that perhaps not be enough to give them the victory? . . .

CHAPTER II.

INFORMATION

"MACHINE-HANDS? Here?"

"Yes, here! In the Shops! Ready for work: six thousand in the west shops, disembarked from the *Cincinnati;* six thousand in the east, disembarked from the *Baltimore!* Carried in and set up last night. Tried out this morning—that is the smoke which you saw unexpectedly. And tomorrow, from seven o'clock, they take on the work in place of the striking workmen, who, *ipso facto*, because of the strike, are permanently dismissed. You have attacked. The Governor parries."

The speaker was silent. And Pietro Ferrati, who was listening, did not reply. In the face of this news which had just hit him he was like a man struck down by lightning.

There was a long pause. Then the same voice continued, with a throb of strange emotion:

"The Governor has parried, and I am very much afraid, Pietro, that the return thrust may be fatal. That is the reason why I, his daughter, have rushed here to betray his secrets to you! But it was as if I saw in his hand an axe raised over your head. Oh!

Pietro! I love you . . . I love you, my darling;
do not despise me for this!"

Yes, the speaker was in truth Eva MacHead Vohr.
And, for the first time indeed, losing her head in the
double torrent of her conflicting emotions, her filial
devotion, and her devotion to her lover, both equally
desperate, the proud girl had fallen from her high im-
partiality, fallen to the depths of treason. And dashing—as she herself described her action—in spite of
herself to the aid of the vanquished, in this terrible
duel between two beings who composed her whole life,
her supreme anxiety was not of calling down the
paternal wrath on the vanquished, but rather of suffering the contempt of the lover she had just tried to
save.

Conqueror, conquered. The struggle, scarcely begun,
really seemed finished. The weapon of the strike was
lamentably broken at the first blow struck. Twelve
thousand machines, conceived by a single brain, rose
suddenly on the field of battle. And that was the end
of the one hundred and forty thousand human combatants, whose purely muscular efforts counted for
nothing any more. Zero!

Crushed by the terrible discovery, Pietro Ferrati
gazed silently at the sleeping city of which, on the
morrow, he would certainly have ceased to be master;
the city which, besides, would kill him without a doubt,
would crush him or would stone him, as the mob always
does to those who have made, for their sake, a fruitless
effort. And he tried to collect the morsels of his

thoughts, pulverised by the unexpected and deadly shock.

When she had said, "Do not despise me!" he had kept quiet. His prostration choked the words in his mouth. He had only put his hand on his mistress's shoulder, and pressed his fingers into her flesh until he bruised it. As tragically unhappy as she was in her despair for him, for a second a smile of joy had parted her lips, pressed tightly together.

Later, without thinking what he was saying, and only to break a silence which was becoming intolerable, he asked her casually:

"How do you know all that?"

"From your brother," she replied.

Mechanically he stammered his surprise:

"Does he talk as much as that? Or only to you? . . ."

"Oh!" she said, "he has always been very intimate at the Palace, and on very good terms with me . . ."

Suddenly she became embarrassed. She was not at all anxious to describe the skillful coquetry which she had used to compel Andrea this once more to betray the secrets he should have kept, even from her. Besides, she was aware of the suspicions she had little by little aroused in him, suspicions which recently had grown keener. And she would not have believed it likely that Andrea, after having given her fairly copious information about everything she had wanted to know, might have watched her actions, her conduct, and perhaps have surprised her as she left the High Palace at night for the Low Palace.

The Italian race does not disdain these surveillances, especially between the sexes, which other people of different morale would call espionage. A matter of climate, matter of sun! The more in love one is, the less scrupulous. It is noteworthy that America, this leveler of the various peoples who compose it, this crucible in which are indiscriminately melted Latins, Saxons, Celts, Germans, Iberians, even Slavs, and from which come out, all in the same pattern, nothing but Yankees—America, if she stamps with the same outward appearance all these diverse beings she refashions, respects, on the other hand, for a fairly long time— several generations in fact—the inner life of each and every one. At first sight there is nothing more alike than two Americans, sons, this one of a Tuscan, that one of a Scotchman from Perth, or of a Frenchman from Lyons. Yet there is nothing more unlike, when you know their lives. In any fairly important circumstance, each one of them will not resemble his neighbour in the least, although alike enough in appearance, but much rather his father, and all of his father's ancestors. The climate, so quick to change a man's skin, takes years to change his blood, and centuries to modify the *neurones!*

However, Pietro was staring fixedly at Eva. The sense of the words which she had spoken carelessly a little while ago had little by little penetrated his armor of torpor. And suddenly the bitter waters of jealousy overwhelmed him. His suffering as a conquered Socialist leader was swallowed up in the agony of a suspicious lover.

He turned away his head suddenly, then said jeeringly:

"Andrea looks very much like me—don't you think? —A woman made that mistake—once."

The Scotch blood of the MacHead Vohrs had two full centuries of "Americanization." Eva MacHead Vohr in all normal circumstances was a pure Yankee, daughter of a man from New York, granddaughter of a man from Baltimore, and great-granddaughter of a man from Boston. Only in extraordinary cases did she betray any of her Highland descent, which went back to the most ancient of ancient Scotland; it was stern, headstrong, obstinate, superstitious at times, but always noble. But in all that Scotland, that of the time of the clans, of the bards and of second sight, there was nothing to compare with Italian wiliness, flashing like a Tuscan stiletto. Pietro Ferrati's insinuating allusion made Eva MacHead Vohr turn red with anger.

"Just exactly what do you mean?" she interrupted sharply.

"Nothing," he answered, "just what I said."

They were silent. The misunderstanding of two beings who love each other, and of whom one suspects the other, can never in the world be dissipated.

Pietro Ferrati and Eva MacHead Vohr were like this, from this moment until—until the end of their story. Between them a shoot had sprung up, like those shoots from fig trees which spring up between stones cemented together in the Roman style, and which disjoin and break into ruins the most lasting monuments.

The suspicious lover gave way, however, before the leader of an army in danger. Perhaps the shock his love had undergone helped to give back to Ferrati, delegate from the Council of the Order of Anarchy, a little of the calm indispensable to the desperate measures which circumstances, desperate in themselves, called for.

For a while Eva was no more for Pietro than the spy which, after all, she had agreed to be. What she suffered besides, all this time, one can imagine, no words can describe.

"So then, in all, twelve thousand machine-hands? That ought not to be enough."

" 'They' say so. The machines do not work eight hours, nor even twelve . . . but twenty-four!"

"But there must be someone to oversee them!"

"One man oversees several of them. We have more foremen and supervisors now than we need."

"But twelve thousand machines don't come from nowhere! And yet no one could foresee . . . "

"Your brother foresaw. My father gave the order."

There was a ring of pride in these words. Followed then a painful silence; Eva sobbed without tears:

"Why must each of these men, men like these, tear out a piece of my heart!"

She leaned her two clasped hands on her lover's shoulders, and forgot herself so far as to implore:

"Pietro, Pietro . . . my love! . . ."

But it was as if she had not spoken. Pietro Ferrati had not heard, or did not want to hear. He was dreaming, he continued to dream. He was as if plunged in his revery, and only came out of it, or rather jerked himself out of it, to ask brusquely:

"That's right, the police? Did they think of them? Have they been reinforced? By how many men?"

"I don't know," said Eva.

Then she hesitated and fought with herself before daring to add:

"Do you want me to find out?"

"No!" said he, impetuously. "You are mine, I will not permit you to . . ."

He did not finish. She did not know whether he was forbidding her to get information, or the means of procuring it.

CHAPTER III

REFLECTIONS

FROM the Blocks to the Shops the electric trams ran four double lines, all placed on tracks. Two tracks had been laid out on the Natural Island; two on the Artificial Island; and these four lines were the only ones which lay to the north of the Shops, on all the territory of the Siturgic, with the exception of the main line of eight tracks which connected the Siturgic with the mainland by the right bank of the Mississippi. But this main line did not touch the Blocks; on the contrary, it circled around them, to cross the Ninth Mouth far to the west of the Artificial Island, on viaduct sixteen miles long. To march from the Blocks on the Shops the army of workmen and its leader had, therefore, only four lines, the shortest of which was from eight to ten miles long, and the longest about twenty-five. This difference was explained by the extent of the gigantic factory, so vast that, from the first shop to the last, the Eighth Mouth flowed over fourteen miles.

To march from the Blocks on the Shops! That is what they had to do, indeed! Engaged without any turning back in their unavailing strike, the strikers perceived too late the frightful *impasse* from which they could not get out. Every combatant always sees three outcomes of his battle: victory, surrender, death!

And there was no surrender for the strikers of the Siturgic. To whom should they surrender, when the enemy refused quarter? Certain at first of success, the delegate from the Council of the Order of Anarchy had not even renewed parliamentary relations with the Government of the Siturgic after the affair at the Mill. Since the Siturgic had foiled his calculations, and had suddenly bobbed up, not only undefeated but actually triumphant, the situation was turned against the strikers, who did not even know that MacHead Vohr had secretly discussed with Washington the conditions of a possible subsistence for the four hundred thousand defeated strikers, and their fathers, mothers, wives and sons and daughters. Lacking an exchange of ambassadors, the strikers knew nothing of this port of safety which was opening for them. For Pietro Ferrati, who had heard something of it himself, was careful not to publish it, his personal interest and his passion for leadership both driving him rather to urge the mass of dismissed workmen towards the most extreme measures, the most uncompromising violences. That being the case, and since the machine-hands which had appeared unexpectedly had endangered the whole enterprise, changing the promised victory into probable disaster, there was nothing left but to attack the cause itself of this fatal change—the machine-hands. To destroy them, and in order to destroy them, to go first

and find where they were, no other plan could retrieve
the battle in doubt. Where they were! In the Shops,
after all. To march from the Blocks to the Shops, in
spite of the police; to carry the Shops by storm; to
destroy the machine-hands, and nothing but the machine-hands; to respect especially the rest of the
machinery, indispensable for starting work again—
that was the ultimate goal of the strike. Such therefore was the worse than hazardous undertaking which
Pietro Ferrati had to manage successfully, on pain of
having driven to despair and to death those who had
attached themselves to him, and on pain of being driven
there first himself. For a conquered leader, whether he
has a conscience or not, does not survive his defeat,—
either the poorly shepherded troop kills the bad shepherd, or the shepherd takes the lead and punishes himself for the crime of having made a mistake.

"Do you think they will be crazy enough to attack?"
Just Bellecour had asked Ralph Athole, on their return from a reconnaissance they had made together
of the possible battlegrounds, to the north of the
Shops, the length of the first of the crosslines which
intersected the four railroads.

Each one of these railroads was barred, on the right
and on the left, by improvised trenches, each oblique,
the two of them forming a recessed angle in which any
troop advancing would have been caught between the
crossfire of eight machine guns. An army corps would
not have got out of it.

"It is insurmountable, look!" insisted Bellecour.

"Right, my dear fellow!" replied Athole, smiling in his usual manner. "But then do you suppose that these good people will be wise enough to starve to death, without kicking over the traces, just to please us?"

MacHead Vohr, an hour later, gave the deciding vote.

"They will certainly be crazy enough to attack. But I still hope that we can hold them in check. And perhaps they won't starve to death after all, if Washington and Buenos Aires come to an agreement quickly enough on this case. . . ."

In the general interest, much more than that of the strikers, the Governor was, in truth, working perseveringly to persuade the American Republics of the advantage which compromise and moderation presented in this matter. To offer some occupation or other, whether fictitious or not, to give work, whether alms or not, to the human arms dispossessed by the invading Machine, was without doubt a free charity. But it was nevertheless a wise charity. (The word "humanity" rarely passed MacHead Vohr's lips.)

"Assuredly," he even said, and as if excusing himself for the side he was defending, "these men who are of no use to society have ceased to be men, since they are incapable of adapting themselves to their age, incapable of following the middle course of the progress of humanity; assuredly the law of Darwin condemns them, without respite, to death. Just the same, Nature does not proceed by leaps, and selection itself is only operated in general by a series of successive repressions. I consider that it would not be successful and even that it would be a blow at Nature, and even a regrettable one—this sudden repression of about three hundred and seventy thousand human lives."

CHAPTER IV

Convulsions

INARTICULATE, monotonous, monosyllabic, but reiterated indefinitely, and nearer the cry of a wild beast than a human clamor, the roaring of the mob on march rolled across the countryside! It was a sort of *Hou! hou! hou!* gloomy and terrifying—gloomy enough to arouse terror and terrible enough to make one flee! Under the lowering sky, an autumn rather than a spring sky, the sound did not rise, but seemed rather to smash on the plain on a level with the tall grass. Four columns, each one at least four thousand strong, were advancing down the four lines, from the Blocks towards the Shops. And not one of these breasts could do anything more than make a painful effort, from time to time, when the legs could hardly take one more stride. For they were utterly exhausted, these men accustomed only to work with their arms and their hands. Exhausted from having already walked so far, desperately fatigued by the thought of having still farther to walk—of not being half-way to the goal. Calculated at the best, and reduced as much as they had been able to reduce it, the shortest distance to traverse was nevertheless more than seven miles.

And there were many more women, old men and little
children than grown men in this disordered, unarmed
crowd, which was just the same an army, and which
was marching on the enemy just as in times gone by,
the armies of soldiers.

. . . To march on the Shops, in spite of the
police . . . to take them by storm . . . to
destroy the machine-hands . . .

And, to do this, it took one hundred and twenty
thousand men, women and children, a third of the entire population of the Blocks, marching helter-skelter
in four columns, without any communication between
the columns except this rumbling which was like a lugu-
brious sigh, and which was heard from one road to the
other, and even above the noise of the Eighth Mouth,
in spite of the more cheerful uproar of its waters.

One hundred and twenty thousand combatants instead of three hundred and seventy thousand; Pietro
Ferrati, still almost master of his army, in spite of
the terrible blow his authority had suffered by the unforeseen appearance of the machine-hands, had judged
this human mass dense enough to overwhelm, without
striking a blow, all the police, machine-guns and armored trains included that the Shops could get together.
There could be no question of a formal struggle. Just
Bellecour had made no mistake in this. Four army
corps, minus artillery of course, could not have chal-
lenged the four cross-fire entrenchments which barred
the four routes at the elevation of the first crossline.
One does not struggle against an adversary, invisible

and capable of furnishing, in ten seconds' firing, more
balls than the Blocks numbered breasts.

But neither soldiers nor police fire willingly on an
unarmed mob; still less on a mob of children, old men
and women! To advance to the point of the bayonets,
to parley, to dispute; and under cover of the discussion, to get around the policed sections by the wings,
too weak to cover effectively all the territory of the
Shops, whose four sides exceeded twenty-two thousand
miles—such was the tactic on which the delegate from
the Council of the Order of Anarchy had decided. It
was a tactic whose excellence history has demonstrated
hundreds of time! If, on July 14, 1789, the guns of
the Bastille had fired on the populace of France, the
Bastille would not have been captured. But it would
have been at the price of a hecatomb before which
Governor Launay recoiled. He died of it, for that
matter, he and all his people. For one always pays
with one's life for the scruple of hesitating to take
another's life while there is still time.

Four high clouds of dust marked the march of the
four columns. From the terraces of the High Palace,
nearly twenty-five miles away, MacHead Vohr, surrounded by his staff, saw these clouds, like plumes of
smoke that signal the arrival of steamers and iron-
clads, before their masts have appeared above the
horizon.

"There they are," announced James Galbraith, who
had followed the Governor's gaze.

MacHead Vohr considered it superfluous to reply.

He had taken the spy-glasses and was searching the distance.

"A lot of them, those people!" murmured Ralph Athole, speaking to himself.

"And even if there are, what of it?" said Just Bellecour who had overheard him. "Just the same I imagine you do not admit that they will swallow up our four dozen machine guns and our seven armored trains? They are unfortunate children who must have their fingers burnt because they are going against all the natural laws, against all common sense based on all the experience of the centuries. Athole, the more they are the better they will see the uselessness of numbers opposed to selection, of body opposed to spirit. They will understand. And they will resign themselves to accept the charity which Society offers them, since after this they will be incapable of existing by their own efforts."

"You have a fine mind," replied Ralph Athole coldly. "Do you really believe that a man ever considers himself incapable of arriving by his own efforts and by his alone, at no matter what goal?"

"I know there are fools in the world!" said the Lyonnais.

"And I do not know whether there are any wise men!" retorted the other.

The seriousness of tone excluded all idea that he might be joking.

At this moment several ladies came up on the terrace. This was Miss MacHead Vohr's day "at home." Mrs.

Galbraith, wife of the councilor on Public Works, and Mrs. Fairvice, wife of an engineer-director, Mrs. Allanway, wife of one of the specialists, who collaborated with the laboratory councilor, George Torral—all had been invited to tea. And, the news of a possible outbreak having arrived, all these ladies had begged their charming hostess to take them up to the top of the Palace, to the terraces from which one could see, perhaps hear, or at least know what was going on.

Eva MacHead Vohr, marvelous in her air of calm and worldly indifference, had acquiesced. Now they stood there looking out across to the Shops in the distance. Four mother-of-pearl opera glasses were trained on the northern horizon; and, cunningly, they had drawn near the group which surrounded MacHead Vohr, to lie in wait for the words that perhaps the leader or his lieutenants would let fall in a moment of distraction.

"For the love of God!" had exclaimed Mrs. Allanway, who loved emphasis and the speech termed "ejaculatory!" "Dearest Eva! Take pity on me, and tell me if you have any idea what this band of wild beasts think they are going to do at the Shops. These beasts, whom the Governor with his genius has suppressed the need of! From now on they will have nothing to do but fold their arms, and American philanthropy will feed them for doing nothing! Do they want more than this? Then what, if you please?"

Eva, all smiles, replied:

"Dear Mrs. Allanway, you haven't the slightest bit

of vanity in you, and so you can't guess what a lot of
vanity others have. But if you will just count up on
your pretty fingers everything the Church considers a
capital sin, you will see that one of the ugliest is called
by that name . . . yes, 'vanity' or 'pride' . . .
Add to it this one, 'envy'! . . . The two things
are enough to show us how the useless workmen of this
poor Siturgic are not absolutely satisfied to owe their
bread to public charity from now on; and, on the other
hand, are very much irritated at not having any more
jam to spread on this bread, which will not amount
any longer, as the Bible says, to what they used to
earn by the sweat of their brow."

"You could make me believe that black is white!"
exclaimed Mrs. Allanway enthusiastically.

She threw her arms around Eva's neck. The young
girl let herself be embraced complaisantly, disengaged
herself at last with a slightly nervous gesture; and,
perhaps to keep up appearances, she picked up her
opera glasses again, immediately training them on the
high yellowish clouds which were slowly rising from
the horizon.

"What extravagant people men like that are!" announced Mrs. Tresham, who had only just come up
on the terrace; "to want to destroy those machine-
hands! Why! My husband was explaining the mechanism to me only yesterday, and they are certainly
the finest effort and the most productive result of the
entire human thought, concentrated for two or three
centuries . . . excuse me, I learned Mr. Tresham's

beautiful expression by heart . . . 'the most productive result of the most beautiful effort of all our thought, concentrated for two or three centuries on machinery!' . . . Imagine wanting to destroy that, and also the good that humanity can gain from it!"

"Oh! Mrs. Tresham!" said Eva who appeared to be quite fascinated, "how right Mr. Tresham is! And how charming of you to give us the opportunity of enjoying such a concise expression, most certainly coined for you alone! But, unfortunately! do you remember that the boatman of the Weser . . . is it the Weser? . . . I am so ignorant! . . . do you remember that the boatmen of some river—I don't know which—smashed to pieces the first steam-boat of the unfortunate Denis Papin, this Frenchman who preceded our Fulton?"

"They didn't prevent steam from triumphing," cut in MacHead Vohr, who had just joined them.

All the women curtsied. At the Palace, Miss Mac-Head Vohr played the rôle of Princess Royal fairly well. But the Governor played to the life the rôle of Emperor.

"Governor," said his daughter, "here are all my friends, trembling like leaves at the thought of the disasters those poor people can heap up in their path."

"They are right," pronounced MacHead Vohr coldly.

"What?" questioned the young girl, and only a close observer might have detected a quick change in the suddenly troubled voice. "What? Governor! . . . you are not going to frighten us. . . . I

mean, to pretend to try and frighten us . . . First
of all, we all heard these gentlemen a little while ago:
it is impossible, they all said, for the strikers to force
those barriers which you yourself have erected to prevent them from going any farther . . ."

"Perhaps they will go farther, in spite of these barriers," retorted MacHead Vohr.

And suddenly a mysterious emotion, terrifying because at the same time deep and contained, made his
voice tremble:

"Eva, my precious darling, I implore you to tell
your father the whole truth! Come, tell your poor old
father, my love! Eva, I implore you! Why are you
anxious for the strikers not to force our barriers and
for there to be no bloodshed?"

The father's voice quivered. The girl trembled all
over.

Did he know? The question suddenly struck Eva in
the very bottom of her heart.

Did he know? Who could have told him? Andrea
Ferrati, perhaps?

Bewildered, confused, Miss MacHead Vohr suddenly
perceived, as in a blinding flash, that this man, Andrea
Ferrati, loved her—dared to love her! . . . In love
herself with someone else, she was indignant, then bewildered. If he was capable of loving her, why not
capable of spying on her and of betraying her? . . .
Yes, and in spite of the fact that he knew the man she
loved was his own brother, the brother he adored?

. . . Are men anything but slaves of frailty, the
playthings of their instincts, governed by fate?

Yes, MacHead Vohr knew. Suddenly, she was convinced of this, she was certain of it.

MacHead Vohr knew. And he did not doubt it.
There was no room in him for any doubt. But he did
not believe it.

His daughter? No. Impossible!

He loved her too much, that was all there was to
it! She could love a man, a man who was not he, he,
MacHead Vohr?

No. Again impossible!

Just the same he had questioned her.

Doubt is a steel file that bites into the soul of iron.

Yes, he had questioned her; and Miss MacHead Vohr
could only reply with a gesture. The paternal glance,
plunging into her very soul, dissected her alive. A
torturing silence followed.

But, by the clemency of chance, a new arrival had
just appeared, Andrea Ferrati. He was returning from
"the front," that is to say, the protective trenches.
And, as was fitting, he went straight up to the Governor in his haste to make his report. At the same
time, just as Ferrati was about to address him, he saw
Miss MacHead Vohr, took in her pose and the Governor's, and knowing himself culpable, perhaps, was
worried.

Miss MacHead Vohr gave Andrea Ferrati a flaming
glance. Andrea Ferrati had certainly been running.
He mopped his forehead.

"Well?" demanded MacHead Vohr, who, with a supreme effort, had become simply the Governor again.

"Well!" said Ferrati, speaking in too loud a voice . . . "things are getting pretty serious . . ."

At the Chief's imperious gesture, he suddenly lowered his voice. A colloquy followed, of which Miss MacHead Vohr caught only this phrase, which was spoken by the Governor energetically, but in an almost grieved tone:

"Poor people! forcing our barriers; it is as if they were forcing the bars of their own tomb . . ."

Having said this, the Governor had broken off the interview. Andrea Ferrati, finding himself alone, retreated a step, as if he had wanted to leave the terrace furtively. But, as he was about to get in the elevator, he found Miss MacHead Vohr just ahead of him, and barring his passage.

"Oh!" he exclaimed, "Miss Eva . . . pardon me!"

"You may well ask my pardon!" she retorted furiously.

He looked at her. She shrugged her shoulders.

"Enough of these pretenses! What have you told my father?"

"I? . . ." he cried, as if choked with indignation. Then getting hold of himself, with his Italian adroitness: "Oh!" said he, "first of all, I beg of you: what have you done that I could report to him? Have you confided some secret to me which I might have been led to betray? Which one, if you please? Or could you, by chance, suppose that I am a simple spy in the pay of the Governor? Would you do me, would you do him, this extraordinary injury? Do you think he has his own daughter spied upon? Do you admit that I accept the wages of a policeman? If so, Miss Eva, you would be singularly guilty in suspecting other people of such abominable things. Are you then—how do I know?—the friend of the rebels? of *a* rebel? . . . But no! I have not said anything . . . only your insult made me forget myself . . . and I ask your pardon . . ."

As he was speaking, his assurance returned. And his last words, clipped short as they were, were the result of the wisest diplomacy. Nevertheless, she was not taken in by it.

"It is useless!" she said, boldly. "You know what you know, and I know that you know it. I have only one question to ask you. Answer me, and then silence! What did you say to my father?"

"What could I have said to him?" he retorted, audaciously. "Where there is nothing, what king would keep a right? Now of course there is nothing, is there?"

"Coward!" she hissed.

The duel existed, in America, in the year 199—. Andrea Ferrati could reply, truthfully:

"I did not hear what you said. A man could not have spoken that word without dying. A woman will not be able to shout it loud enough for a man's ear to catch."

This was becoming a war of phrases. Eva MacHead

Vohr lost the little remnant of cool-headedness left her.

"Coward!" she repeated. "Coward, who knows that Pietro Ferrati's mistress will not slap Andrea's face!"

She had spoken very low. And at this moment everyone had stopped talking. Then, there was a great uproar on the terrace. And, for the space of a breath, Eva thought that her confession had provoked that uproar. For the girl it was a second of hell. But the instant afterwards she was undeceived. No rattle of machine-guns can cross twenty-five miles of intervening space. But, no matter what the distance, watchful spy glasses easily discover the blue smoke of a salvo. All those who were looking from the High Palace towards the horizon at the north had sent up a great cry simultaneously: with the gray masses of dust clouds which designated the four columns of people on the march from the Blocks towards the Shops, four jets of blue smoke had suddenly mingled. The machine-guns had spoken.

"At this second many men are dead," cried serious Mrs. Galbraith, as if in spite of herself. At times she had a sense of realities.

"Many other men will perhaps live longer because of the death of those you speak of," replied Ralph Athole gently.

Silence held all spellbound on the terrace. The souls of those men who had just died, now freed, were perhaps passing that way. . . .

Impetuously Miss MacHead Vohr had seized Andrea Ferrati by the wrist.

"So then, you know. . . ."

But he, more violent, interrupted her at white heat.

"So, you know—you, my brother's mistress—you know that I love you! You know it, you knew it, and, never, not even by a word, nor by a sign. . . ."

"What!" she cried, controlling her voice, however. "What! you dare to pretend that I, I should have confided in you! Confide a love so noble that if you spent your whole life dreaming of it you could never understand it?"

"You say that to me? I, who love you and have never spoken, because I was so afraid of finding you less than any dream? . . ."

This was his reply. And, at this moment, what he proclaimed, he would have sworn before God on the Day of Judgment.

He was none the less a man of highest honor. All his life was a proof of this. The human race is only the plaything of the climates which have weighed on it for some twenty or thirty generations.

They did not understand each other; and, reciprocally, they despised each other. She thought she ought to insult him again, and, in doing so, to draw a sign from him:

"You are too vile to be more than your brother's half-brother! At least redeem what there *is* left to redeem of your shame! Why did my father say what he said? Is that unhappy populace, for whose safety Pietro Ferrati has consecrated his life, risking a final catastrophe, by trying to force the barriers which the

Governor has erected between them and their goal?"

She was so beautiful in her haughty appeal that Andrea could not refrain from turning traitor once more.

"Ah!" he cried, "you cannot even foresee what that catastrophe would be! Not even my brother, with all his genius, could imagine it! . . ."

"Good-bye!" she said.

She flung herself into the elevator. Surprised by her swiftness, he saw the door slammed in his face.

Down there, on the cross-section trench, the mass of the people who had come up had spread out to right and to left, even beyond the wings of each machine-gun post. The posts had at first held a truce, when the columns had come up to them. There had been explanations, without violence, a fairly long time. But each column was at least three or four miles long. When the head stopped, the rear had still pressed on. As a result, men, women and children were now spread out over the two sides of each route—spread out so completely and effectually that the posts had soon seen themselves surrounded, outflanked, and each column submerging and overwhelming each barrage, the police officers were, in the long run, in the desperate alternative either of seeing all measures taken to prevent the strikers from reaching the Shops, outplayed, or of having recourse, on the spot, and almost without warning, to force.

To force. That meant, to the machine-guns! . . .

The necessity arose, suddenly. On the Artificial Bank, at the right side of the second route, a troop of little boys and girls, running as far as they could, crossed the line of the machine-gun barrage.

"If they come on sixty paces more, they will enter into our dead zone and no longer will be in danger from our cannon," observed one of the gunners to the officer of the police.

"Bugler!" cried the officer. "Sound the warning!"

The notes rang out shrilly. Girls and boys, who were running joyously on the meadow, nine or twelve hundred feet to right and to left of the road, did not hear anything, or at least did not understand. And, all together, they continued to run gaily without even dreaming of their peril.

And yet there was peril, terrible peril. If the range of the machine-guns was passed, nothing could stop the people from dashing towards the Shops to destroy the machine-hands there. It was impossible for the police to let them go ahead. One cannot exact suicide of anyone.

"Bugler!" cried the officer again. "Warning!"

Once more the bugle-call died away. And terror seized the crowd which was beginning to realize what was happening. Not, alas! the crowd down there which was pushing beyond the permitted boundaries, but the one which remained back on the road and heard, saw, understood. . . .

"You aren't going to shoot down those poor little

ones?" cried a man whose breast was pressed against the mouth of a machine-gun.

"Will they stop?" anxiously inquired a gunner who was manning the gun.

"Murderers!" howled the mob. But too soon. There is nothing more infuriating than an unjust reproach.

"Murderers, eh?" one of the policemen repeated furiously. "Who is it who will do the murdering in a little while if we let those worthless fellows gallop ahead?"

And, without any order, smarting with anger at the insult which redoubled the danger for him, he pulled the trigger.

Among all the contagious diseases that medicine has ever discovered, murder is the most prompt to become epidemic.

A gunner had fired. Ten gunners fired. And it was a hecatomb of corpses that piled up, to right, to left, all around the second route, less than a mile wide, to three hundred or six hundred feet deep. The green plain was stained red. And, at this moment, headlong flight upset these thirty thousand men where death had ploughed its furrows. The turncoats did not stop until they had reached the Blocks, six miles away.

But, to right and to left, neighboring columns, which had advanced the length of the first, both on the third, and on the fourth route, were not stopped as the second column had been.

Guns heard from a distance and shots in the immediate vicinity are two very different affairs.

Everywhere men were parleying, at the mouth of the guns. Suddenly the fusillade, burst out on the second route, resounded again. And this time the effect was doubled: everywhere the machine-guns cracked: everywhere the masses of strikers rushed against the cannon simultaneously. At barrage posts one and four, the machine-guns carried off the victory and drove back the assaulting columns. At post three the police were beaten back, overwhelmed, annihilated. Three shots sent three seconds too late. Half a dozen strikers having been thrown down, the thirty thousand survivors hurled themselves upon the police, too humane to have defended themselves when there was still time, and heads cut off were brandished on the end of poles. Beside themselves, this mob of thirty thousand human furies turned into beasts by this victory without a struggle, rushed in a torrent, by road, by slopes, over all the plain, towards the undefended Shops. . . .

And, less than a half-hour afterwards, while eighty thousand bewildered fugitives rushed to the Blocks, mad with horror, and crying defeat, thirty thousand furies, drunk with their victory, stormed towards the Shops, intent upon killing everything they could find!

It was exactly five minutes after midnight, this Monday, April 9, 199—, on the terrace of the High Palace, when Miss MacHead Vohr's guests began to notice her absence. . . .

CHAPTER V

Block 216, Post 32

AUTO, airplane—it did not take Eva fifteen minutes to go from the terraces of the High Palace to the terrace of Block 216.

Pietro Ferrati was naturally not there. In the apartment on the twentieth floor whose windows looked out on the Ninth Mouth, Miss MacHead Vohr found only one of the delegate's secretaries. She knew this man, by name Faraway. He did not hesitate to give her all the information she wanted.

"The delegate," he said, "is necessarily down there, 'at the front'! You can imagine that after the terrible disappointment about the machine-hands he was not sitting on any bed of roses. All the 'loud mouths' in the Blocks fell on him, accusing him as one man of treason, of standing in with the enemy! God knows what! They are not men, those beasts! . . . You can get nothing out of them, neither reasoning, nor understanding. . . . The chief, betray the Cause? As if he had not sacrificed everything for it, as if he would not be a damned sight happier, if he had stuck to the right road! Oh! I beg your pardon, Miss! You can't think like me, of course! But, just the same, now that you see clearly through all the hellish mess, don't you think a man of as fine a calibre as the delegate is throwing pearls before swine when he gives up absolutely everything in order to untangle their affairs and get them out of the hole they're in? As if the four hundred thousand brute beasts of the Block were worth the little finger of a Pietro Ferrati!"

He shrugged his shoulders, seized with lively indignation over the revolting absurdities of the mob. He concluded at last with the information she was begging for:

"Of course he had to take up the challenge. A little while ago, he himself marched, at the head of the columns, on the Shops! He is down there now!"

"But where, down there?"

"How do I know? He went off with the men of the second group, by the route on the Artificial Island, the nearest to the water. . . ."

At that moment the telephone bell rang.

"Eh, what's that?" said Faraway, as he took off the receiver.

He listened. Eva MacHead Vohr saw his face beam with pleasure.

"Hello? Yes, it's me!" he said. . . .

He was listening now, punctuating the conversation with exclamations of delight.

"Oh! . . . Oh! . . . Fine. . . . Only this column? . . . And not the others? . . . So, everybody is in flight, sir, except you, and just the same, it doesn't make any difference? . . . Well, at last you've done

it, eh? . . . You forced the barriers between you and
the goal? . . ."

All of a sudden she remembered. She herself had
used those very words when she questioned Andrea
Ferrati so closely, before rushing to Pietro's aid. . . .

She had said: "Are they risking a catastrophe, in
case the strikers force the barriers which the Governor
has set up between them and their goal?" . . . And
Andrea Ferrati, chosen secretary of the implacable
MacHead Vohr, had replied: "You cannot imagine,
neither you, nor anyone else, nor even my brother,
what this catastrophe would be!"

A violent trembling shook her all over from head to
heels.

She leaned against the wall. On the greasy red
Turkish cloth, her aristocratic hand, long and nervous,
made a spot of beauty.

"Faraway!" she called in a hoarse voice, "Faraway!"

The secretary had hung up the receiver. He hurried
to her:

"Yes, Miss MacHead Vohr?"

"Does he know . . . the delegate, does he suspect
that there is another danger?. . ."

"What danger? . . ."

She looked at him, dismayed, mute. What danger?
She herself did not know. But, with a jerk, she pulled
herself together:

"Just one thing. Where is he?"

"He is telephoning," said Faraway, "from post
32 . . ."

The telephone map was spread out on the table. Eva took it in at a glance. Telephone post 32 was where the second route crossed the third intersecting line—to the north of the Shops, therefore, but south of all these police defenses interposed between the strikers and the machine-hands which the strike wanted to destroy. Between Pietro Ferrati and the catastrophe predicted by Andrea, there was therefore not a single barrier left.

No barrier? Then what? Death? or worse? . . .

She was terrified.

The map on the table was a confused mass of curves, underlinings, inscriptions. Although expert in archeology, even indeed in history, Miss MacHead Vohr knew little about geography when it came to recognizing an aerial route.

"On the whole," she asked, "to get to this post 32 from here. . . . How do I do it?"

"See for yourself," said Faraway, taking the protractor and the flat ruler: "you must steer to the South 124 degrees East . . . 24 South by the compass[1] that is thirteen miles exactly."

"And . . . 'he' is there?"

What need to name people, when one thinks of them as if there were no one else in the world?

"He was there when he telephoned me," replied Faraway.

He picked up the receiver:

---

[1] The author apologizes for not having had a magnetic map at his disposal when he wrote this passage, and of having met the difficulty with a deflection chosen by guesswork.

"Hello! Post 32 . . . the delegate from the Council of the Order? . . ." ,

"He is leaving."

"Hold him!" cried Eva.

"Who is speaking?" they asked.

Without even hesitating, the daughter of the Governor betrayed herself.

"I! Eva MacHead Vohr! I am coming by airplane, hold the delegate! Matter of life or death! Just a moment and I will be there!"

Without a word of good-bye to Faraway she rushed up the stairs, arriving ahead of the elevator. Ten seconds later her airplane took off, and headed straight for S. 24 E., without observing the most rudimentary precautions as to height. . . .

CHAPTER VI

Eve, Abel, Cain

OF THE four columns storming the Shops, only one had triumphed. But one was worth as much as four! Little did it matter that thirty thousand, or sixty thousand, or one hundred and twenty thousand adherents of direct action had, only a little while ago, faced twelve thousand machine-hands to be destroyed. The victory was neither more nor less certain. At the most the police might perhaps be able to cut off the tunnels under the Mouth and to preserve, for a time, the six thousand machines of the Natural Island. As for those of the Artificial Island, it was as if there was already nothing left of them. . . .

At least, everybody thought so at the Blocks, at the Residences and elsewhere. Everybody, except perhaps Andrea Ferrati, Ralph Athole, one or two other persons . . . and MacHead Vohr. . . .

Pietro Ferrati himself no longer doubted complete success now. His battle seemed to him already won. Victorious, the second column had at first abused its victory as is the custom, by massacring to the very last man the police at the station of the conquered barrage.

Their heads, cut off, brandished on the ends of as many
spikes, preceded the rabble of the conquerors towards
the Shops, still three good miles away. At a third of
this distance Pietro Ferrati, who marched at the head,
had been very careful not to risk uselessly his regained
popularity by protesting against the savagery—atrocious but human—of the slaughter and the severed
heads, had continued to lead the column until all danger
seemed clearly passed. Then—and it was at telephone post 32—he called a halt, long enough to send
to the Blocks a first bulletin of the victory gained. It
was a question, in his mind, of how to forestall the dis-
orderly return of the three repulsed columns. In this
way, the fugitives would be brought together and prevented from scattering disorder, desolation, terror on
all sides. On the other hand, overtaken themselves by
the news of the success of the triumphant column, they
would return instinctively to the principles of order and
power, instead of to those of mob rule. This was correctly calculated. Nevertheless, his message trans-
mitted, the reply which arrived from Eva MacHead
Vohr did not fail to surprise Pietro Ferrati, to upset
him also. . . . And, although he was already somewhat
behind the head of the column, which had continued to
advance towards the Shops, still nearly two miles away,
he decided to wait for the airplane announced, and to
make a clean breast of this affair. Miss MacHead
Vohr, coming to join him in broad daylight—it was not
yet five o'clock—and shouting her name into the receiver of the first telephone at hand, was doing more

than she had ever done, more than he had ever asked
or permitted. No doubt it was a serious, vital reason
which inspired such temerities in the most fervent, but
the wisest, of lovers that Pietro Ferrati had ever
known.

"I will wait," he concluded, speaking to himself. "Besides, the airplane will be here before the last strag-
glers of the column have gone past me."

There again, he had calculated correctly. Eva's
plane arrived less than a minute later. The tail of
the column was still far from having reached the telephone post. Pietro Ferrati, who was scanning the
northern horizon, saw the black wings before he heard
the throbbing of the propellers. And he did not de-
tect another throbbing, nor catch sight of other wings,
arrived this time from the south. A second airplane
was hurrying up, flying five or six thousand yards
higher than Miss MacHead Vohr's plane. Consequently this plane recognized the other but was not recognized by it. The first plane landed directly, the wind
blowing from the south. The second, having at first
straightened out, came down in spirals, then landed
alongside the first. Miss MacHead Vohr had just leapt
to the ground. Pietro Ferrati was running up to meet
her, when he stopped amazed, exceedingly annoyed also.
The airplane from the south had touched ground, and
Andrea Ferrati got out of it.

The old habits of childhood outweighed the lover's
instinct. It was to Andrea that Pietro spoke first.

"You!" he cried, "you here! But understand that in the end I shall not be able to save you any more!" . . .

"It is to save you, it is still to save you, that I have come!" cried Andrea, interrupting him. And he added: "To save you, to save her, and to save the others too . . . yes! even to save the others!"

Eva, however, was looking at them both; and doubly hurt that they had at first neglected her—both of them had neglected her!—she had folded her arms on her breast and kept silent.

Andrea saw her then. And he turned from his brother to run to her. She was hurt again and even more by this: it was not the one she loved who came to her first!

"Eva!" exclaimed Andrea. "This is where I find you again! What horrible madness! Ye Gods! The Governor, the Governor! What would he say?"

"You were already his spy. Are you his valet now?" she threw at him like the sting of a whip; "his valet, you, the brother of this man?"

She jerked her chin towards Pietro. Andrea drew himself up haughtily:

"I am a man," said he, "who does not change sides; and a man who, while doing all his duty, is in addition forced to save the situation for those in the other party, as much as he can without betraying his own. That is what I am! You have known those who were less particular."

Already Pietro had stiffened in his turn. If Eve had

died before the day of the first crime, Cain would never have slain Abel.

"Those who change sides," said Pietro, "are those whom truth has touched. And those, who are the future, are not in the habit of losing. It is therefore superfluous to save the situation for them. Society has not ceased to progress. And now comes the hour when it will gain the world."

"Here," said Andrea, "here comes the hour when all of you, if you do not stop, are going to die!"

Eva trembled violently.

"Andrea!" she cried, imperiously, "you know something! Tell us what you know!"

He turned his back on her to watch the column which was filing past, running now, running at full speed, in their haste—now that they were victors and had forced the barriers and conquered the police—to reach the Shops, and to destroy those ogre machines, devourers of workmen; those murdering machine-hands!

The *hou! hou! hou!* of this unchained mob rose steadily, momentarily growing more terrible. To the degree that it approached its goal, it increased its pace.

"The dead run swiftly!" exclaimed Andrea Ferrati involuntarily.

He looked at this galloping mass with a kind of horror.

"The dead?" repeated Pietro, without understanding.

Eva, so pale ordinarily, had become the color of

earth. Under the rouge on her mouth, her discolored lips chattered.

"What!" she said, "it is against those poor beings. . . ."

Andrea bowed his head.

"Well?" asked Pietro.

"Death to all, if they break one machine," pronounced Andrea very low.

He seemed to be afraid to speak aloud; afraid of the words he was saying. Perhaps he actually was afraid. . . .

Pietro responded.

"For heaven's sake, shut up!" said he, "and keep these old wives' tales! Are you trying to make her faint?"

He had put both arms around Eva. She drew herself up:

"Me, me faint? Ah! don't be afraid, dearest. . . ."

She used the endearing term proudly, looking defiantly at Andrea.

He felt himself defied. Hot anger stirred the blood in his veins.

She, however, had replied, still speaking to Pietro:

"But be careful! what he says is not a fairy tale! Oh! be careful! . . ."

Pietro looked at Andrea.

"I have told you," repeated the other, more reserved. "Death to all if they break a single machine. The Governor. . . ."

"Death? What death?"

And without giving him time to reply.

"Andrea, come!"

He took his arm away from Eva, and placed his two hands on his brother's shoulders.

"So they sent you to frighten me, didn't they? By the blood of Christ! I would not have believed that of you! Ah! no . . . it is not you—there speaks the blood of your mother—"

Andrea's mother had detested Pietro. Andrea knew this, but he had adored his mother none the less, and he still adored her. Pietro's double injustice revolted him.

"Thanks!" he said, bitterly: "that is my reward for having risked my life again for you, and for her! . . . No matter: they sent me, in truth, not to frighten any one nor even to warn whoever it might be, but to snatch both of you out of here, she . . . the daughter of the Governor . . . and you . . . my brother . . . at once, quickly! . . . before it is too late . . . she, and you too, yes! . . ."

Stupefied this time, Pietro had let go of Andrea.

"It isn't true!" said he, hesitatingly; "the Governor does not know that she is here. . . ."

"Fool!" cried Andrea, "do you imagine then that I have not told him, that I have not confessed, explained everything, betrayed all! . . . yes, betrayed: when I knew that, perhaps before a quarter of an hour, there would be nothing more here but corpses?"

"You betrayed? You? . . ."

"Miserable coward!" cried Eva. "Ah! I knew, I knew well that it was he. . . ."

She seized Pietro by the wrist.

"But what are you waiting for then—to kill him?"

"At once!" exclaimed Andrea, baring his chest; "kill me, and kill her with the same blow, by preventing me from saving her!"

He had folded his arms.

"Ah, indeed? You have not yet understood? How many times must I repeat it before you will understand? In a quarter of an hour perhaps, unless you stop, unless you can stop this horde which is rushing on madly, everybody here will be dead!"

"Dead? But how? For God's sake explain, if you can! Aha! you can't? You don't know? Ah! Liar! So that's what you have come to, you, you. . . ."

"You don't believe me?" said Andrea dully.

He had foreseen many possibilities, but not this one.

"How do you expect me to believe?" replied the other harshly. "A lie like that? . . . when you're telling one, make it a big one, you poor child that you are!"

He became excited.

"Really, your danger must have driven you all crazy! What? old MacHead Vohr couldn't find any better way than that to save his miserable machines: to send word to me—to me, already master of the Shops!—that if I use my victory the lightning is going to strike me? . . . For it would have to be lightning, at the very least! . . . and what lightning, to shatter at one blow, thirty or forty thousand men! . . . I have almost that number of men here. . . ."

With a sweep of his arm he embraced the column which was still filing past, innumerable, running in wild confusion now, as men run to destruction. Not a man had stopped to give a single glance at this extraordinary trio, their commander-in-chief, one of the engineers from the factory, and the daughter of the ruler of the Siturgic. The truth is that nothing mattered to anyone now except this promised land in sight, the undefended Shops and the machine-hands to be destroyed. . . .

Andrea followed Pietro's arm with his eyes. And those words haunted him: running as men run to destruction. . . . Of all his brother had said, he had heard only two words: "Your danger. . . ."

"Our danger . . . the danger to us?" he repeated, aghast with horror.

To tell the truth, he knew only this: a little while ago, MacHead Vohr, searching for his daughter, and no longer finding her on the terrace, had rushed to him and had ordered him:

"Go and bring her back!"

"But she will not want to. . . ."

"Go! you poor fool! . . . Quick. . . . Before the first ranks of their column have reached the first of my machine-hands, *there will no longer be a living being between the Shops and the Blocks.*"

He had gone.

Three days before, in his presence, MacHead Vohr

had already said, speaking to Ralph Athole, who was
deploring the probable massacre of several hundred
strikers, the machine-guns of the police would mow
down:

"Let us hope that instead of several hundreds, the
deaths will not be several hundred thousands."

"Oh!" had objected Ralph Athole, "we don't yet
know how to kill men by hundreds of thousands today. . . ."

"Tomorrow is not today!" MacHead Vohr had replied.

This was all Andrea Ferrati knew. But that was
enough for him and, for Eva MacHead Vohr, it would
also have been enough. For Pietro, however, it was too
little.

His column, thirty thousand men, women, old men,
children, equaled thirty thousand victors; behind these,
three hundred thousand others were already pouring
out of the Blocks, now that the barrier had broken.
And all these were headed for the Shops. Therefore,
one more hour, and not one of the six thousand machine-
hands of the Artificial Bank would exist any longer.
Another hour and the same thing would be done to the
six thousand machine-hands of the Natural Island.
Consequently, before night this diabolical and unexpected turn of events would be removed, wiped out,
and the strike would become all-powerful once more:
"Labor," that is to say, Anarchy, would have check-
mated "Capital" which means Order . . . or rather,

Law. Indisputably nothing in the world, not even lightning, would stop, could possibly stop this multitude,
this incommensurable horde, irresistibly launched and in
sight of its goal.

"No!" he cried again; "no, I do not believe you. Get
out of here now, go and tell them so."

"You don't believe me! You are going to keep her
here and kill her?" Andrea hurled at him, pale with
emotion.

Pietro turned towards Eva.

"Eva, do you want to go? . . ."

But she was already angered.

"Never! I am where I should go. Go, Andrea, and
do your work: report to the Governor that his daughter is here, in the front ranks of those he would strike
down . . . and let him strike if he dare! . . ."

"You see that you are killing her!" repeated Andrea.
"And so this is all your love for her amounts to, eh?"

"Your love would have been different, I suppose!
But confess now that you love her! . . ."

They were all talking together now, each one listening only to the promptings of his own passion.

Andrea, suddenly, became excited:

"Yes, I love her!" he cried, "I love her and I admit
it!"

"And you love her so much, that you would go as far
as to take her away from here, if you could, eh? So
much that you would take her back down there, to re-
store her to her father at this price?"

"Cad!" cried Andrea at this insult.

The other continued.

"You would even kill me, the better to save her? To save her from me, especially?"

"Of the two of us, you are the murderer. I, whom she does not love, I, who cannot serve her, I refuse to flee alone: and you will kill me in killing her."

He looked at Eva long and deeply:

"Eva, I love you more than he does. You have chosen badly."

She answered Pietro, as if she had not heard Andrea:

"Do spare me his insults," she said with disgust.

The injustice of lovers is supreme.

Suddenly the *"hou! hou! hou!"* which kept time to the race to destruction was interrupted, cut off short, subjugated and submerged by a more formidable clamor, a gigantic clamor in which sounded all the triumph of the populace's gratified savagery. It rang like a "view-halloo!" And it needed no explanation: the column had just reached the machine-hands: the column was going to begin its work of destruction. . . .

Pietro looked at Andrea haughtily:

"Well?" he began. . . .

But almost immediately he stopped; Andrea was no longer looking at him. Andrea was no longer looking at Eva. . . .

In the very marrow of the bones of every man who comes from religious Italy, there exists a foundation of belief, no matter how far he may have traveled, no matter how many other countries he may have lived in. Because Andrea's mother had suckled milk from a Tuscan nurse, the naïve faith of this nurse welled up from the heart to the lips of Andrea, about to die and seeing his death. . . .

Andrea had thrown himself on his knees, forgetting his anger, forgetting even Eva. And a supreme supplication burst from his lips:

"*Sancta Maria, gratia plena, ora pro nobis peccatoribus! Nunc, et in hora mortis. . . .*"

Pietro, stupefied, had no time to think. Eva was looking at Andrea, who, in that moment, had in advance detached himself from the world. Suddenly he seemed beautiful to her. Perhaps, in this second, she understood that she had indeed chosen badly, ...

CHAPTER VII

A MAN

THE one hundred and fifty chief engineers were present. And, likewise, the fifteen directors, the five councilors, and the Governor; the five councilors, all of them, for a wonder. Athole, Tresham, Bellecour, Galbraith, and Torral—George Torral who, this time, had not sent his excuses.

Sixty years ago, at the time of one of the great wars which, at the beginning of the Twentieth Century,[1] plunged all Europe in flames, blood and ruins, a Frenchman, an engineer at Saigon, Indo-China, had deserted rather than fight. Not from cowardice: the man was brave. Not from the standpoint of pacifism: the man was not crazy, and knew that war is one of the vital instincts of the human animal, as of any other animal for that matter. But from the standpoint of civilization: this man was a man; and, profoundly imbued with individualistic ideas, he felt himself more akin to an Englishman or to a German of his own social class than to a Frenchman of the hereditary aristocracy or of the unintelligent plebeians. Logical with himself, he had therefore refused to take his part in a national

---

[1] This was written in 1920. The author writes *wars* in the plural. Pure presentiment.

war which he detested. But he would very willingly have fought in a civil war which could have brought him in opposition to those he considered his real enemies, were they proletariat or gentlemen.

To desert was the only way then, as it has always been; to escape from the territory of the belligerent nations. Germany and the Philippines, everyone knows, were neutral in the war of 193—. A Hamburg liner carried George Torral from Saigon to Manila. Later, when peace had come again, George Torral emigrated to the United States; France had become forbidden territory to him. In the States, he started life over again; and this life was soon more brilliant than the life of his youth had ever been. The engineer Torral was one of the most expert metallurgists of his time. Had he been a naturalized American, America would have quickly recognized him. A number of great enterprises fought to get this incomparable man who knew everything, and imagined, invented, achieved much more even than he knew. He was well known, then celebrated. Nevertheless, his celebrity did not bring him riches. Like many of his compatriots, Torral lacked neither intelligence nor cleverness; and he was even deep, as are also many Frenchmen: deep, but clear; which is the reason why imbeciles denied that he had depth. Furthermore, he did not lack a practical mind, any more than a brilliant mind, which could help him to take advantage of all his other powers. But he did not do this because he lacked something else, something which is generally lacking in all France: concentration; in other words, the cement which holds together all the virtues and all the human powers, to transform them into fame and fortune. Without concentration the most inspired man will never be anything but an adventurer, sometimes illustrious, always unfortunate. George Torral, therefore, who was just this type of man, had, about 197—, passed his sixtieth year; and in spite of his great reputation, he was living in New York rather as a Bohemian than as a famous old man. Perhaps imminent justice was making him expiate in this way, before absolving him, the sin of his youth which had been formerly his desertion. . . . He himself had certain days when he believed so. One day he even admitted it.

It was one morning in the Albany bar; the Albany bar, at that period, was perhaps the most frequented of the noonday "eating-houses" in New York. Amusing joint where many people of most varied minds lunched every morning on oysters, steaks and cocktails. As a rule, George Torral, solitary and morose, bolted down his dozen Blue Points, while disdainfully despatching with a glance the latest newspapers—one paper a minute. To read twelve times, from the *Herald* to the *Tribune*, the same news, the same puerile account of a supposedly new process of making aniline dye, should be enough to disturb the digestion of an Eleventh Blue Point, fresh and fat. George Torral declared so, speaking aloud, but to himself:

"As if exactly eleven years ago, I had not discovered and published the chemical secret which puts aniline out of business for good and all. . . ."

He thought a moment, then added:

"If there is a God, I am obliged to confess that He is making me pay dearly for my peccadillo of having refused the idiotic duty that was offered me in 193—, at the time of the French and English war—that wretched war which killed my poor Fierce, whom I would have made an intelligent man of in the end!"

He referred to a very old friend of his, killed in battle at sea, June 30, 193—.

Now, it happened that as George Torral, the sexagenarian, finished cursing heaven in these terms, a man younger than he, who was lunching alongside him at a table separated only by the glass partitions which have made the Albany bar famous, straightened up:

"Are you really," said this man speaking through the glass of the partition, "are you really the man who invented the counter-aniline?"

"Yes," replied George Torral.

"Ah, George Torral, then?"

"The same. And who are you?"

"James Fergus MacHead Vohr. Do you know me?"

"Yes. You made your fourth billion yesterday."

"Correct. You know me. And I know you equally well. You have never made any money, though."

"No," agreed Torral, "and yet I would know how to turn your four billions into forty."

"Strange," said MacHead Vohr, "I was thinking the

same thing this very moment. Do you want to do it?"

"Yes," said Torral.

The only thing he had learned from Americans, after thirty years in America, was not to split hairs.

"How much will you take to work for me?" said Mac-Head Vohr.

"For you, like your lackey?" said Torral. "Well! five per cent on everything I do, and you bear all expenses."

"Done!" said the Wheat King.

But at that time he had not yet become the Wheat King. He was infinitely far from being it. But if he had sized up Torral, Torral immediately sized him up.

From that hour Torral was a rich man. Sure of the morrow, freed from that fear of the future which is the original vice of the Frenchman, Torral made one profitable discovery after another, while, by making use of him, MacHead Vohr started to pile up his billions. Between these two formidable men understanding engendered friendship. Next to his daughter, George Torral was the one MacHead Vohr loved most in the world. Later, the Wheat King—as he had now become—was, in addition, made Governor of the Siturgic which he had just formed. The new-born factory, from its first cry, stretched its infant arms and enfolded half the world in its embrace. And, immediately, like Philip of Macedon, two thousand three hundred and fifty years ago, calling Aristotle to the cradle of Alexander the Great, MacHead Vohr called George Torral to the cradle of his giant daughter.

Since then George Torral, now entering on his nine-tieth year, though always hale and hearty, lived at the Siturgic, without ever leaving it. The Isolated Tower —this ancient building erected not far from the High Palace on the Artificial Island—was at the same time his dwelling and his office; his laboratories—the twenty-seven floors of the building ("nine only," he said; "I count like the Chinese: nine floors, each one a trinity, like God!") comprised twenty-one experimental labora-tories, observatories and charging rooms, all arranged to make the most modern installations in Paris, Boston, London, Warsaw, Glasgow and Chicago, green with envy; and six annexes reserved for garages, servants' quarters, storerooms, warehouses, offices, and all that modern life has invented. George Torral called him-self a civilized man, therefore an egoist. The most in-telligent, therefore the most subtle.

The one hundred and fifty chief engineers were there-fore gathered together and, with them, the fifteen direc-tors, the five councilors, and MacHead Vohr; George Torral, the last to enter, went straight to his chair, sat down, and, even before the meeting was opened, took out from under his coat a little machine. . . .

CHAPTER VIII

Professor Torral's Lesson

A LITTLE machine. . . .

It was very little, indeed . . . prismatic and rectangular. Twenty centimeters long by ten wide and fifteen high. It was of mahogany, with here and there divers turnkeys with little touches of ivory. Glass bulbs surmounted the top, and steel tuning forks extended from one of the sides.

George Torral, seated, put one hand flat on the green cloth-covered table, and with the other caressed, almost with tenderness, the little machine he had placed in front of him, very carefully. . . .

It was Monday, May 9, 199—. Quarter-past five had just struck.

"The meeting will come to order!" MacHead Vohr had said. "Athole, how far have the strikers gone?"

"Two hundred yards from the northeast corner of the West Shops!" the even voice of the privy councilor had replied.

MacHead Vohr had then turned towards Torral.

"You have time?"

"I have more than necessary," Torral assured him.

Whereupon, George Torral stood up.

271

Many of the chief engineers had never seen him, he
so seldom left his Isolated Tower, his lair. They looked
at him curiously. Before all of these men of America,
he appeared extraordinary and different from them.
Very different, and quite extraordinary; so little, so
mean, so deformed, with his thin legs and arms, his
curved back, his head too large and his hair too long
and shaggy; a high, thick mop of hair which formed a
toupet above his over-large forehead—a forehead which
bulged like the top-sail of a clipper running before the
wind. His gestures were frequent, but abrupt. His
eyes, sunk in the depths of their sockets, under the
shelter of bushy eyebrows, darted lightning glance on
lightning glance without interruption. Weak, lean,
ugly, in contrast to his audience of robust, athletic
youth who, even if they worked with their brains at
least had learned how to relax and rejoice in their
bodies—he, George Torral who all his life had ignored
the fact that he had muscles, was the personification of
pure intellectual development.

He addressed himself solely to the Governor, disdain-
ing or ignoring the one hundred and seventy other men
who were listening.

"Governor, excuse me if I recall to you first of all
my words of twenty years ago . . . yes, my words on
the first day of our acquaintance. Do you remember?
You had just engaged me, enrolled me under your flag,
in your pay? and you had said, 'I want to work better
than anyone has ever worked yet.' I asked you, 'What
do you want to do?' You said to me, 'To make life.
. . .' Do you remember? . . . Then I said, 'If you

intend to work to make life, and **if you want** me to help you, I must work on my part . . . and I must prepare to make death.' I have worked, Governor. I have searched. I am prepared. I have found the solution. And I had been ready for a long time when you explained to me, eight days ago, to what a pass your idiots of workmen were threatening to plunge your Siturgic. I told you: 'All right, they will go where they want to; but they will not go where you don't want them to. Because if they tried they would not succeed. I would stand in the way.' You did not ask me anything more. I thank you for having had confidence in me. I repeat to you today what I told you that day: they will go as far as you will permit. No farther. As soon as you wish, I will stop them."

"How?" asked MacHead Vohr.

They looked at him. Several of the engineers noticed that he was pale.

"By killing them, naturally," said Torral.

He began to laugh, and added:

"Oh! I am not bloodthirsty, and I have never wasted time trying to find a way of changing fools into wisemen. I have tried to find the way to change the living into dead. I have searched and I have found it."

"Radical remedy!" said Athole gently.

"Illegal!" declared Bellecour with decision.

But Torral, who suddenly straightened up, looked them up and down one after the other:

"What's that?" he said, "you are still bothering about morals? Good principles? Honest and puerile citizenship? Puerile especially?"

He shrugged his shoulders in a gesture at once crude and expressive.

"No humbug, eh?" he asked, becoming again a Parisian of the faubourgs. "Rough on you, this weakness! But you don't catch me in that trap any more! I'm on the other side of the fence!"

He jeered.

"Excellent! So these gentlemen haven't forgotten their catechism yet? Excellent, I repeat, but deplorable! And a thousand pities, for we are not going to agree very well! For my part, I have swung about. I don't turn the other cheek any more when I am slapped: I show my fist—or, rather, I show lightning, for I have learned to make use of it. . . . What more just usage than to strike down those who, less intelligent than I, therefore less worthy of living, have not been able to control it as I have done, and don't know, as I know, how to handle thunder? Those who only know how to bark, and who just the same try to bite? To bite with their poor little teeth, the teeth of miserable little brutes?"

He tapped on his machine. At the top of the parallelopiped, three or four of the glass balls shone suddenly, with a singular violet light: and one of the tuning forks of the side vibrated, giving out the note f-sharp.

"Hey there!" he said, quickly pressing both hands on two ebony handles that were attached beside each other on the back of the instrument.

Then he finished:

"When I bite, now, I bite with those two teeth there. Two false teeth, but long ones."

He showed the two handles, which he was pressing with both hands. He laughed:

"I assure you that it would be unwise to fool with these two toys . . . to fool with them both at the same time . . . before you were quite at home with the apparatus. . . ."

Someone pushed open the door and ran towards Mac-Head Vohr. With a gesture MacHead Vohr stopped him:

"They are . . . " began the man, speaking low and gasping for breath.

"Where?"

"Almost at the Shops . . . that is, they were . . . it took me some time to come down here. . . ."

"Almost there?" repeated MacHead Vohr.

He arrested Torral's attention with a jerk of his chin.

"More than twenty seconds, Torral . . . let us say thirty, all included. . . ."

"Oh!" said Torral, "that is twenty-five too many!"

He took his machine up in both hands. It was heavier than one would have imagined to look at it. He carried it to one of the French windows which looked towards the horizon at the north. . . .

For the event, they had opened all communications between the Moorish room and the Louis XIV drawing-rooms. . . .

On the windowsill Torral rested the oblong box. A

liquid compass was fastened to it; its two sights, placed one in front of the other, were located between two rows of bulbs with glass tops. Cogged wheels controlled the double marking of a suspension dial. Torral attentively trained the apparatus on the heights; then, manœuvering the marking for direction, he covered in a horizontal sweep one hundred and fifty degrees of horizon, in the space of one second.

"All ready!" he said, turning towards MacHead Vohr. "Governor, whenever you wish?"

A silence followed.

Tresham, production councilor, had drawn near Torral and was examining the machine on the windowsill.

"What is the principle?" he asked.

Torral looked at him, slightly contemptuous.

"Perhaps you know the postulate of synchronic vibrations?" he asked rather haughtily, "and the theorem of visual cones? Both are incorporated in this instrument. This is only a generator of N rays to differentiated vibrations with reflector and lens, to which I have joined a transformer on rolls. The tuning fork and the bulbs are there only to verify the exactness of the synchronisms, either in the order of the sounds, or in the order of the lights. In this way I change a certain ray of the frequency (N^t) to another ray of the frequency (NX^{ty}), x and y varying respectively, at my will, between the limits $\frac{x}{1}$, $\frac{x}{2}$, $\frac{y}{1}$, $\frac{y}{2}$. If the radiation thus obtained is filtered through my mirror, then centered through my lens, I produce a visual cone whose center may be thrown on whatever sector I please, creating on all its geometric ground a center of attraction for all the vibratory movements in the world—in particular, for the movements of the frequency $V = \int v,$ which constitutes the phenomenon called life, and the movements of the frequency $M = \int m,$ which constitutes the appearances called matter or substance. In this way I attract, from point to point, all that is material illusion and all that is living illusion. But with a force, therefore with a variable velocity, since it is the activity of the reverse of the root of their absolute quantity. The equilibrium of a living body is immediately destroyed by it: *ergo,* this living body dies; also the equilibrium of dead matter is broken: *ergo,* this matter dissociates and disappears. Nothing simpler—though I had to puzzle over it and dozens of little problems whose solution helped the creation of an apparatus for practical demonstration. This one...."

He tapped his fingers on the little parallelopiped of mahogany, ivory, glass, bronze, ebony and steel.

"This, this bit of mechanism! It did not take more than six hours for my two helpers to assemble these pieces, following my draft directions. But this draft took me not less than twelve years to complete. It was not muscles, it was brain that did the work!"

He threw a glance at the assembly:

"The Governor has often expounded to me, as he has to you, without doubt, his very correct theory on the law of Darwin. Those who cannot or will not adapt themselves, are condemned to death and executed by the holy law of selection. For once, we ourselves will ac-

complish the object of the execution, and that is all!
. . . Kindly admit then that *this* represents the guillotine of the Law of Natural Selection. Nothing less,
nothing more. And since this Law demands it, we are
going to cut off some heads."

"How many?" bluntly questioned the Lyonnais, Just
Bellecour

"Oh!" said Torral, doubtfully, "how do I know? . . .
As many as will be necessary, that's sure! A few more,
it might well be."

This time the silence was terrible.

Merciless as were these men, who all, in a spirit of
sycophancy, had modeled themselves after their chief,
MacHead Vohr, whose own heart would have cut diamonds, they were troubled when Torral had finished
speaking. It took the prudent Athole (prudence equals
audacity) to break this silence, heavy as death, which
hung over the assembly:

"Have I understood correctly?" asked Athole; "the
suppression of all life that comes within the radius of
your machine, involves the dissociation of material illusion. . . .?"

"Naturally!" said Torral, with the satisfied tone of
a professor whose demonstration has been understood
by his best pupil. "Naturally, all living matter modi-
fying its frequencies is dissociated. You have grasped
the result we are interested in, very clearly. Four
hundred thousand dead, but not one corpse. No trace
of dissociated bodies will ever be found."

He began to laugh, and his laughter sounded like the rattle of a skeleton.

"How much simpler that is: no cemetery!"

At that moment the man who had come in before returned:

"They are there!" he cried.

"Where?" asked MacHead Vohr.

"At the Shops. They are breaking dow   le doors."

MacHead Vohr motioned with his chin towards Torral again.

"Torral, all ready?"

"All ready!" said Torral. "Give the word!"

MacHead Vohr's voice had trembled. Torral's voice did not tremble.

But just as MacHead Vohr, conquering his emotion, was about to give the command, one of the telephones fastened to the pillars of the Granadan room rang.

Some one took off the receiver. Through the loud speaker a voice called:

"MacHead Vohr?"

"Here," replied the man who had taken off the receiver, after a glance at the Chief.

"Tell him his daughter is at the head of the strikers, with Pietro and Andrea Ferrati . . . yes! there, where they are going to smash the machines. . . ."

It was Eva's voice. And every man present recognized it. She herself, of her own accord, had conceived this supreme gesture, this filial blackmail, in the hope of saving her lover. . . .

CHAPTER IX

"Beware the Axe!"

THE door of the shop, battered by the mob, fell in and split into flying pieces of metal and splinters of wood. Twenty strikers hurled themselves through the opening, shouting triumphantly. This was the first shop to be invaded: shop 00.016.

After they had entered, the victors stopped short, surprised, a little worried: the shop was empty—absolutely empty; neither foreman nor boss was in sight. In the place of the enemy, the workmen saw only the machine-hand that belonged to this shop; machine-hand 10,006. For that matter, the machine-hand was running; the other machines also. Shop 00.016 was a bread-making shop. Under the guidance of the machine-hand, hydrators, kneaders, and yeast-makers turned regularly, overseen, accelerated or retarded by the reflexes of the little steel shock-absorbers whose grooved sticks, first of all, wrapped around each other, then stretched out on all sides, ran from top to bottom and from bottom to top, from right to left, and from left to right, in a mixture of copper and of bronze, of gutta-percha, of rubber, of silk. No sign of man anywhere! And yet the baked bread rose in full pastry

molds and fell in beautiful order on the movable plane
of the stoves. The doors opened, shut, opened again.
Once baked, the batch of bread passed from the stove
to the machine that brushes the bread with butter, from
this machine to the coating-machine[1] and finished by
piling up in layers one on top of the other in the bins
of the rolling pavement, whose regular motions carried to the storerooms in the sub-cellar, hot from the
oven, the holiest and the only eternal manna of
humanity. . . .

Not a sign of a man. . . .

The Governor's orders, in truth: and certainly, an
imperative order, if there had ever been one: from three
o'clock in the afternoon, all the non-striking personnel
of the Shops, of the transformation and of the transit
units: all the men from the docks, the piers, the lighters,
the cargo-boats, the loaders: all those of the administration, of the laboratories, of the police, of the auxiliary service, of the secret service: all the chief engineers, engineers, officers, bosses, sailors, police, foremen, supervisors, artisans . . . in short, all who worked
with their brains, not with their arms; all who had
therefore not participated in the present strike, who
had not revolted . . . had been obliged to evacuate
hastily, not only the city of machines, but even the

---

[1] In 199— the methods of bread-making were still quite primitive, as we
have just seen. To knead the bread, make it rise, bake it, coat the round
loaves, necessitated as many successive operations; therefore, as many
distinct machines. Finally, the coating-machine intervened to keep the
fresh bread from hardening as it grew old. The simplification of all these
processes dates only from 201—.

Residences, those of the Artificial Island, as well as those of the Natural Island. *"Under pain of death,"* ran the telegram immediately posted on all bulletin boards, and repeated fifteen thousand times, on the fifteen thousand electric boards of both banks, *"every-one must withdraw immediately, and all work must cease south of parallel 20 degrees, 11 minutes north, parallel figured by a straight line running from the High Palace to the Low Palace and passing through the Isolated Tower."* These three buildings were indeed situated in the same latitude. There was no explanation, but the very strangeness of the order assured its prompt execution. "Under pain of death," had terrified everyone to such a degree that, in many of the shops, the foremen, fleeing as fast as their legs would carry them, neglected to stop the machine-hands. As the provisions for the principal machines were not exhausted, there was nothing to stop the machine-hands from functioning. Deprived only of a surveillance, in most cases superfluous, the machines continued working, controlled by their normal directors, the machine-hands. Everything went smoothly, especially in shop 00.016, from about three-thirty until exactly five-thirty. . . .

At five-thirty, in shop 00.016, an accident, the first for that matter, occurred: the invasion of the shop (which was functioning perfectly without any other than purely mechanical labor) by the mob of rebellious human labor. . . .

Twenty men had entered, each one of whom had just walked twelve miles or so; twenty men who had braved the police fire, and who had seen their own blood—or worse, the blood of their own people—run red; twenty men, therefore, exacerbated with fatigue, and thirsting for immediate revenge.

And yet they stopped short, utterly surprised by this peaceful industry, by this human economy, which the evidence before their eyes symbolized for them. For a moment, the injustice of their meditated act, the injustice of this destruction they had come to accomplish, the injustice and the folly of their rebellion, this rebellion against progress, against the march of centuries . . . against the very rotation of the earth! . . . for a moment, all this flashed across the mind of each and every man. But only for an instant, a momentary flash! The other injustice, that which the world committed against them, the injustice of the cruel natural law which must be gratified; the injustice of the earth which ought not to turn since, in turning, it crushes; this second injustice in their eyes effaced the first. They advanced. One of them, an Englishman—by name Harry Wind, orator and leader, and brave too, since as under-delegate from the Council of the Order he had been one of the first twenty to force door 00.016 — walked straight up to the machine-hand, which was working away at its task, and faced it with a magnificent gesture. Realizing that he was about to speak, the other men crowded around him, those who were already there, and those who were pressing behind him. With folded arms, they stood in a circle about the machine-hand, which kept on working silently, and the man who was going to speak. Harry Wind took a deep breath and swelled out his chest.

"So here you are," he said, "you fellows who are trying to steal the workman's bread from him and even want to take it out of his mouth! There you are, famine-maker! Murderer of women and children! Devil that has brought desolation to our men!"

An oven door opened badly. A reflex of the machine quickly rectified the error. The sliding plane slipped back, the door opened again . . . and the batch of bread sizzled, in beautiful round loaves already browned and smelling delightfully of pure flour.

The machine had replied. The man felt the severity of this reply and was annoyed.

"Dirty beast!" he cried, "dirty lying beast! Wait and see. . . ."

He stepped back, and took a kind of start, throwing one foot behind him. He wore enormous hobnailed shoes, heavy iron clips in front. He leaned to the left, bearing all the weight of his body, ready to let fly a furious kick at the machine. . . .

But, suddenly, he lost all desire to destroy. . . .

CHAPTER X

The Worst Agony

"GOVERNOR MacHEAD VOHR?"

"*His daughter is at the head of the strikers, there where they are going to destroy. . . .*"

Of the one hundred and seventy engineers who had heard these words, not one of them had failed to recognize Miss MacHead Vohr's voice.

And there was not one of them who did not turn white.

Motionless in the depths of his armchair, James Fergus MacHead Vohr at first had not stirred, like a man struck with paralysis.

For three days, because of Andrea Ferrati's desperate betrayal, he had known. But he had known without believing. Not for a single moment, in all these three days, had he believed that it was true. And not even a little while before, on the terrace of the Palace, when he had questioned his daughter. Not even after she had replied. Only, now, when he had just heard her voice, that voice whose sweetness symbolized for him all the joy he had ever known, all the joy he might ever have dreamed of. And this voice had spoken the words he had just heard.

Now, at last he must indeed believe.

285

An in spite of that, George Torral, Councilor at the Laboratories, as cruelly indifferent as a surgeon's knife, had placed his hand on the ghastly machine:

"At your orders, Governor!"

Ralph Athole intervened quickly:

"Torral, pardon me; your apparatus kills, or rather annihilates everyone who comes within its radius, doesn't it?"

"Everything that is alive, yes!" said Torral.

"And you can neither restrict nor limit the zone of destruction?"

"No."

"Everyone down there then, who is really alive. . . ."

"Will be dead in a few minutes. That is right."

"Without any possible exception?"

"Without any exception. How do you think there could be any exception? That is impossible. The idea is childish."

All those who were listening, instinctively looked questioningly at each other.

James Galbraith went up to Torral quickly.

"Do you know that, down there, there is . . ."

But, from his place, Just Bellecour interrupted him, drowning out his voice.

"Do you know that, down there, besides our one hundred and forty thousand strikers of whom many certainly are irresponsible, there are one hundred and fifty thousand women, twenty thousand old men and forty-five thousand children, who are all innocent?"

"No, of course not," replied Torral, "I know nothing about it. How should I know? I am not the executive councilor! Moreover, what difference does it make to me? And what difference does it make to all of you?"

Just Bellecour counted:

"One hundred and forty, plus one hundred and fifty, plus twenty, plus forty-five. . . ."

"Pshaw!" said Torral, interrupting him, "what if that would make three or four hundred thousand living beings to kill? Haven't you lived long enough to know that, normally, every week a good million of men die, and I don't know how many billions of animals, all less evil than you and I?"

Ralph Athole had come up to Just Bellecour. He touched his shoulder.

"My dear fellow, I conceive your horror—if I may say so, your holy horror—at killing, in cold blood, so many men, so many women, so many poor little ones, all unquestionably innocent . . . (and so much the more innocent because I don't believe in free will). Certainly, this is a most ghastly affair! But have you thought that, by their folly, these unfortunates would risk causing . . . what do I say, would risk causing . . . would cause, would positively cause the worst famine, and not only among four hundred million other men, women and poor little ones, all innocent, also, all even more innocent? Have you thought of the old men, of the sick, of the convalescents, of the women in child-birth, of the new-born babes, of all the weak, of all the helpless ones for whom *famine* signifies *death?*

Have you, last of all, realized that the fact of the strike is a capital crime, when the strike becomes the murderer of a whole country? . . ."

"I have realized," cut in Just Bellecour impetuously, "that I will not have anything to do with this sacrifice!"

"Come! bring water, a basin, a napkin!" proposed Torral, ironically, "like our friend, the late Pontius Pilate, wash your hands of it!"

"Instead of that, look at that man there!" advised Ralph Athole.

He pointed to MacHead Vohr.

All, to be sure, had spoken very loud. MacHead Vohr, however, had heard nothing.

It is said that, in the last seconds which precede their end, those who are about to die and who are conscious of it, relive one by one, with meteoric rapidity, all the hours of their lives, from the first to the last, from the one they have just begun and will never finish, to the one which, on the other hand, they finished with their first infant cry, but which had begun without their volition. In the same way, MacHead Vohr, in this moment worse than death, relived many past hours— all the hours spent by the side of the only being he had ever loved or rather adored—his daughter; and even adore was too poor a word to express his feeling for her.

He saw Eva as a baby, taken by a smart nurse for a ride in a little carriage drawn by goats. The carriage might have stepped out of a fairy-tale by Perrault. The goats' hoofs are gilded. But crossing the avenue, the baby takes fright. The police, who have recognized the fairy-like equipage, block the quadruple files of motor cars on both sides.

Who, in New York, does not know that the Wheat King would ruin Wall Street rather than suffer an impertinence to this little weeping creature, all smothered beneath her robes of old English point lace?

A little girl who runs in the park at San Diego, with the golden fleece of her loosened hair flowing down her back. MacHead Vohr has just arrived from Chicago in his private car, the *Eva*, beating the records for speed. And from a long way off the little girl sees her father and rushes to him, her hair streaming after her like the tail of a comet. Behind MacHead Vohr the footmen are carrying a huge mechanical toy: a toy railroad which runs on one hundred yards of rails: Miss Eva had wanted to have her own line, a real line, with locomotives that whistled! . . .

Boston. The University of Cambridge. The Stewart prize, awarded to the young girl whose thesis, on the ancient history of the people of the Orient, wins the majority of votes from the University committee . . . Miss MacHead Vohr . . . Music . . . the march from *Lohengrin.* . . .

And then the High Palace. The terrace. . . .

"Tell your poor old father!"

Silence.

An airplane flying away.

Oh! the sound, *real*, crackling, of a heart too over-flowing with love, of a tortured father whose heart is being torn to shreds. . . .

Hadn't someone said just now?—

"What difference does it make to me?" . . . Did someone really say that?

It is true, indeed. . . . It doesn't make any difference to many people. . . .

MacHead Vohr struggled in the depths of an inexpressible night. Other words plunge into this night and pass near him, vibrating so strongly that, in spite of himself, he hears. . . .

"Four hundred thousand men to kill, possibly. Four hundred million other men to save from hunger, certainly."

Is it true that Christ stumbled three times in mounting His Calvary?

Tumult. Men rush forward. In rising to go from his armchair to the window where Councilor Torral has placed his machine, Governor MacHead Vohr has stumbled against a crease in the carpet and fallen. . . .

At that moment, a telephone in the room, another telephone, rings and a voice calls:

"Board of Engineers?"

It is Ralph Athole who takes down the receiver and answers:

"Here."

"Shop 00.016 is invaded. The other shops on First Avenue are either forced or are going to be. . . ."

Governor MacHead Vohr is still lying on the floor. Two chief engineers have taken him by the arms. He starts to get up.

But, before he is on his feet, he gives the order, he has given the order . . . oh! with what a terrible voice, pitiable, sobbing! . . . but just the same he has given the order:

"Torral! Go ahead!"

CHAPTER XI

A Black Hole

"*NUNC, et in hora mortis nostrae! Amen. . . .*"
The prayer was said. And the hour had not yet struck, the final hour. Surprised that he was still alive, Andrea Ferrati did not get up immediately; what was the use, only to fall his full length on the ground, the second afterwards?

Still another second passed and Death did not come. Andrea Ferrati got to his feet, astonished.

His brother, troubled, had watched him pray. He saw him stand up afterwards. He saw his amazement. At last he began to believe.

"Andrea!" he cried, suddenly, "forgive me! I forgive you . . . I doubted you, but . . ."

Andrea held up his hand to impose silence.

"We have no more time! I forgive you, too! Of course, I love you. . . ."

Eva had not taken her eyes from their faces.

"I loved her, too, in a different way," said Andrea again, motioning Pietro to look at her. "At the point where we are now, that is no longer very important . . . in a little while we shall be allowed to love each other, all three of us, in the same way . . . in the only way. . . ."

292

Miss MacHead Vohr was not religious.

Brought up by her father in the Methodist church, the ugly harshness of the Protestant ceremony had first of all shocked and then repulsed her. She did not believe in anything. The terrifying mystery of human life, isolated apparently between the two dead eternities of the before and the hereafter, the mathematical impossibility of a limited consciousness—that chance would place in the midst of a limitless unconsciousness, as if it were feasible to divide something by nothing, or everything by any old thing—had not troubled too much her woman's mind, subtle, but futile. She had said, as so many others say: "I will see well enough when I get there. . . ."

And she saw. . . .

At first, an imperceptible changing of conditions around her. Solids appeared to her less certain; the gaseous more tangible. There was a tree in front of her at several hundred feet. She saw it less distinctly, and was not exactly sure that it was a tree, nor even that it was anything at all. The air, on the other hand, the invisible air that was between this tree and her, suddenly became perceptible to her, . . . sensible to the touch, opaque. She shivered, understanding that all this matter, non-existent for her, the second before, existed now with so much force that her own body, already weakened, would never make its way through it. . . .

She saw that . . . then . . .

Then, having turned hastily towards Andrea Ferrati

. . . towards Andrea, not Pietro . . . Why? . . . a formidable instinct forced her to this change, this supreme division of her thoughts . . . both from her anxiety, and from her desire . . . having turned towards Andrea . . . she saw him only faintly. . . .

And yet, very clearly! Oh! with a terrifying clearness, but without color . . . that is, gray . . . a light gray, a pearl gray, which, besides, had become the color of everything around her, the color of everything. . . .

The contours were sharp, however, in this uniform grayness which she was touching, was feeling, was tasting, much more even than she saw it. . . .

A black hole, immense and swirling, divided the gray. Eva. . . .

And yet she was still herself! Herself and nothing but herself:

Eva leaned over the black hole.

Above, a question hovered:

"What do you want, before?"

She said, hastily:

"This: my last wish. . . ."

The question waited. . . . Eva tried and could not find it. No more names. No more things. All her memory was flying away below.

"Bah!" she said.

The black hole grew larger, became an immense abyss. Eva plunged into it. There was nothing more.

CHAPTER XII

Death Simplified

"BUT where are they?" asked Just Bellecour, the executive councilor, nervously.

"They are no more," said George Torral, councilor at the Laboratories.

He shrugged his shoulders. Ralph Athole placed his manicured hand on the Lyonnais' shoulder.

"Didn't he explain to you that his machine dissociates all living substance? There could not be any corpses!"

He tried to laugh.

"If I were a fool of an anti-clerical, like the majority of their leaders were, and as almost all of those poor creatures were, I would say, nevertheless, that when it comes time for the resurrection of the flesh, God will have trouble in recognizing them. . . ."

The Shops, from which they were just coming out, were all in order, except for the doors, most of them battered in. But of the human beings who had broken in these doors, not a trace. Autos, under imperative command, had just turned in the direction of telephone station 32. The first to arrive behind the Governor's carriage, the councilors got out of their limousines and looked at the scene, which had been ravaged; trees, like men, had disappeared.

"There are two fine beasts," said James Galbraith, "who were in luck to have their stable situated on the right side!"

He pointed to the Governor's golden chestnuts. Mac-Head Vohr, for some unforeseen caprice . . . he was so little given to caprices . . . had ordered the antique barouche, the ex-antique barouche of Miss MacHead Vohr, to continue the inspection of the territory the strike had passed over. And, from the Shops to station 32, the carriage had preceded the file of official motor-cars along the second route of the Blocks.

At station 32 the Governor had stopped and alighted. The station was on a little hill; a mole-hill more or less. The Governor had ascended it, and stood there, alone. Formerly, his favorite secretary Andrea Ferrati would have been with him, near him, and without doubt Mac-Head Vohr would have leaned on the shoulder of this man he loved, and whom, secretly, he had perhaps des-tined for his daughter. But Andrea Ferrati was no more. And Eva MacHead Vohr was no more. . . .

Motionless on the top of the little hill, his tall figure, formerly so straight, now bowed, James F. MacHead Vohr was scanning, with meticulous attention, the earth that his child's last footsteps had trod.

Nothing. No sign. But yes, a few imprints. Mac-Head Vohr stooped. In this spot two men had walked. Their feet had sunk into the damp ground, while they stood facing one another. A little above, some smaller tracks were also visible. And these were the tracks that MacHead Vohr looked at to the exclusion of all others. . . .

At the foot of the little hill Athole, Galbraith, Tresham, Bellecour and Torral were grouped. In the distance directors, chief engineers, and the rest were looking on, respectfully.

"After this blow," murmured Galbraith, "the Governor is no longer Governor. The office is open."

"And you are clearly designated," said Tresham, bowing before Athole.

"I?" protested the Scotchman.

"Unanimously!" confirmed Galbraith.

Bellecour had not spoken. Torral was looking in another direction. Athole continued:

"Gentlemen, the victor today, the 'solver' of the affair . . . and may the gods forgive me if I use the most idiotic word that has been coined for a hundred years! . . . the man, after all, who stands out from these actual events, is not I, it is this man here!"

He pointed to Torral. Torral, who had not heard, understood just the same.

"A mistake, Galbraith! The succession is not open the least bit in the world!" he said ironically, "and if it were, I shall be ninety-seven years too old!"

"You are not so old as MacHead Vohr!" said Athole pointing to the Governor, who had bent towards the ground, and did not straighten up.

"Possibly! but don't forget that, if he dies of this, it will be I who have killed him!"

"That matters infinitely little to the ungrateful world," retorted Athole; "the king is dead, long live the king! And you are the king!"

"By right of ingratitude, then?" asked Torral ironically. "It makes infinitely less difference to the immemorial people. The Empire to the worthiest, said Alexander Magnus. Whereupon you have my vote, Athole. I resign. Ninety-seven years! You don't realize it! Nothing worse than too frequent elections."

"This man," said Just Bellecour, pointing to Mac-Head Vohr, "cannot stay in any case. I consider he has done his duty. But it was his duty to be an assassin and four hundred thousand times an assassin. His greatest reward could not be more than absolution pure and simple. For the rest, the centuries will judge."

"The centuries?" said Torral, infinitely ironical.

"The centuries are God, for those who believe, of whom I am one. Four hundred thousand innocent people wiped out, it is a heavy weight in the balance. . . ."

"Four hundred thousand innocent people? Say, rather, four hundred thousand useless people! My dear fellow, the Holy Selection, as Torral calls it, is a Moloch, but a material Moloch, therefore inevitable. The strong devour the weak. And we ourselves besides were not the strong, but only the instruments of Power. We could not rid ourselves of the terrible necessity. It is not we who killed: it is the Law that killed through us. And MacHead Vohr was only the executioner, irresponsible . . . innocent."

"Four hundred thousand condemned to death in one

of the scales, and his daughter in the other? Why not, indeed? Your scales seem to me reasonably balanced," said Torral, still ironically.

"God will judge!" repeated the Lyonnais.

Perhaps he thought of his native plain, above which rose the four massive towers of an almost eternal basilica. Torral, whose thoughts were elsewhere, looked at him disdainfully.

"God?" he said, questioningly.

"Gentlemen, in any case, it doesn't matter to us," cut in Athole. "We have certainly seen much of it: but, on the whole, what we have seen was much more courageous than suicide."

"Athole!" someone called.

It was MacHead Vohr. Athole went forward.

"Stay there!" commanded the Chief.

Athole stopped.

"This," said MacHead Vohr, marking with his finger the hillock where he stood, "tomorrow this will be surrounded by a grill of cast steel, without a gate. No one will ever enter here. For the rest, I give you my power of attorney, Athole, while waiting for Washington to ratify the choice I have made of you to succeed me. This morning I sent in my resignation as Governor. It was all too heavy a burden for me."

"That I will never believe," said Athole courteously.

"You will have a suitable commemorative plaque put on this grill," concluded MacHead Vohr. "From this moment, you are Governor. No need to name a successor for the secret service, the executive councilor will assume his task and yours. The interior relations as well as the executive department are enormously simplified. I imagine this was the last strike that will ever be attempted on the planet. For me, it leaves only one regret—that of not having known how to stop it save by sacrificing the most precious blood of my veins. But better that many men perish rather than all men! Now, Governor Ralph Athole, govern the Siturgic even better than I have done; and may God prevent its being at the price it cost me!"

"So be it," said Athole. "For the remainder, if I am obliged to, I shall do as you have done. Just the same, Heaven preserve me from it! Governor MacHead Vohr, if you permit, I intend to take your advice in all matters."

"Useless!" said MacHead Vohr. "My life is over."

"I beg your pardon," said Athole, "you are right!"

THE END

SCIENCE FICTION

An Arno Press Collection

FICTION

About, Edmond. **The Man with the Broken Ear.** 1872

Allen, Grant. **The British Barbarians:** A Hill-Top Novel. 1895

Arnold, Edwin L. **Lieut. Gullivar Jones:** His Vacation. 1905

Ash, Fenton. **A Trip to Mars.** 1909

Aubrey, Frank. **A Queen of Atlantis.** 1899

Bargone, Charles (Claude Farrere, pseud.). **Useless Hands.** [1926]

Beale, Charles Willing. **The Secret of the Earth.** 1899

Bell, Eric Temple (John Taine, pseud.). **Before the Dawn.** 1934

Benson, Robert Hugh. **Lord of the World.** 1908

Beresford, J. D. **The Hampdenshire Wonder.** 1911

Bradshaw, William R. **The Goddess of Atvatabar.** 1892

Capek, Karel. **Krakatit.** 1925

Chambers, Robert W. **The Gay Rebellion.** 1913

Colomb, P. et al. **The Great War of 189—.** 1893

Cook, William Wallace. **Adrift in the Unknown.** n.d.

Cummings, Ray. **The Man Who Mastered Time.** 1929

[DeMille, James]. **A Strange Manuscript Found in a Copper Cylinder.** 1888

Dixon, Thomas. **The Fall of a Nation:** A Sequel to the Birth of a Nation. 1916

England, George Allan. **The Golden Blight.** 1916

Fawcett, E. Douglas. **Hartmann the Anarchist.** 1893

Flammarion, Camille. **Omega:** The Last Days of the World. 1894

Grant, Robert et al. **The King's Men:** A Tale of To-Morrow. 1884

Grautoff, Ferdinand Heinrich (Parabellum, pseud.). **Banzai!** 1909

Graves, C. L. and E. V. Lucas. **The War of the Wenuses.** 1898

Greer, Tom. **A Modern Daedalus.** [1887]

Griffith, George. **A Honeymoon in Space.** 1901

Grousset, Paschal (A. Laurie, pseud.). **The Conquest of the Moon.** 1894

Haggard, H. Rider. **When the World Shook.** 1919

Hernaman-Johnson, F. **The Polyphemes.** 1906

Hyne, C. J. Cutcliffe. **Empire of the World.** [1910]

In The Future. [1875]

Jane, Fred T. **The Violet Flame.** 1899

Jefferies, Richard. **After London; Or, Wild England.** 1885

Le Queux, William. **The Great White Queen.** [1896]

London, Jack. **The Scarlet Plague.** 1915

Mitchell, John Ames. **Drowsy.** 1917

Morris, Ralph. **The Life and Astonishing Adventures of John Daniel.** 1751

Newcomb, Simon. **His Wisdom The Defender:** A Story. 1900

Paine, Albert Bigelow. **The Great White Way.** 1901

Pendray, Edward (Gawain Edwards, pseud.). **The Earth-Tube.** 1929

Reginald, R. and Douglas Menville. **Ancestral Voices:** An Anthology of Early Science Fiction. 1974

Russell, W. Clark. **The Frozen Pirate.** 2 vols. in 1. 1887

Shiel, M. P. **The Lord of the Sea.** 1901

Symmes, John Cleaves (Captain Adam Seaborn, pseud.). **Symzonia.** 1820

Train, Arthur and Robert W. Wood. **The Man Who Rocked the Earth.** 1915

Waterloo, Stanley. **The Story of Ab:** A Tale of the Time of the Cave Man. 1903

White, Stewart E. and Samuel H. Adams. **The Mystery.** 1907

Wicks, Mark. **To Mars Via the Moon.** 1911

Wright, Sydney Fowler. **Deluge: A Romance** *and* **Dawn.** 2 vols. in 1. 1928/1929

SCIENCE FICTION

NON-FICTION
Including Bibliographies,
Checklists and Literary Criticism

Aldiss, Brian and Harry Harrison. **SF Horizons.** 2 vols. in 1. 1964/1965

Amis, Kingsley. **New Maps of Hell.** 1960

Barnes, Myra. **Linguistics and Languages in Science Fiction-Fantasy.** 1974

Cockcroft, T. G. L. **Index to the Weird Fiction Magazines.** 2 vols. in 1 1962/1964

Cole, W. R. **A Checklist of Science-Fiction Anthologies.** 1964

Crawford, Joseph H. et al. **"333": A Bibliography of the Science-Fantasy Novel.** 1953

Day, Bradford M. **The Checklist of Fantastic Literature in Paperbound Books.** 1965

Day, Bradford M. **The Supplemental Checklist of Fantastic Literature.** 1963

Gove, Philip Babcock. **The Imaginary Voyage in Prose Fiction.** 1941

Green, Roger Lancelyn. **Into Other Worlds:** Space-Flight in Fiction, From Lucian to Lewis. 1958

Menville, Douglas. **A Historical and Critical Survey of the Science Fiction Film.** 1974

Reginald, R. **Contemporary Science Fiction Authors,** First Edition. 1970

Samuelson, David. **Visions of Tomorow:** Six Journeys from Outer to Inner Space. 1974